St. Martin's Paperbacks titles by Meg O'Brien

I'LL LOVE YOU TILL I DIE
A DEEP AND DREAMLESS SLEEP

A DEEP AND DREAMLESS SLEEP

MEG O'BRIEN

St. Martin's Paperbacks

For

Luella Wilcox

Who has blessed me with her extraordinary gifts of friendship, patience, wisdom, and love

A DEEP AND DREAMLESS SLEEP

Copyright © 1996 by Meg O'Brien

ISBN: 0-312-95775-0

Printed in the United States of America

St. Martin's Paperbacks edition/July 1996

10 9 8 7 6 5 4 3 2 1

CHAPTER 1

Whidbey Island, Washington

According to the *Whidbey Island Journal* this morning, the investigation into Beth Lambert's death is being reopened. The banner headline stretches, an accusing finger, across the front page:

> YOUNG ISLAND WOMAN'S DEATH NOT AN
> ACCIDENT?

I sit on my dock reading this, and all the old emotions come rushing back, all the memories I'd thought buried in a year of grief and learning how to live without Beth. For a year I had railed at fate: *How dare you do this? Seventeen is too young to die—the heart barely broken in, the soul a mere promise of what it may one day be.*

Fate, of course, had nothing to do with it. When someone dies that way there are always reasons, and the reasons seldom bear close inspection.

Beth's body was found last summer in a wooded ravine near her home. Cause of death, according to the county coroner, a broken neck sustained in a fall. There was no reason to suspect foul play. Beth was known to everyone as a happy, well-adjusted young woman from a "good family." She had no known enemies and was excited about attending school in the east that fall. Her death occurred in the middle of one of the worst storms ever to saturate Washington state. The ferry from the mainland had shut down. Emergency services were in short supply; deputies and volunteers were out shoring up homes along the beaches and checking downed utility lines. Citizens manned CB radios, the only means of communication left on the island.

It was assumed Beth had run out into the storm in search of help; there were minor burns on her face, and a portion of the Lambert mansion was found the next day to have severe fire damage. The blaze seemed to have started from a kerosene lamp and spread quickly. Inspectors said later that this must have occurred during a time when the rain had stopped but the winds were still tearing through. "Once that front window blew, it wouldn't have taken long."

It was assumed that in the darkness Beth dropped her flashlight, tripped on a rock or root, and fell into the ravine.

But now the papers are saying that official police records in the case of Beth Lambert are missing. Specifically, autopsy photographs and pages from the coroner's report.

Pete Shelton, Island County Sheriff, is quoted as saying, "I'm sure they were simply misplaced when we moved our offices in March." But suspicions have been raised, and the papers are hinting at a cover-up.

That means that yet again there will be an endless round of questions. They will come to all of us who knew Beth, just as they did before, and this time they will poke and pry into every dark, tragic corner until satisfied they finally have the truth.

But truth is an elusive thing, I've learned. I'm not certain I even know what it is anymore. *Oh, Beth. When they come to me what shall I tell them? What would you want me to say?*

CHAPTER 2

Beth Lambert came careening into my life one warm June day, tripping along the path through the woods from her own house to mine. She was thirteen then and had moved here with her parents just after school was out. They bought the old Hiller estate, a large white Colonial originally surrounded by thirty acres of lush grass and trees. The Lambert contractors, hired to build on a wing, had first destroyed the grass with their bulldozers, then replaced it with rolls of sod from a discount house.

"I'm so *booored*," Beth complained good-naturedly that day. "My mother's talking to the decorators, and my dad's in Seattle at work, and I saw your corral . . . Oh shoot! It's not a corral, is it? I thought you had a horse!"

She had been crestfallen upon closer examination of my vegetable garden—which, in fact, was a corral until my dappled mare, Allegra, cashed in. Allegra had no obvious disease, just closed her eyes one night while I was away studying law at Harvard and died. I always felt she did it to teach me a lesson for having more important things on my mind.

My mother did much the same thing five years ago—more or less up and died. She did have a disease, but for her there would be no hospitals, no probes, no drugs to delay the onslaught of the hideous cancer growing in her lungs. She went to her people in Northern California, and there on the rancheria in Mendocino County they burned smoke, held ceremonial dances, told stories round the fire. Friends came from many states, honoring my mother's work for Native American rights. They brought gifts and tokens, and when my mother decided the time was right she lay down on a bed of deer-hide, smiled at me, closed her eyes, and departed.

I was twenty-nine then, and on the long drive home to Washington I beat my fists on the steering wheel, cursing the heartless moon. I thought Katherine Wing had gone off far too soon, and like Allegra, had done it to teach me a lesson. I was with a law firm in Seattle before my mother died, a "bright young associate," they called me, both feet on the ladder, eyes on the stars. There was little time or patience for the hourlong drive and ferry ride to Whidbey—even less for listening to the old tales, or the guilt my mother ladled out along with her meals. "I thought when you became a lawyer you would help us!" my mother would cry—again and again.

My argument then was always selfish, always much the same. "Let it be. Where are the reporters now, Mother? Where are the movie stars? Indian rights are a hopeless issue. No one cares anymore."

"Oh, Naomi . . . you have strayed so far from my side," she complained one night over a bubbling pot of leek soup.

"The cub must walk from its mother. You told me that."

"But you don't even use your own name!"

What she said was true. Years before at Harvard I had added an "E" to Wing. Thinking—and yes, I will admit this, though it grieves me now to do so—that it somehow seemed more elegant. Less Indian. Why must I, I had reasoned, in a new age, a new time—the first in our family to go to law school—be saddled with the old stories, the old angers, old pain? I had grown up with it always before me, coloring and tainting everything I learned, said, did.

Why can't I simply be me, I had rationalized at twenty? Naomi Winge, attorney at law, a woman who will one day live in a high-rise apartment on a hill in Seattle, with a classy view of the Sound.

It was a foolish dream, I know that now. One can never be "simply" anything. There are always battles to be fought. A price to pay.

I am thirty-four now. Hard to believe how much life, and death, has been packed into these past five years. I look at myself in the mirror and see the same face, though a bit more worn. My hair is still dark and long, with only the occasional gray strand. The eyes tell the story, however. The eyes have looked upon too much grief.

When Beth Lambert came into my life three months after my mother died I gathered her in, like a gift. When Beth herself departed last year it was a punishment: I didn't deserve the gift; I'd betrayed it. That is the truth that comes knocking at my heart, night after endless night. I try not to let it in, but often a memory will strike without warning, a blast of cold air that brings with it a cry: *"You had a hand in it, Naomi. She might be here now, if not for you."*

I'm not certain that blast of air isn't really my mother knocking on my heart, ranting in my ear. Katherine Wing, in life, could be avoided. In death she is everywhere.

I will tell you something, though I've never told anyone else: my dead mother tried more than once last year to warn me of Beth's impending danger. Perhaps you won't believe me, and if so, I would be the last to blame you. But I know what I know. It began quite normally, the way my visions generally do. One moment I was alone, and the next my mother was there, a slight, ghostly figure at first, no more than a whiff of air, an impression that something not quite of this world had entered my presence. Generally, the hairs on the backs of my arms stand upright. This time they damn near froze there, like the bristles on the back of a polar bear.

I had been weeding, upturning earth, and thinking—for no reason I could explain—about the coldness of death, and of graves. When I felt that unworldly presence I turned abruptly, worried not by the vision, but because, as it took shape, it clearly became my mother. In the four years since she had died, Katherine Wing had not been what one might call a silent specter. To not speak out and bluntly, was never her nature in life . . . nor did she restrain herself in death.

It might have helped, I suppose, if she'd been your everyday ghost, drifting about ethereally, disappearing around corners without a word or a by-your-leave. Rather, my mother was, in death, as she'd been in life: a thorn beneath my toe—or, as I'd been inclined during one of her visitations to put it, one phantasmic pain in the neck.

When she appeared in my garden on Whidbey three weeks before Beth died, my mother wasted, as usual, no time. Nor did she refrain from dramatics. She came dressed in the buckskin leggings, beads, and feathers of her ancestors and mine, and when she spoke her voice was like thunder mixed with the music of the spheres. "There are terrible signs in the heavens tonight," she warned without preamble. "Naomi, I saw the child, Beth, dressed all in white. She held a round ball in her hand and from it shone light, and in that light I saw the child herself crossing the River of Ghosts to her ancestors' side. You must warn her, daughter! You must warn the Lamberts."

I'd been having visions since childhood, scenes of ancient times and long-dead relatives, many of whom I'd never known. As a child I told no one, figuring I had enough problems already, enough strikes against me on a mostly white island stuck in the middle of Puget Sound. I didn't want to be any more different than I already was. So I denied the visitations when they first began. Later, my mother said, "I knew you were having them, Naomi. You couldn't fool me." When I complained that I could use a good night's sleep once in a while and I wished they'd all learn to nap, she would say reprovingly, "It's your heritage as an Indian, Naomi, to see these things. You can't get away from it, no matter how hard you try."

Finally I came to accept the visions and even welcome them. There were times in my lonely growing-up years when it was even comforting to speak with an aunt who had long-since passed. People I'd never met in life appeared with helpful messages, and more than once some accident was averted by a thoughtful grandmother or uncle.

When my mother appeared last summer, however, to warn me about Beth's impending death, it shook me.

I tried to deny it at first. "I don't believe you," I said with much scorn, as I knew my mother and her hidden agendas far too well. "What sort of trouble are you trying to stir up here?"

Katherine Wing, no more than five feet tall, seemed at least ten in her outrage. "See for yourself!" she cried.

With that she placed a vision before me, and though I tried to avert my eyes, it wasn't possible. Thrown before me like a film on a screen was my beautiful Beth, lying in a ravine, covered with dirt, sticks, and leaves. She was on her side in a fetal position, crying. Her head was at a strange angle, and around her neck was the butterfly necklace she'd been wearing for at least three months before she died. She was holding it fast to her lips.

I'd wondered about the necklace and asked her, one day in my garden, "Where did you get that? It's very nice."

"I bought it at the secondhand shop in Langley," she said, though she didn't meet my eyes. "It's not expensive or anything, I just liked it."

She was hiding something, I knew. And I wondered if, in fact, Curt Lawrence had given her the necklace. But then why not just say so? Her parents knew she was seeing Lawrence and approved of him as being from "one of the best families" on the island. Why lie about the fact that he'd given her this small and not inappropriate gift?

"Why a butterfly?" I asked, trying to draw her out. "Any special meaning?"

Beth only shrugged, rubbed her back, and looked away. Picking up a spade, she began to help me furrow rows for lettuce and beans.

That was in May. In August my mother laid this vision before me and claimed it to be of the future. My heart twisted in agony at the tears, the fetal position, the pitiful young body covered in dirt and leaves. Stooping down, I tried to touch Beth, to hold her in my arms, but there was nothing there, of course, just air. "Beth," I whispered urgently, "Honey, what's wrong? What happened?"

She turned her eyes to mine, though her head did not move, and it was then I realized that her neck was broken. I drew in a harsh breath, and she said to me clearly, "Black . . . feet."

I was confused. My eyes went involuntarily to her feet, but they were clad in her usual Nikes—white, not black. At any rate, I was certain this was not what she meant. I shook my head. "I don't understand."

Her voice was soft and very far away. "I'm sorry, Naomi. I didn't mean it." She began to fade.

"Beth," I cried, "it's all right. Lie here, lie still. I'll go for help."

"I can't. Oh, Naomi, it hurts so much."

A hand went to her abdomen, the other out to me, and within moments it was all that was left of her. I grabbed for the hand, my fingers clutching, but they tightened on themselves as the last vestiges of Beth disappeared and there was only me, on my knees in the dirt in my garden, sobbing.

Time passed that day in August, and slowly I came back to myself. My mother was standing before me, arms folded. "You see?" she demanded. "It's just as I've told you. You must do something to prevent this, Naomi."

I struggled to my feet, wiping tears and dirt from my face. "You have outdone yourself, Mother," I cried. "How could you bring such a monstrous scene to me?"

"Don't you want to know? Isn't it best to be warned?"

"It would be, if it were the truth. But I can't trust you. How do I know you didn't just create this hideous illusion to frighten me?"

"Now why on earth would I do that, child?"

"You and I both know why. You want me to go to Beth's father and fill his mind with so much fear, he'll forget everything else." I brushed my hands off on my jeans. "Mother, I've filed the necessary papers every step of the way. Leave it to me. I can keep Lambert Enterprises from buying the Wintu lands, and—"

"My dear daughter, just how long have we been waiting for this matter to be settled? Five years is it, now? Five years, while you—"

My mouth tightened. "Don't say it. Don't you dare say it."

She was silenced, though sullen. And I was angry, terribly angry that she had used Beth in this wild attempt to disarm Adam Lambert and thus further her political cause.

Of course, I should have listened. I can only say my perception was blurred; the relationship between my mother and me was so confused in those days, I did not always see things as they truly were.

It is a pitiful defense, I know.

My mother, at any rate, did not give up. A week later she appeared in jeans and denim shirt, the way I remembered her from the seventies, when I was sixteen. She was marching back then for the American Indian Movement. Marching to Washington, to Alcatraz, to Wounded Knee wearing beads and buckskin, and sometimes even a headband. In truth, she looked less like a Wintu and more like one of those young white hippie dropouts who were so hot to be Indians in those days. My classmates at Whidbey High laughed when she passed on the street. I was humiliated, horrified. I refused to watch her on the nightly news.

But here she was again, looking so real, so alive, and I couldn't flick her off now as easily as on TV. I was at my easel that day, working on a great snowy owl in charcoal. "You are wasting time, Naomi," she said quietly, "and there is little left. You must tell Adam Lambert that his daughter is in danger." Her breath, an icy mist, cooled my cheek.

I dropped the charcoal, heard it land with a thud on the bare wood floor. "Tell me what's supposed to happen, then," I demanded. "How can I believe you when you tell me only part? Why are you playing these games?''

''No games! There are things that cannot be spoken aloud, daughter. To speak them is to make them irreversible. Once the Great Spirit hears . . .'' She shook her head sadly, folded her hands as if in prayer, and rolled her eyes.

''Oh, Mother.'' She was wearing me down, making me believe it. ''What if I do go to Adam with this? Will you promise not to take advantage of it? Will you ease up about the Wintu land, while we find out what's going on?''

Here I swear she looked as crafty as ever, as sly. ''It's your land too, Naomi, the land of our people. And Lambert Enterprises wants to destroy it.''

Tears sprang to my eyes. ''Sometimes I wish I'd never heard of Lambert Enterprises. Mother, can't you leave me in peace, even now?''

''What peace?'' Katherine Wing cried. ''What peace is there when none of us rest?''

In my remembrances of Beth, I swing back and forth between her life and mine. Her mother and mine. My mother and me.

They were obvious from the first, the problems in the Lambert home. Not that Beth complained, other than the typical teenage comments about being bored, or feeling put upon for having to clean her room. Even then she would smile, so I'd know she didn't mind all that much; therefore, it was more in the body language that one could spot the real trouble, if one were looking for it. The biting of nails, shadows behind the eyes, a spontaneous laugh that dwindled off into a forlorn smile.

I didn't see that at first, of course. What I saw that first day was a child who came up to my shoulders, a leggy teenager who still thought in some ways she was nine rather than thirteen, her wheat-blond hair tangled from somersaults and climbing trees.

"I like you, Naomi," she said in her forthright way. "May I come back tomorrow? There's nothing to do at home."

I didn't think I had much to offer in the way of entertainment, so that took me by surprise. Though I'd inherited Crow Cottage three months before from my mother, I was still living then in Seattle, in that classy high-rise I'd always wanted, near the Pike Place Market. I came home weekends to the island, though, driven by some sense that there were things here I might learn about myself, my mother, and our seemingly disparate—though actually quite similar—lives. I had begun to enjoy my weekends here, and even, oh-so-belatedly, the hour-long trip by freeway and ferry.

Still, what had I to offer a child like Beth? First of all, no horse. And certainly no rolling green lawns or imported marble fountains, such as the Lamberts were putting in. Crow Cottage sits on a smallish piece of land on the edge of Puget Sound. It was built years ago by Arn Jensen, a retired ferryman who had lived with the Amish as a young man and remembered their love for fine craftsmanship. He built Crow Cottage with native fir, using pegs rather than nails. The cabinets are cherrywood, the windows both stained and beveled glass.

"You'll never find a warped piece of wood here, or a squeaky floor," Jensen told my mother the day she looked it over. "Hate like anything to sell, but you know how it is. My knees freeze up all winter, and every time it rains..." Jensen peered down at me then, through glasses that were so spotted with fingerprints, you had to wonder how he could see.

I was ten, my father had just died, and I was suddenly afraid of all strangers. I wanted my mother to reassure me that I'd be all right in this new home, away from my friends in Seattle, away from all the familiar streets and comforting city sounds I'd known since I was born. I reached for her hand. But my mother had the habit of gesturing wildly as she talked. More often than not I found myself holding air.

And so it was on this day. My mother and the ferryman continued to dicker, and I stood impatiently by in my Sunday best. Finally I slipped off to the side and sneaked up the loft stairs. There I found a round stained-glass window: a bright yellow tulip surrounded by green leaves. I tiptoed over, inched the window open, and peeked through, looking down to the field in back.

What I saw down there was more wonderful than Seattle, more salutary, even, than my friends. It caused my heart to beat like a thousand drums, wiping thoughts of all else away. I inched back down the stairs with only a glance at my mother and the poor doomed ferryman. He didn't stand a chance, I knew, not a prayer. Quietly, I left through the front door. It wasn't that I felt I was doing anything wrong—only that I treasured my discovery. I didn't want to share.

It was spring, I remember, and I made my way through knee-high grasses and tall yellow wildflowers to the back. There was a bit of open meadow before the woods began, and in that green open space was a fence—its four long rows of horizontal boards white and gleaming. Within it stood my prize. I crept over to her on the balls of my feet so I wouldn't frighten her away. Then I reached out and touched her soft, warm nose. She nuzzled me and whinnied. She did not fling herself about, ignore me, or dash away.

As I stood there stroking the muzzle of that gray-and-white dappled mare, I told myself it was only the sun streaming through cedars, not love, that made my eyes tear, making me seem to cry. Still, when I looked up and saw my mother watching me from the long row of windows inside, I could tell she knew the truth. In another ten minutes she'd bought the cottage, and the mare, for a song. It was a good deal, too. In all the years I've been back and forth, either living in or leaving Crow Cottage, I have never known the floors to either squeak or warp.

There were, instead, other kinds of damage. One does not put a stubborn, know-it-all, teenaged lawyer-to-be in the same small house with a just as stubborn, full-blooded Indian-activist mother for eight years and expect harmony. *Survival of the fittest.* That's the way it seemed between my mother and me.

That's why I understood when Beth Lambert came knocking and wanting to stay. Her father, Adam, owned a large timber company; he commuted to his office in Seattle six days a week. Beth's mother, Susan, was a return student at the University of Washington, carrying a full schedule to earn a master's degree in economics. Both parents were tired at night, tense. I came to learn that they took their frustration out on each other—and sometimes, either verbally or through indifference, on Beth.

My new little neighbor fell into my weekend routine easily. She liked to sit and watch me paint, and often she helped me gather herbs from my garden at the end of the day. Together we would clean them, boiling the nettles for tea, hanging the basil and oregano to dry. I loved to cook back then, and often we'd make dinner together. Beth would set the table and keep watch over boiling pasta as I sautéed basil, garlic, and tomatoes for the sauce. Both of us ate with gusto, our appetites honed by the work in the garden, the hot sun, and fresh air.

After the dinner hour, temperatures on the island frequently cool, and we often wound up in my living room by the wood stove. "It's so cozy here," Beth said the first evening we did this. When I close my eyes I can still see her snuggled into the padded window seat, her face flushed from the warm fire and the food.

I remember looking around and thinking that my little cottage must seem simple to Beth's eyes. It had probably cost Katherine Wing less to decorate all of Crow Cottage than Beth's parents had paid for even one of the faux marble statues she'd described in her house. But what my mother lacked in luxury she made up for in color, bringing in Native American art from every corner of the nation. Though full-blooded Wintu herself, she was curious about other tribes, collecting artifacts and studying their customs. As an activist she was working for all Indians, she said, and should know who she was working for. At one point during the seventies, when AIM was at its most explosive, she even took in people. Wherever they came from, if they had Native blood and were working for the cause, my mother fed them and gave them a place to sleep for the night. I would lay in my loft bedroom snuggled under a down comforter, listening to the rise and fall of voices below, soft as rain on the roof. I don't specifically remember stories that were told regarding the Movement, but at twelve I knew names like Mad Bear Anderson, Essie Parrish, Stella Leach, and Leonard Crow Dog. I absorbed them like a sponge from that bed in the loft, under the hypnotic spell of my mother's voice mingled with a stranger's, the sound of rain, the scent of dark-brewed coffee, and the flap, flap, flap of a mimeograph machine spitting out flyers next to the kitchen sink.

As for Beth and me, our nights were more serene. Beth loved music, and had her own piano at home. As a substitute, I'd found a lap harp in the second-hand store in Langley, which I would pluck at rather ineptly, while Beth sang. She had a high, sweet, and terribly off-key voice. It was hard sometimes not to smile as she reached for a note with all earnestness and vigor, only to have it fall flatter than a mushroom beneath the heel of a running deer.

It's the blonde hair I remember best, however, the way it shimmered and brightened my garden, my every room . . . the way the rainbows from my beveled glass windows touched it with red, green, or blue, especially when she laughed and shook it free of its elastic band. It pains me still that no matter how hard I tried to capture those precise shades of wheat on canvas, I never could. Thus I have no worthy memory of

Beth on canvas, nothing to study on winter nights when the short days have gone and there's nothing to do but remember. Every weekend, all that first summer long and then throughout the winter, Beth came to my door. "May I come in?" she would ask, though she knew she was welcome. She used the formal "may" just the way her mother, Susan, had taught her. She always asked if there was anything she might do to help, and unlike many thirteen-year-olds, she seldom pouted. Rather, she was bright and curious, always poking into things. Now and then her voice held a trace of loneliness. It was a big house over there for a child alone, and though a housekeeper came to cook dinner and clean at three, Beth was left to fend for herself most of the day. It was safe enough on the island—or so we thought. Safe from strangers, rapists, murderers.

"Her *spirit* wasn't safe," my mother's ghost has railed at me so many times since. "Why didn't you protect *that*, Naomi? The child's *spirit*!"

When the end came for Beth last August it came with the wind crying through the tops of the fir trees, clouds scudding low over the islands at an alarming rate. A freak storm, the forecasters called it. Rain came down in torrents on my roof. It upturned boats all along the Sound and closed the car ferry from Mukilteo. The storm cut off all aid from the mainland—and it cut off, too, Beth's mother and father as they struggled, in blind panic, to get home to their daughter from Seattle.

The deer huddled close to my cottage all that day, the mother and her two yearlings. They stood beneath the large old cedar by my kitchen window, their sides touching for warmth and reassurance. Even for the deer, this was a wild, angry day.

For Beth, of course, every day held the potential for anger. I knew this by now. This, and so much more.

If one could only know how easy it is to lose someone, how fragile young life is, a mere green tendril fighting to take hold. Not a day would be wasted, not an hour.

It is easier, of course, to see these things from outside the family womb.

CHAPTER 3

It is still early morning. I have digested the *Whidbey Island Journal* along with coffee on my small dock, and now I sit before Pete Shelton, sheriff of Island County. He looks over at me, a curious light in his eyes. Pete's known me since fifth grade, when he and I were the only Indians in an all-white class at the private school our parents had put us in, thinking to give us the best education possible. As far as book learning was concerned, they were right. By our classmates, however, we were both teased mercilessly for being, in some way I never clearly understood, different.

Certainly we dressed, spoke, and behaved like all the rest. We struggled to fit in, but to no avail. I spent a lot of years angry, believing they discriminated against us simply because we were Indians. When I was older I came to understand that it wasn't race so much as our parents who were the problem. Pete's had moved to the island from the Snohomish reservation in a time when Indians were even less welcome than they are now. Shortly after, we moved here from Seattle. My father had been shot before my mother's eyes during a dispute with a utility company over the razing of timber lands. The utility company was ordered to "recompense" her for her loss, and with the modest sum she received, she bought Crow Cottage. Then my mother, who had said she wanted out of the Movement—who had moved to the island, in fact, to retire and recoup—did instead regroup. She organized and marched all over Whidbey, often with a small, ragtag band of hippies behind her. She printed angry political flyers, distributing them throughout the islands. This tiny woman who had been somewhat shy when my father was alive, became loud and abrasive. Obsessed. People here were just sort of easing out of the fifties and sixties, and for the most part they were farmers—*Happy Days* stock—not asking for much but a quiet life, a color TV, and a new Amana freezer. My mother's attempts to convince them they were living on stolen Indian land were not met with joyous hurrahs.

Given that, it wasn't surprising I never got invited to classmates' homes. But then, neither did Pete. Eventually we made up for this by doing things together, like riding horses down on the beach at night when the tide was out. I'd gallop ahead on Allegra, my dappled mare, enjoying the wind on my face and the freedom. Pete would often lag behind, and I'd turn to find him dreaming, gazing up at the sky as his Appaloosa snorted and stomped, eager to get going. That was Pete, head in the clouds, heart in . . . well, who knew where?

Because my mother insisted, I took him home to the cottage to meet her. Pete, who still had relatives on the reservation, was fresh meat, she hoped, for her cause. *"Get 'em while they're young,"* she'd say, having learned her lessons well at the Bureau of Indian Affairs Christian schools. She would snag Pete at the dining room table, going on and on about restitution and reclaiming the ancestral lands. Pete would nod, look agreeable, and later I'd laugh, embarrassed, and say, "She really is a nut about that," expecting him to agree. Sometimes he would, and other times he'd answer, "She's pretty noisy about it. But I don't know . . ."

When we were sixteen, Pete and I decided to make love. That's just how it happened: we decided one day. All summer long we'd been casting new eyes at each other, and whenever our hands or bodies would accidentally touch it was like a three-alarm fire. By this time we had been friends for so long, it only seemed natural (at least to me) to talk about it.

"A lot of kids I know are doing it by now," I said over a cup of coffee at Joe's Cafe in Langley. My voice was nicely steady, but my grip on the white coffee mug shook. I did that to myself a lot in those days— pretended to be cool, offhand, when all the while my insides were jelly.

"Just because everyone else is doing it, that doesn't mean we have to," Pete answered somewhat nervously.

Already, "Just Say No." The lawman in training.

"Well, then—what are we supposed to do? Ignore the way we feel?" I shamelessly slid the toe of my boot up the hard inner line of his thigh.

The year was 1976, and Pete's shiny black hair was a statement of the times. It hung in two traditional braids to his waist, bound at the ends by bright red cloth. Long hair was "in" for everyone, as was the natural look—so of course I'd cut mine short and slicked it down. Pete, however, wore a suede vest his grandmother had made for him on the reservation. The scent of animal hide mingled with sweat; we'd just come in from riding. I wanted him badly in that moment, there in that too-bright cafe with its worn linoleum floor, chipped water glasses, and unshaded bulbs. I am ashamed to say I used tradition as my argument, much as I scorned it for other reasons then.

"In the old days it would have simply happened," I lobbied earnestly. "People would have been happy for us, there would have been ceremonies and dancing. It's only the white man who said it was wrong— the nuns, the priests, the missionaries. Do you want to be like them?"

All the while the toe of my boot worked its way along his thigh. Pete didn't pull away. Instead his eyes locked on mine, and he sat very still, a flush rising as that toe found what it was looking for.

We went back to the beach, to a sheltered cove we'd discovered as children. Above it rose a hill, and atop that, in sharp relief, a centuries-old Snohomish ceremonial rock. Our lovemaking was awkward at first as the recently grown-up part of us held back, felt suddenly embarrassed, said it might be wrong after all. Then suddenly Pete let out a boisterous *whoop!* that relieved the tension. He laughed, pulling me down onto the sand, and we rolled about a bit, giggling, before we quieted and came together.

I don't remember pain. I only remember a ceiling of stars and Pete's reassuring words, his gentleness. I remember the sand at my back, and grains of it between our lips. I wrapped my arms around Pete's neck and held him close, tasting the sand, tasting his tongue, and I remember feeling secure then, and cared for, filled to the brim with something I didn't even know I'd been missing. I remember thinking to myself, *This is what I've always wanted—at last.*

We went on like that the rest of the summer, first the customary ride on the beach, then the playful lovemaking. It was as if, together, we hurtled backward to that ancient time I'd used in my argument—doing what was natural, right, and innocent, the way it was meant to be. Sometimes we would finish with coffee at Joe's, where we would discuss things, argue, challenge each other's views. I loved to argue. Between Pete and my mother I was building my skills for debate, and though I didn't know it yet, for the law.

Pete always saw me home at night, and more often than not my mother would snag him and begin her proselytizing anew. She was in Seattle a lot that summer, organizing a rally to release Leonard Crow Dog from prison. "You should come with me," she said quite often to Pete (having given up on me). "See for yourself." I heard this once from the bathroom where I'd gone to wash sand from my back, and I stood there looking into the mirror, feeling more all-of-a-piece and happier than I'd ever been. "Naomi," I said to that image in the mirror, "you are the luckiest girl in town."

But Pete's moods changed after that. He became withdrawn, and I saw him less often. One night when we were riding on the beach I turned around and he was gone. Vanished. "Pete?" I called softly. There were no waves, and my voice traveled loudly over the sand.

Pete didn't answer. At first I was simply curious, but then I felt afraid. A wind came up and tore my hair in every direction. I shivered. "Pete?" A moment later I heard hooves pounding, then a savage shriek, an *"Iyiiiiiii!"* that slammed from hill to surrounding hill. Pete came tearing across the sand on that Appaloosa, his black hair flying free of the braids. As he drew near I could see the sharp angry planes of his face in the light from a half moon.

He drew up short when he saw me, as if he'd forgotten I was even there. "Where were you?" I asked, still frightened, but more of him now than his disappearance.

He pointed, wordless. I followed his gaze to the top of the hill, to the Snohomish ceremonial rock, where— he had once told me as he stroked my face, my lips, my breasts—men had become warriors. Another shiver rolled down my spine.

"We used to *own* that beach," he said. "It was *ours. Our* land, *our* trees, *our* water, *our* sand!" When I tried to reason with him that we lived in a new time now and should try to blend in, he simply looked at me sadly and shook his head. "You just don't get it, do you?"

That's when I knew I had lost him to my mother.

Pete looks at me steadily now through his new glasses with the round black rims, the kind that are quite stylish with the yuppie brigade. His look makes me squirm, as if he knows things about me that even I don't know.

"Where did you go?" he asks.

"Oh . . . drifting."

"Thinking about Katherine?"

"I suppose. And you."

He shakes his head and a lock of short dark hair falls over his forehead. He brushes it back. "You were jealous of a shadow, Naomi. There was never anything . . ." He lets it go, but I know. *Physical.*

"She took your soul," I say. "That was what mattered to me."

"And what about yours, Naomi?"

I don't say, *I escaped before she got mine.* I am no longer sure this is true.

"I heard you were reopening the Beth Lambert case," I say with an air of casual interest.

His steady look never wavers. "Possibly."

"Everyone knows it was an accident, Pete."

"Do they?" He takes the glasses off and rubs his nose, then his eyes, as if weary.

I watch him a long moment, remembering the battle he waged to become sheriff on an island that said it would never happen—not for an Indian. But Pete, once grown, was always liked. He became an ombudsman between the whites and Native Americans on the island, helping to sort out problems and arrive at peaceful compromises for all concerned.

It probably didn't hurt matters that he was tall and nice-looking. Leaders in this country must be tall, it seems, and an attractive appearance certainly helps. But the corker—the thing that swung the votes in the end—was that the only other person who ran for sheriff that year was a woman. Whidbey Island announced its choice: it preferred an Indian to a woman.

His hand comes away from his eyes, and I see that they are red.

"Your vision's getting worse, isn't it?" I say. He always had trouble reading the blackboard in school. As sheriff on a small island, it's probably just as well he's never had to draw a gun.

Pete sighs. "You know, Naomi, the Snohomish believed that if you didn't paint your face black after you killed someone, you'd go blind."

"Really? Have you killed someone?" I ask, surprised.

He hesitates. "Maybe."

"Who?" I am thinking a bank robber, a kidnapper, yet I haven't read anything about this in the *Journal.*

He shrugs. "Sally Ann."

I can't help smiling. "Sally? Your *wife?* Last I heard she was very much alive."

"She doesn't seem to think so. Says I've stolen her youth."

"In what way?"

"Well, first off, she says she could have been a ballerina if she hadn't married me and had three kids."

Sally is cute and short, but she weighs nearly as much as Pete, and always has. She has never been known for her light-footedness.

"You had a fight?"

He nods.

I laugh softly. "She's grouchy, that's all. You know how she is when she gains a few pounds."

"No." Pete says, "it's different now. This is serious."

Sarah Bernhardt, they called Sally Ann in school, I remember. Vivid, overly dramatic. Not a dishonest bone in her body, but she did love playing her part to the hilt. Pete married Sally after he tired of my mother and her causes, after he came back to Whidbey and settled down. I was at Harvard then.

Pete rubs his eyes and looks away. "Naomi . . . what if she's right? What if I am killing her?"

We let that sit, each of us thinking our own thoughts. "Well," I say finally, "maybe you should paint your face black while there's still time."

He laughs, and for a brief moment his expression softens. Behind it I see the young boy again.

The phone rings on Pete's desk, and he swivels round in his chair to talk in a low, confidential voice. Then he puts the receiver down, swivels back, and looks long at me. I feel he is judging me—my clothes, the jeans and denim jacket, the work boots . . . my long dark hair tied back in a red kerchief. Gone are the Seattle power suit, the heels, the makeup. It doesn't seem to matter, since Beth. Only the land matters, the hoeing and weeding, the turning over of soil and the burial of thoughts beneath.

"Remember when we used to ride horses and do everything together?" Pete asks suddenly.

"Of course."

"Did you know that back in the old days, in the Kaska tribes up in Canada, if a girl played with boys or boy-type toys, she was designated a male for all time?"

"I seem to recall hearing that."

The truth is, I remember my mother telling me this. *"Women were allowed to be strong, then, Naomi—to be warriors."*

"Allowed?" I had argued. *"Do you hear yourself? How many were not 'allowed?' You call that freedom?"*

But Pete is going on in that instructive way he learned at my mother's knee. "The girl's parents would tie a pouch of dried bear ovaries to her belt, and she'd ride and hunt with the men. If a male even tried to touch her, he'd be severely punished."

"Seems like the bear ovaries would take care of that," I say.

He doesn't smile.

"Okay, Pete. Just what are we talking about here?"

He gives another shrug. "I just wondered. You carry symbolic bear ovaries on your belt these days, Naomi? Seems like a long while since I saw you with a man."

I try to laugh it off. "Oh, I get it. You think I became a designated male from all those years of hanging out with you?"

He shakes his head. "I know better."

I look away, and see that rain is streaming against the office windows. *Rain, sun, rain, sun.* If you don't like the weather, we say here, just wait, it'll change. Meanwhile, there are espresso stands on every corner. You can count on caffeine to bring you up, we say as well. Never the sun.

And never a man.

I clear my throat, which has become dry as dust. "About Beth . . ."

"An interesting segue."

I meet his eyes. "Could we stop this, please?"

And to my great relief he leans back in his green metal chair, folds his arms, and looks and talks like a cop again. "What do you want to know?"

I stand and begin to pace. "First of all ... to my knowledge, Beth's case was closed shortly after her death. With no evidence to the contrary, it was assumed she had fallen into the ravine by accident."

"That's right. There hasn't been any real new evidence, if that's what you mean."

"Then why reopen the case?"

"I'm not at all sure we will. The newspapers, as usual, have jumped the gun. But Lambert sent someone to review the files."

"Adam Lambert? Beth's father?"

"You got it." Pete looks at me from beneath black-as-night lashes that shield his thoughts, then says, "You heard from Lambert lately?"

I glance out the window. "No ... why would I?"

"You were pretty close to the family."

"I was close to Beth."

"Right." He leans forward and places his palms on the desk. "Okay, Naomi, I'll give it to you straight. I was about to call you, anyway. Yesterday, I had a little visit from Lambert's attorney."

"Not Travis Hartmann?"

"One and the same. He wanted to review the files on Beth's accident, and I had no reason to stop him, so I said okay. I gave the guy everything I had, put him in a room, and let him go at it. About an hour later I'm coming back from lunch and Hartmann corners me out on the steps. He starts complaining in loud tones, all about missing autopsy photos and coroner's reports. I try to explain some things got mixed up when we moved the offices in March. I tell him that probably what happened is the missing reports are just in another box, still in the warehouse. We'll find them, I say. But Hartmann won't listen." Pete studies my face. "I guess you know how that can be." When I don't respond, he continues. "So anyway, he starts demanding a reinvestigation. Claims there's some sort of conspiracy here in my office to cover up what really happened to Beth. Timmy Dix happened to be here from the *Journal*, taking it all in, and the next thing I know it's all over last night's paper." He pauses. "Naomi? You okay?"

I have sat back down in the chair and rested my forehead in my hand, for I'm feeling very tired suddenly. I look at him. "Pete, surely this will all blow over. Once the missing files are found . . ."

He shakes his head. "I wish that was all there was to it. This morning first thing I get a call from Hartmann. Naomi . . ." He looks at me warily.

"What? What is it?"

"Uh, look, I know this is crazy. But Hartmann says the mother, Susan Lambert . . . he says she's accusing you of having some hand in the way her daughter died."

I am silent. I have no answer for this.

"Naomi? She wants me to arrest you."

Pete has scoured up a cup of coffee for me. It is dark and bitter, leftover dregs, but I swallow it down gratefully. "Better now?" he asks solicitously. "Damn, I thought sure you were about to faint there for a minute."

"I'm all right. But Pete, what does Susan think I did?"

"Hartmann says she talked to Beth just before the phones went down on the island that day. She said Beth was on her way to see you, and the more she thinks about it, the more she's certain you and Beth argued. She claims you did something to her, or she wouldn't've run off that way. Hartmann says if he finds what he expects to find in the coroner's report, namely bruises or some other evidence of a physical altercation, he'll insist charges be brought against you. Either way, he says Susan Lambert is demanding the right to confront you in a court of law. He says if criminal charges aren't filed, she'll bring a civil suit against you."

I am on my feet again. "I don't believe this! And you, Pete. You know the kinds of emotional problems Susan's had. Don't tell me you're putting any stock in this."

"Not me. But you're a lawyer, Naomi, and you were trained to look at the facts. The facts are, one, you were close to Beth. Some might even say too close. No, don't go looking at me like that. You know it wouldn't be the first time Susan Lambert accused you of stealing her child. Emotionally, that is."

"Did she say that this time? That I stole Beth?"

"Hartmann said it for her. Said you 'seduced' Beth away from her at a young, impressionable age. Naomi, if she starts talking like that to the press, there's no telling how it'll end."

"Pete, this is crazy."

"Yeah, well, fact two. We're in an election year, and this kind of thing makes good political fodder. Old

Willie Putch is hot after my job, and he's already in there stirring things up, hoping to make me look bad. The press got to him last night, I hear—too late for his comments to make it into this morning's paper. But you can be sure we'll read all about it in tomorrow's. How my office, and probably me personally, are in some sort of cover-up to keep the truth about the way Beth died from her poor grieving family."

"But why you, personally? Pete, what exactly is Putch saying?"

"I'll know for sure when I get up tomorrow morning and read the *Journal*. But I can tell you what Hartmann's saying, and Putch's complaints are probably along the same lines. Hartmann says it's well known you and I were involved years ago, and that we're still friends. He says if I did see anything out of the ordinary at the time Beth died, and you had something to do with it, I'd have covered for you. In fact, Susan Lambert claims that's exactly what I did."

"But that's impossible. There was an inquest. The coroner gave his report then, and there were no findings of foul play."

"And so we're at fact three. Hartmann says if Beth had had that accident at any other time but during that storm, and if we all hadn't been so overworked, there probably would have been more questions asked about the way it happened. Unfortunately, he's right."

To that I have no comment, as I know it's true.

"Even so, Pete, no one's going to listen to Susan Lambert's ravings. She isn't well."

Pete studies me through narrowed eyes. "Yeah? You hear that from Adam Lambert? You talk to him lately?"

"No. I did have lunch with an old friend last month, someone I worked with at Robinson-Leigh. She does legal work for a competitor of Lambert Enterprises, and she said she'd heard that Adam and Susan separated a few months ago. Surprisingly, Susan left him— not the other way around. It's also rumored she's in counseling, but that it doesn't seem to be helping."

For several moments I lean against Pete's window sill, looking out and thinking. *Hartmann is Adam Lambert's personal lawyer. Does Adam know what Travis is doing? Does he know what Susan's up to?*

"Naomi . . ."

I turn.

"You said at the inquest you didn't see or hear from Beth that day. You told me that too. It was the truth, wasn't it?"

I glance away. "Of course."

There is a brief silence, following which, Pete sighs heavily.

I smile, but my lips feel tight. "I'm sure it'll all work out."

He looks unhappy. "I'm not so sure. Naomi, this whole thing has a real bad feel. Why don't you talk to Adam Lambert, see if he can get his wife—or ex-wife, whatever—to let up?"

"No. I can't do that. And I shouldn't have to. Once the autopsy records are found—"

Pete's eyes flicker.

"What is it?"

"Maybe nothing. It's just that I was up all night looking for them, and I can't find them anywhere."

"But surely they'll turn up. It's as you said, they're packed away, misplaced, but you'll find them."

He doesn't respond.

"Pete? What's wrong?"

"I don't really know. Just a hunch. Nothing I can talk about right now."

A long moment passes as we both look at each other. I could press for more information, but something tells me to leave it alone for now. I glance at my watch. "Well, I should be going. I've got a lot of thinking to do. I assume I'll hear from you quickly enough if Susan makes some formal move to have me charged?"

"Of course." He gives me a glum look and I turn and head for the door. As my hand touches the handle he says, "Naomi?"

There is something in his voice. I stiffen and turn back. "Yes?"

"One other thing."

"Okay. Hit me with it."

"Hartmann also said to tell you that if we don't comply with Susan Lambert's request to reopen the case, she'll be forced to tell the press the whole sordid story." Pete stares down at his hands. "Sorry. Those are his words, not mine."

"The whole . . ."

"That you stole her husband . . . not just her child."

CHAPTER 4

I leave the station in Coupeville and am driving home, wondering: Can Susan really do this to me? The only answer I come up with is yes, of course she can. And she'd be well within her rights.

My hands are shaking on the wheel. "We never get away with anything," I can almost hear my mother saying. "It comes back, bad or good. All things must be balanced."

I should have remembered that, of course—I with my law degree, and Justice with her scales before me every day.

So this is how it happened, and I tell you this without apology, as there is nothing so wasted as an apology when the harm's already done. I will say only that we believed what we did was right. We even told ourselves our affair would be good for Beth—that if we were happy, she would be too. Our happiness would (we said) create an energy, like an aura, that would extend itself to her.

I met Adam Lambert through Beth, that summer when she was thirteen. She had been coming over nearly every day, and then one Sunday afternoon she brought her father with her. "Sorry to come unannounced," he said, smiling, "but I didn't have your number. And Beth couldn't remember."

I had been painting all day. I was disheveled, my face and hands smeared with oil paints, my living room a mess. But I told him he needn't apologize and invited him in for coffee. We sat by the bay window, where I have two comfortable chairs looking out on the trees and the Sound. The sun was going down, and it filtered through the trees, creating rainbows through the beveled window panes. Beth had left us alone to talk, and we could see her along the shore, stooping down to pick up shells and caterpillars and harmless snakes, whatever she could find to interest her curious mind that day. Adam and I watched her a moment, then glanced at each other and smiled.

"I just wanted to make sure Beth isn't making a pest of herself," he said. "I know she's been over here a lot."

I assured him she was not a pest, and studied him through the steam from my coffee. He was not at all what I'd expected: the tough-as-nails robber baron. Though his shoulders were broad, and he carried himself straight and tall like any captain of industry, he was rather thin. His light brown hair clung to his scalp in tight curls, and he nervously ran a hand over it that day, as if unsure of his welcome in my home. His eyes, though, were a soft, warm, gray, and there was in them a bit of Beth's sense of adventure.

On this particular Sunday evening, I didn't at least consciously think of Adam Lambert as someone for me. He was Beth's father, the husband of her mother, and I wasn't the type to have an affair with a married man. In fact, I'd always felt that women who did so were less than smart—not much more than a convenience, and why couldn't they see it?

So we drank our coffee and watched Beth play, and talked about the fact that the weather had been unusually warm this year, and wasn't that nice for Beth, who loved so much to be outdoors. He said the deer had been a problem for the gardeners, and I said fire the gardeners and load up on Irish Spring. He laughed, looked at me curiously, and I said no, really, it works, and told him my mother's recipe for putting pieces of soap in the toe end of socks and hanging them on stakes around the garden. "For some reason, it works," I said, laughing. "The deer won't come near."

I asked about Beth's mother, and he said that Susan was studying economics at the University of Washington, and since she was returning to college after so many years at home as a wife and mother, it was difficult for her. Adam said he had gone to college for a master's in business, then taken over his father's company while Susan raised Beth the first few years. Now it was her turn. He seemed to support her in this, yet a shadow crossed his face. And before long he stood, thanked me, said, "I should be getting back," and went away.

Beth waved to him as he headed down the path, "No later than ten," he called. "Remember."

"Okay, Dad," she answered, giving me a smile and a conspiratorial wink behind her father's departing back. We both knew there were fresh-picked black-berries waiting to be rinsed in the sink; Beth had spied them the minute she walked through my door. We'd be making pies until way after ten.

We both also knew by now that her tardiness would not be noted. Her father, as she had told me, would be working in his study, door closed. Her mother might or might not be home. Often she stayed late at the university to study, and Beth had told me how she'd come home late, her nerves frayed, and would fly off the handle at the smallest thing. More often this occurred when Beth was home, rather than when she was not.

"I think it makes her nervous when I'm around," Beth said. "She really likes being alone best."

Beth seemed so old a child when she said this . . . an old soul, understanding her mother's flaws and ac-cepting them. Therefore it seemed a harmless enough arrangement when Beth took to spending her time with me. I had the child—whom I was coming to love as if she were my own—and Adam and Susan Lam-bert had their work.

There is no way to explain what Beth came to mean to me. Until she arrived in my life I hadn't given a thought to how little space children take up in the world. Sometimes after we'd worked in the garden that first summer, we'd come stomping into the kitchen covered with mud. Beth would run up to the loft, get into one of my long, clean flannel shirts, and I'd wash her T-shirts and socks out by hand. Then I'd lay them on the grass to dry, and be stunned at the sun shining on white, so little white. Children have small things . . . small shirts, small socks, small needs. They don't seem to demand much, only your total time and absorption while you are with them. A listening ear, of course, for the stories of so-and-so in school, of the new cute boy in class, the great new tape at the music store in the Everett mall.

Often throughout that next year I'd be thinking about other things . . . like whether it was time to set the daffodils into the ground or sow seeds for the annuals. But Beth would bring me back. "Are you listening, Naomi? I just asked you a question." I'd smile and say, "I heard it on some level. Now tell me on this one." And I'd listen in earnest, responding with the "Oh no's," and the "Oh, I don't believe it's!" she required.

She shocked me sometimes with her adult ways. She asked me about my relationship with my mother, and when I'd give her an abbreviated version, she'd call me on it and make me tell her the *whole truth*. That was the away she put it. "I want the *whole truth*, Naomi, not some make-believe version you've convinced yourself of."

She seemed to know—possibly because she was living it herself—how one must break away from one's parent, and yet how one longs for the parent to hold one still.

"I think it will be all right for your mother and you," I said often that summer.

Then, shortly before their first Christmas on the island, Adam and I met one Monday morning on the ferry ride to work.

"Naomi!" he exclaimed, coming up to me on the observation deck with a pleased smile. "I've been hoping I'd see you here."

I swear, as God and the Great Spirit are my witness, I did not know until then that I'd been hoping for it too—that I had in fact been casting my eyes about on my daily commutes to and from Seattle, looking for that brown hair above the crowds, the warm gray eyes, the smile.

We sat inside, in a booth by the windows, sipping espresso. We talked about Beth as we had before, and I assured him once more that she was no problem; we were in fact doing fine. I asked him how Susan was, and he said, "About the same," and I wondered if Beth had let on that she'd told me about her mother. The same haunted expression I'd seen at my cottage crossed his face again, but he smiled quickly and said he'd heard that Beth had had a great time with me the week before at the planetarium. "She knows all the constellations now, and she's demanding a monster of a telescope for her next birthday—which, as you may know, is on Christmas Day, so I suppose she'll get it."

"Well, better that . . ." I smiled and spread my hands in a shrug. We both knew what other teenagers were doing on the island. There weren't a whole lot of ways to pass the time through the long winter months, and both drugs and alcoholism were on the rise.

"That's true," he said. "I have a lot to be grateful to you for, Naomi."

A look passed between us, broken only by the sound of the ferry engine gearing down as it docked. We were already at Mukilteo and would have to race back down to our cars. He ran to the second level, I to the first, and we barely had time for a good-bye.

The next Monday morning we ran into each other again. We both laughed and spoke the cliché, "We've got to stop meeting like this!"

Of course we didn't stop. I began spending more and more weekends on the island; we "ran into" each other on Fridays, then Mondays, again and again.

I will not even pretend our meetings were by accident, as in retrospect, and given all that happened later, it seems a minor sin that I actually plotted them in advance. I'd wait certain Friday nights in a nearby Seattle lot, until Adam's black Mercedes passed and pulled into line at the ferry. I'd slide my Nissan somewhere into the row of cars behind him, and then come across him by "accident" upstairs, having coffee.

I do not know how I came to be this person—I who had formerly scorned such things. How could I go so quickly from being an intelligent corporate attorney all week, to a silly lovestruck woman on Friday nights? How could simply sitting across a table from a man cause such tremors inside my skin and make my mouth go hot, then dry?

We talked about other things besides Beth. Common business problems, our schooling, the way we'd grown up. We looked for things to agree on philosophically, unwilling to strain that first tenuous bond with disagreement of any kind. But as our faith in that bond grew, we began to challenge each other, not with any real heat, but for gentle exercise.

Then one morning at my desk at Robinson-Leigh, I had a telephone call from a former associate of my mother's, a Wintu attorney who had worked with her before her death to prevent the razing of the ancestral lands in northern California. They had won that case. But did I know, she asked, that a large Seattle timber company, Lambert Enterprises, was now making a bid for the land? It did not look good this time. Lambert Enterprises had a flotilla of excellent attorneys behind it.

"I should warn you . . . we may come to blows in court," I said to Adam on the ferry that day. "That land you're trying to buy in northern California belonged to my mother's ancestors."

His dark brows lifted in surprise. "Tell me about your mother."

I almost shrugged it off and said, "You don't really want to hear about that." But my mother's dying was still fresh in my heart, not even a year past. And I thought, surprising myself, *The stories need to be told. It's time.* So I told him—sitting there a hundred and seventy years later, drinking espresso on a picture-postcard ferry in this beautiful Sound, surrounded by islands and quiet and peace. I told him how the whites had discovered the Wintu in the Sacramento Valley in 1826, and how that was the beginning of the end. Four short years later Oregon trappers brought malaria to our valley, wiping out more than seventy-five percent of the Indians. "My mother's people were too few and too weak after that to fend off the white occupation. White settlers brought in cattle and sheep. They overran the land, destroying vital nutrients the Indians needed to survive. Goldminers came and polluted our fishing streams. And as if that weren't enough, in 1850 the whites held what they called 'friendship feasts.' They invited the Indians, poisoned the food, and killed over a hundred and forty Trinity Wintu. After that, hundreds upon hundreds of my people were systematically massacred by the good fighting men of the United States Army."

I realized, as I told Adam Lambert this story, that sometime in the months since my mother's death, her people had become mine, in spirit as well as in fact. "In Old Shasta," I continued, my voice beginning to shake, "miners burned down our council meeting house and murdered three hundred. Then, after the Wintu were effectively wiped out, only a handful of us left, they herded us together and forcibly marched us, naked and starving, hundreds of miles to the Mendocino coast. Mothers and children were separated. Many died."

Adam made a low sound of shock. I didn't give him a chance to speak, but continued. "Even that wasn't enough. In the seventies, three dams flooded Wintu territory. Most of the land my people had lived on was wiped out. Gone."

I sat back, finally, my breath and nerves shot. I missed my mother more, suddenly, than I would ever have dreamed, and rued the fact that I hadn't been to see her more often while I'd lived in Seattle. In my sky-high aerie above the Pike Place Market, I had had a few years of success, of growth, of total independence—or so I'd thought. One is never independent of one's mother. Or her dreams.

This struck me that day as it had on no other. The knowledge filled me and overflowed me, making me cry. I was shocked, horrified at the display. But through it all came a bright, rhythmic singing through my heart: *I'm back Mother. I've come home.*

"They raped us," I said, hearing her voice reach across the River of Ghosts and meet my own. "They raped our land."

It was then that Adam first touched me. It was innocent enough, a hand reaching across a table to another hand in comfort. "I'm sorry, Naomi," he said, holding my cold fingers. "I suppose I've been deliberately blind. I didn't know any of this."

Of course he did not—even after all the battles my mother waged, all the marches, all the flyers, all the slogans. American Indian rights were a popular, romantic movement for awhile, claiming a great deal of media attention. A lot of people, including whites and well-known entertainers, signed on. Eventually most of them signed back off. The reporters and camera crews disappeared.

"There may be something I can do," Adam said. "Believe it or not, I don't have the final say about land purchase. It's up to my board. But I'll look into it further. There may be a compromise our stockholders would accept."

I nodded and took a deep breath, settling my nerves. Reaching for my cold coffee I only then realized that Adam was still holding my hand.

"You can let go now," I said, smiling a bit awkwardly.

He didn't move. "I don't think I can," he said.

We didn't come together right away. But I knew weeks beforehand how it would be, that Adam would know by instinct the spaces I'd want him to fill. I knew he would come to me one night and that we would do what it was in us to do, no matter the consequences.

I knew so many things . . . I with my woman's sureness, I who knew so much that year. What I did not know was that because of us, Beth would die.

CHAPTER 5

I have taken the off-shoot road that leads to the Sound and my cottage. Less than a mile before reaching my own driveway I pass the Lambert mansion. It sits empty, the burned-out portion covered over with piles of lumber and heavy sheets of plastic that flap loudly in every storm. The semicircular driveway is now deserted, the grounds untended, the tall, many-paned windows boarded.

There have been contractors here recently, however. I've seen their trucks, and equipment leans against a south wall, covered with tarps. It has occurred to me to wonder whether Adam is getting ready to move back in. Or will he sell?

I look away, my thoughts steady on the road ahead. Deliberately, I shut out Susan's accusations regarding my responsibility for the way Beth died. Within minutes I am at my own drive, not much more than a narrow track through the woods. My cottage can't be seen from the road; it nestles on a low bank, and by some quirk of nature it was spared in the storm last year. My mother swore it was protected by my paternal great-grandfather's spirit. My great-grandfather was a Wintu chief, or rather leader, as they were called. It was a position passed down from his father, but only—by custom—because he was talented enough for the job. Aside from being liked by everyone, and being a good talker, a chief had to prove himself as a great singer and dancer.

I've often thought I got my love of talking and music from him. But I've never been one to dance.

It is because my cottage is isolated in this way that I am able to remain here since Beth died, I believe. There is healing here—in the trees, the garden, the water, the owl, the deer. Whether there are also ancestral spirits is not an issue. I will take healing any way I can get it these days.

Once back at Crow Cottage, however, it is not so easy to forget the ghosts as it was before my visit to Pete. I feel driven to get my hands in soil, and in my loft bedroom I slip into faded, too-large but comfortable cotton pants that bag in the seat. Next I pull on an old T-shirt with green and brown spots that look much like camouflage, but are actually grass stains and mud. There will be sturdy, waterproof Wellingtons to slip into downstairs, by the kitchen door. For now I pull on socks and quickly pick up around the loft, as I'd been too rushed to think of it earlier. Dirty clothes are tossed over the railing. I follow them via the ladder-like stairs, scooping them up and carrying them to the small washer I've added to the bathroom.

Next I make a pot of dark coffee, which I will put into a carafe to take out to the picnic table next to my vegetable garden. As the coffee brews I quickly clean up downstairs. It helps when my cottage sparkles so that all the countertops and woods catch whatever sun there is. When the inevitable rain begins, I go around lighting candles on the sills of the bay window, the bookcase, the dining room table. Without all this, without light to relieve the shadows, I tend to slip into depression. This past year I have been known to sleep for entire days, huddled in bed and waking only now and then from a nightmare, straining my eyes to see if a waving tree limb is really Beth, smiling, running this way across my lawn.

Still waiting for the coffee, I pass a feather duster over some of my mother's trinkets. On my desktop is her Tsimshian soul-catcher, a long, thin wooden charm that looks oddly like a clothespin with both ends open. This charm supposedly held the soul of a dead shaman, and was placed into a sick person's mouth. The dead shaman's soul was said to enter the patient's body, expelling the demon that had made him sick.

I remember this charm from childhood, though I don't remember my mother ever using it on me. I do recall Vicks VapoRub, chicken soup, and cinnamon tea.

My eyes go to a Cheyenne painted war shield, on the stone wall behind the wood stove. My mother chose it and much of her native decor from a catalog, as if choosing a pair of boots from Sears or L. L. Bean. "Look, Naomi, come see!" I remember her calling out one day from the window seat, where I found her reclining in the sun, a catalog braced against her knees. "What do you think of this Booger Mask?"

I studied it a moment and then said something caustic like, "Not much." To me it was spooky, a skull-face with scars, not to mention the snake atop its head. The ad copy explained that it was Cherokee, and that the term booger came from "*bogeyman*," which was borrowed by the Cherokees from the native language of black slaves.

I gave a loud groan. "Mother, *must* I grow up with that gross thing around the house?"

My mother sighed and went back to turning pages.

Now I look at that mask—which my mother never ordered, but which I myself sent for only a few weeks after she died, in a guilt-ridden, lonely moment—and I remember how difficult a child I must have been. Not at all like Beth, who until those last weeks—

Beth.

Dear God, she is all around me, everywhere. No matter what I do, no matter how many ways I try to distract myself from the pain, Beth is here.

I should never have talked to Pete. In fact, I should know better by now than to read the island rag. There are things one is better off not knowing, and the last thing I need is to be reminded about the night Beth died. Nor do I wish to think about Susan Lambert's accusations, and where this all might lead.

I turn away to the kitchen, blinking. The coffee must be ready. And where *are* those damned boots? I left them right here, right next to the door, I know I did. Where the hell are they?

I find them several moments later outside on the stoop. For a moment I shake my head at myself, feeling despair. It's so hard remembering the common everyday things, since Beth.

The soil in my vegetable garden, because it was once the corral, is rich with natural nutrients. Nearly everything I eat is from this garden, the herb garden by the kitchen, or from neighbors with whom I trade. I dig deep with my fingers into the ground, upturning soil and testing its quality by scent, as my mother taught me to do. Inspecting the backs of lettuce leaves I find the usual pests, and I talk to them, asking them why they are here and what message they bring. This too is my mother's teaching. "If you listen, you will hear their wisdom. You may also tell them you would appreciate their leaving. That way you won't have to spray."

This doesn't always work for me, but I do follow my mother's wishes. Since she suffered from lung cancer, yet never smoked, contemporary medical thinking is that her illness was due to environmental pollution. It was because of my mother that I switched from criminal to environmental law shortly after her death. It was because of her—and her mother, as well—that I fought Adam Lambert, finally, to keep him from buying and razing what little remained of the Wintu land.

My grandmother's name was Sally Jones. And I ask you, what kind of name is that for an Indian, given to her of course, by the white Christian schools? She grew up on the Round Valley Reservation in Mendocino County. It was the only land she knew, though her parents remembered the desecration of their homes in Old Shasta, the murderous "friendship feasts." They raised my grandmother to never forget these things, and when she was of a certain age she became a student of Kate Luckie, a Wintu shaman who lived in the early 1900s. Among my mother's books, handed down by her mother, is a 1935 monograph by Cora Du Bois. In it, she quotes Kate Luckie. I remember only parts, but it is as if those parts are engraved upon my soul.

"When the Indians all die, then God will let the water come down from the north. Everyone will drown. That is because the White people never cared for land or deer or bear . . ."

And, *". . . The tree says, 'Don't. I am sore. Don't hurt me.' But they chop it down and cut it up. God will upset the world, because it is sore all over. Everywhere the White man has touched, it is sore."*

My grandmother, Sally Jones, was not an activist like my mother. She was a quiet woman who prayed to her spirits and held her ceremonies. But she left my mother with one admonition: that she must never let the old ways, the old hurts, die.

So you can see why my mother became who she was. Take a few spirits, a few rituals, add in a Movement that sweeps the country like wildfire, and a husband who's been shot and killed in the cause.

The sun is high overhead now, just beginning its journey west. With daylight-saving, an hour or so past noon. I wipe sweat from my brow and reach down to pull a weed that has sneaked in between two heads of red lettuce. My fingers strike something hard and sharp in the soil. They pause, then expose a glint of metal. Digging furiously, I upturn earth in a sweet, sweet rush of recognition as I see an object half-buried—a gold chain, and on it, a tiny gold butterfly. *Beth's necklace.* I hold it in my palm, my eyes sweeping every inch of it with love and remembering. My thoughts go back to the day I asked her about it and her reluctance to tell me where it had really come from. I somehow knew her story about finding it in the secondhand shop in Langley was not true. And now, again, I wonder—why the lie?

Beth was seventeen. I had watched her grow from an awkward thirteen to the lovely young woman before me. We were here among the vegetables weeding that day, and she was puffing away—complaining about all the bending, holding a hand to her back. I asked her if she was having her period, and she snorted and said, "Why does everyone just naturally assume that if a woman's out of sorts, she's bleeding? That's very sexist of you, Naomi."

With much chagrin, I admitted she was right. I realized something else at that moment, too: how much Beth was changing. I hadn't seen her as often in the past few months. Of course she was busy with school, already applying to colleges and universities for their fall term. Her parents wanted her to go east to Yale; Beth was hoping to be accepted by the University of Washington. I said nothing, but Beth was bright, and I privately believed that Yale would accept her—even as I hoped selfishly that she'd end up right across the Sound at U-Dub.

So yes, she was busier at seventeen than she had been when she was younger, and I thought this was natural enough. I truly did not expect her to make as much time for me. Still, some of her sunniness of disposition had fled. I worried about that, and thought how different things were, now, from what I ever imagined they would be.

Adam . . . how did it go so wrong?

*   *   *

I'd told myself, of course, all those things mistresses
tell themselves and more—the most primary one being that our affair was helping both Adam and Beth.
Five years ago there was all too little joy in that house
with Susan. Her alcoholic, pill-inspired rages, begun
early in their marriage, had been growing more and
more frequent. She wouldn't respond to Adam or his
pleas for therapy for them both, and his hands seemed
tied.

I won't tell you the rest of my reasoning, for if
you've seen any Grade B movies regarding such matters, you surely have heard it all. I won't even bother
to relate my tale in great, sweeping, romantic terms so
that you might then be more understanding of how I
fell into this thing. If you were more understanding
you might then be more forgiving, and the truth is, I
don't want forgiveness. I prefer to feel the pain, to go
deep inside where it burns like an angry red coal and
can wipe out even for a moment the memory of Beth's
trust, and how it was so badly betrayed.

So no, I won't tell you, at least with any thought of
absolution, how Adam and I first came together in my
Seattle apartment with the lights of skyscrapers all
about, the Space Needle like a giant phallic symbol
pricking the sky. And how that made us feel. Or how
the fog came in, mornings, enclosing us, as it seemed,
in a cocoon. How Adam's eyes would happily meet
mine over the breakfast table, our feet in their warm
socks touching, rubbing, as we read the *Times* over
espresso and juice, biscuits, and lacy orange marma-
lade.

I will tell you I learned that love is at its best a
bright, vibrant, caring energy, reaching out from man

to woman, woman to man, and at times even over-flowing to touch and comfort those around it.

I will also tell you what it was like to have Adam as a friend. For above all else, he was that. We talked, that first year, even more than we made love. Adam, a skilled negotiator in business, was adept in the art of personal conversation as well. He had the ability to listen and not feel that he had to fix things, as so many men do, and then get all tense and run because you're "burdening" them with your problems. Adam would listen, nod, make a comment or two. He might ask me what I intended to do. Or if I'd had a bad day and wanted only to rest my head on his shoulder, snuggle in while the world went by, he didn't automatically assume this meant sex. Instead he would hold me, perhaps rub my back and neck. We'd sit quietly like that and eventually he'd get up and go out to the kitchen, fix us something simple, like coffee, or soup, and sour-dough bread.

I asked him once, "Are you like this with Susan?"

"I was. She won't let me near her now."

"Did something happen? Is there some reason she's angry with you?" I was thinking an earlier affair, since when a man is having one, it's a good guess he's either had one before or will again. Otherwise, how could Susan not be happy with this man?

"I don't know," Adam said. "She won't talk to me. I honestly don't know what went wrong."

I could see that he truly did not. And I myself was too inexperienced—or blinded by love—to see that men are terribly unaware of how they hurt women. They simply haven't a clue.

*   *   *

I look off in the direction of the Lambert house, though the woods are thick between us. Between them and me, as well, just before the blackberries begin, is my mother's hedgerow, planted the year we moved into the cottage. There are European hazel, tartarian honeysuckle, and high bush cranberry intertwined. Together, they lend each other a strength no one of them would have had growing alone.

"This is the way we must all learn to live, Naomi," Katherine Wing said on one of those bittersweet days before she died. I remember she was standing out here in her hip-high boots, a smudge of mud on her face, her long dark hair, with its hint of gray, pinned up into an all-weather hat. A hawk flew overhead, and she followed its course to the top of a seventy-foot oak in the woods. There its nest hung in the bare branches, black and spooky, like something out of a haunted house movie.

My mother continued her lesson, one of many she gave out of doors. "The tree doesn't ask if it *wants* to hold the hawk's nest, or if it's smart, or convenient to do so. We need to give to each other, daughter, as nature does. Then we will all have strength."

"Mother, people aren't plants," I said. "Perhaps you expect too much."

"You will learn," Katherine Wing replied, with a sadness in her eyes and on her tongue. *As if she saw the future.* "You cannot hurt another living thing, Naomi, and not suffer harm yourself."

Of course she was right.

I look down now at Beth's butterfly necklace, still gripped in my hand, and I am overcome with sadness so heavy, so thick, it is like a living thing. Yet at the same time my heart lifts. "Did you drop this here that day, Beth?" I whisper softly. "Did some part of you want to leave it here with me, knowing you would soon be gone? Is it a gift?"

The minute that thought is out, however, confusion rushes in.

What is it? What am I remembering?

"*Think, Naomi!*" I hear, clear as a bell. "*Where did you see this last?*"

I whirl about, searching the garden for a form to go with the voice. There is no one there.

"Mother?" I call. She doesn't appear.

But then I know. For I see again, clearly, the prophetic vision my mother brought to me last year before Beth died. I see Beth in the ravine, doubled over and kissing the gold butterfly, then reaching out a hand, a hand I could not feel nor ever will again. My gaze moves back to her other hand, clutching the butterfly to her lips.

And that's it—the message, the thing I'm to understand: *The necklace I am holding now was around Beth's neck when she died.*

But how can that be? How did it get from her body, to me?

Or . . . was the vision in the ravine flawed?

I can almost hear my mother's offended *haruumph.*

A crow skims by overhead, letting out a fierce shriek. Dark clouds move in from the north, and the phone begins to ring inside. Still gripping Beth's pendant I hurry back down the path, wiping my boots quickly on the wood-and-bristle scraper by the kitchen door.

The screen door slams behind me as I reach for the blue phone on the wall. "Yes? Hello?"

No one speaks. "Hello," I say more loudly. "Is someone there?"

My hand on the receiver tightens as the silence continues. It is not a hollow silence such as fills the wire when someone's hung up. Rather, I can hear an ever-so-delicate sound of breathing.

I look down at my other hand, at the gold butterfly cutting into my knotted fist.

So. It's begun again.

"Look," I say, anger flaring. "I know it's you. Don't do this. I'll call the police this time—I swear I will."

There is a click. A dial tone takes over. Grimly, I hang up. Setting Beth's necklace on the window sill over the sink, I wash dirt off my trembling hands, squeezing soap from the funny little black-and-white cow dispenser Beth gave me. Numbly, I dampen a paper towel and wipe dirt from the telephone receiver. Kicking off my Wellies, I leave them by the door.

Moving slowly, unable to think clearly, I head for the shower, stripping off clothes and dropping them in the small square hallway between the kitchen and my mother's old bedroom. At the bathroom door in the hallway I pause, glancing into my mother's room. This is where Beth slept the nights she stayed over, here beneath the slanting beamed ceiling, next to a long row of windows looking out on trees. Propped against pillows are my mother's half-dozen Kachina dolls that Beth so loved. I imagine I can still see her lying here on the bed, curled up in a ball, with one of those dolls in her arms. Her hair would be tumbled, her cheeks damp with tears. Beth seldom stayed over unless there was trouble at home—unless she'd run here to hide.

I turn back to the bathroom. Stepping in, I reach into the shower and turn it on full-force, then stare into the mirror over the vanity as I wait for the water to warm. *It really could have been only one person making that call. But why is it starting again—after all this time?*

I test the shower water and step into the tub. Deliberately, I force myself to focus only on the soaping of an arm or leg. But it's all there, sneaking around the edges . . . the odd appearance of Beth's necklace, Susan's accusations, and now, the phone calls.

I won't go through that again.

Rinsing my hair and body, I dry off quickly. A glance at the clock on the vanity tells me it's five after two. There is still time.

Running naked through the living room and up to the loft, I take a navy blue suit and black Italian heels from my closet. In a drawer I rummage around for stockings and find a pair of off-black pantyhose without runs. Sitting on the bed I pull them onto my still-damp legs, cussing them as they catch. I have not dressed this way in nearly a year. The nylon feels odd against my skin, and once I'm in the suit I find it too light and flimsy after the heavy work pants and flannel shirts I've become accustomed to.

But I am going to Seattle—and I will not go without my "power suit." It has not been that long, and there is still part of me with a foot in that world, a part that cares. I won't be looked at and whispered about by people who knew me "when." *She's gotten odd, you know. Lives on an island and talks to trees. And did you see those clothes?*

In particular, I will not have Adam Lambert think I've let myself go. Or that I've done so because of him.

CHAPTER 6

The elevator takes me swiftly to the twenty-fifth floor. In the thickly carpeted hallway with its soft Monets and vibrant van Goghs I open my bag, pull out a silver compact and check my hair in its mirror. Making one final adjustment, I put the compact away, straighten my shoulders, and enter the office marked DAVID LAMBERT, PRESIDENT.

"I'd like to see Mr. Lambert, please."

The young woman behind the reception desk is no one I know. She asks me if I have an appointment and I admit that I haven't. "Please tell him Naomi Wing is here. It's important."

She gives me a quick look up and down and lifts the telephone receiver, pushing buttons. After a moment she speaks in hushed tones. Nods. Her voice rises, as if reassured. "Yes. Yes, Mr. Lambert. I'll tell her." She hangs up. "He asked if you would mind waiting a moment. He's on long distance, but he'll see you."

I nod and take a seat on one of two cushy white chairs beneath a cherubic Raphael. The floor and ceiling are both sky blue; the effect Susan strove for in decorating this way, Beth once told me, was one of sitting on a cloud. I remember coming here often with Beth, filling in for Susan on museum and art gallery jaunts. "Come with us," Beth would plead. "Mom's home sick, and Dad would like it if you came. You like him okay, don't you?" Her forehead would pucker and I'd give a casual shrug and pretend not to be deliriously happy to tag along with her and Adam, pretend not to be thrilled to be a substitute mom and wife, if only for a day.

The amazing thing was that Beth never guessed. That's how good we became at deceit. Add to that the usual teenage inability to think of one's parents as sexual beings, how could she ever have pictured her father and me together, doing the things we did . . .

With that, there is pain deep in the area of my heart. I close my eyes as I've learned to do and go inside myself, to a small, bright room where all is well. The air conditioning hum begins to fade. Voices in the carpeted hallway, ringing telephones, become a mere whisper. *If only*, I think with one last wave of anguish, *if only* . . . Then even that wanes, and there is nothing but the bright sweet light, and that room where Beth is still alive and . . .

"Ms. Wing? Excuse me, Ms. Wing?" Slowly, I open my eyes. "Mr. Lambert asked me to see if you'd like coffee or tea."

"No, thank you."

"Are you sure?" she asks anxiously. It is clear she's been told to treat me well, and is new on the job. She is doing her best.

"Tea would be nice," I say, forcing a smile.

She looks relieved. "Herbal or regular?"

Please go away. "Herbal, I guess."

That leads to more questions. "Peppermint? Chamomile? Blackberry Zinger?" I am cursing myself for not just taking coffee, but tell her chamomile. When she brings the hot, steaming cup to me several minutes later I breathe in its relaxing aroma, then set it down on a little glass table and close my eyes. Remembering.

The morning after Beth died, my phone call to Adam, thinking we might share our grief. His voice distant and cold. "I realize I haven't been fair to you, Naomi. I told you a week ago we'd have to break things off, but I haven't been consistent. Now I really must insist. No more calls. No more talk. Susan needs me now."

I knew by the stilted way he spoke that she was standing there listening. I also knew it was Susan who'd been calling me for the past week and hanging up. I knew she'd somehow found out about us. Adam knew it by then, as well. He'd been pulling back, erecting walls the entire week. It was almost impossible to get through to him.

Then, suddenly, his daughter was dead. He and Susan both had suffered a terrible loss, and Susan, for her part, was holding on to all she could. I knew something of how she felt, as I felt much the same.

So of course I understood. Part of me, however, hoped he would call back later when he was alone and say something like, "God, Naomi, I'm so sorry. I couldn't say anything else. She's been so devastated about Beth, and she was right there, demanding that I break it off with you once and for all."

I would tell him I understood, that it was all right. We were all hurting, all doing the best we could. Then he would come to comfort me, and to accept the comfort I was longing to give him.

The call never came. Instead, three days later, Travis D. Hartmann, as Adam Lambert's representative, moved in and snatched up the Wintu land that my mother, and finally I, had fought so hard to preserve. He snatched it up before my very eyes, and I confess I made it easy, as my eyes were closed then, swollen-lidded with grief. In short, I did not mind my back, and in law that is fatal. Beth was barely cold in the ground before Hartmann had found a loophole in my latest hurriedly written injunction—written without due thought and under duress the day after Beth died, my fingers shaking so hard I could barely hold my pencil let alone think.

After that I never saw Travis Hartmann, or for that matter, Adam Lambert, again.

Until now. I hear a sound and open my eyes to see that Adam has stepped out of his office. He walks over to me—thinner than I remember, his shoulders oddly hunched forward, as if to protect his heart.

For a long moment he merely looks at me, then without a word ushers me into his office, closing the door behind us. I walk ahead of him to a chair that faces the windows. Gray light streams in, merciless. I blink, and he thoughtfully tilts the blinds to shade my face.

It is these small niceties that rope one in, I remind myself. The larger picture is the one that tells the tale.

"How are you, Naomi?" he asks gently.

I cross my legs and try to act as if my being here is not an unusual event. "All right, I suppose. You?" I note that his short brown hair is silvered now with gray.

He shrugs and sits before me on the edge of the desk. His hands lie loosely in his lap as if they have failed him somehow and no longer know what to do. "Putting one foot in front of the other. I suppose I wasn't doing too bad until recently. But the nearer we get to the anniversary of it, the more difficult it is to believe it's been only a year. Every day without Beth seems a lifetime."

I nod sympathetically, remembering, however, to stiffen myself against feeling too much pity.

"Adam . . . I saw Pete Shelton this morning. He told me about Susan, and what she's saying about me. What's going on?"

He rubs a hand over his forehead and frowns. "I'm sorry. I've been trying to reach you, but I suppose you were on your way here. I wanted to tell you myself."

Moving behind his desk, he sits heavily in the antique office chair his wife had upholstered for him years ago, when they first were married. It is the color of sandstone, and there is a small, almost invisible spot of oil where his head has rested all these years. It is a poignant reminder of just how long he and Susan have been married—in fact, if not in deed.

A few seconds go by as Adam studies a small silver crucifix in a frame on his desk. "Are you praying?" I once asked him, as I was reminded of my mother when she would hold some fetish or other and stare into space. "I suppose," he answered. "Though I'm no longer certain that anyone hears."

It has occurred to me, more than once, to wonder why I have been surrounded all my life by people so devoted to their beliefs, so intent on serving such stern, exacting masters.

Adam raises his eyes finally from the crucifix and says, "Susan has apparently been having nightmares about that night. It haunts her, I think, that she wasn't at the house when it happened. She isn't at all well, and her therapist felt that if we had more facts about that night, a better picture of what might have occurred . . ."

"So it made perfect sense to charge me with some sort of foul play?" I say sarcastically.

He looks pained. "No, not at all. When I sent Travis to study the police files, I hoped only that he'd be able to come back and reassure Susan that Beth's death was a tragic but unpreventable accident. I felt that armed with enough solid facts, he might be able to convince her that even if she'd been on the island that night, she wouldn't have been able to change what happened."

"I see. So instead, Hartmann finds the coroner's records missing and jumps at the chance to make me a villain, not to mention Pete and the entire sheriff's department. Is that it? Nice going. It certainly does let Susan off the hook."

A red flush rises to his cheeks. "I had no idea Travis would leap to that conclusion or that he'd make it public. If he'd talked to me first about it, instead of the press and then Susan, none of this would have happened. I truly am sorry, Naomi."

My smile is humorless. "Well, not to worry, because once Pete finds those records they'll prove me innocent and erase any notion of a cover-up. Only problem is, there you are back to square one again with Susan."

"Naomi, I honestly hope those files are found. But either way, I promise you I won't let Susan go through with her threats. I'll do everything I can to stop her."

"And we both know how good you are at that," I say, then wish I'd bitten my tongue. "Sorry. I don't mean to sound spiteful. But your wife can be relentless."

"We've separated," he says.

"I heard. I guess that means she's over you, right? Oh, except that there's one other little thing. She's calling me again."

He looks disconcerted. "Calling you? You mean phoning and hanging up?"

"Yes."

He frowns. "Are you certain?"

"It's her MO. She just sits there and breathes. Same as before."

He shakes his head worriedly. "I had such hopes that Annie Lowell would be able to help her. It did seem things were going well in the beginning. Annie recommended that Susan have her own place . . . she said it would be good for her if we lived apart, that it would help if she learned to be on her own."

"So much for psychiatry," I can't help saying. "Look, Adam, I don't mean to be glib about this. Susan was Beth's mother, and for that reason alone I'd like to see her get well. But these harassing calls were part of the reason I had such a bad time of it after Beth died. I couldn't work, and I hardly ever slept . . . I even let Travis Hartmann steal the Wintu lands right from under my nose. And when I phoned you for help about Susan you never returned my calls. I finally had to tell your damned machine."

He winces. "I didn't just ignore your messages, Naomi. Please believe that. It's just that I was trying so hard to break things off that last week. You can't know how it was. I'd swear I wouldn't talk to you at all, and then all of a sudden I'd be holding the phone in my hands..." He sighed. "I listened to your messages. They were the reason I got Susan to see Annie Lowell in the first place."

"And the calls stopped." I lean forward. "But now they've begun again, and I'm not going to put up with it. Look, I haven't come here to ask you to do anything about this. I'm just putting you on notice that before it gets out of hand again, I intend to take whatever steps I must to nip it in the bud. It's bad enough Susan is accusing me of murdering her daughter, a child I loved. I won't let her harass me like this as well."

"Are you talking about a restraining order?"

A scornful sound escapes my lips. "Any battered wife can tell you just how effective they are."

"Then, what?"

"I'm not entirely sure. But I'll let you know."

Adam sighs, pushes himself up from his desk, and goes to the window. As he stands looking down on the marketplace of Seattle, I have a chance to study his back, the set of his shoulders, the way he always seems to stand a bit crookedly, as if one leg is shorter than the other. A memory comes back of Adam naked in my shower, Adam at my kitchen stove, Adam tossing another log on the fire, sitting beside me on my sofa as we watch a video on TV, squeezing my hand. I see us laughing together at some joke. And though I know it is good we no longer see each other, know that the pain has been less this past year because I'm not so divided, so frustrated, so damned *yearning* all the time, I must admit that I miss the good moments, the laughter and the sharing. I miss taking walks along the waterfront, shopping at the Pike, attending concerts . . .

I look away, and feel a small shock. My gaze falls on a far wall and a corner niche, where a life-sized statue of the Virgin Mary stands. Beneath it is a photo of Beth. A small bouquet of wildflowers rests in a vase beside the photo. Light from a red votive candle dances across the silver frame, and Beth's lips seem to move, reprimanding me. He was my *father*, Naomi, she seems to cry. How *could* you?

It isn't unusual, I know, for a devout Catholic to have an altar in his home or place of business. Still, this shrine to Beth, so long after her death, strikes me as too much. For some reason, it gives me a chill.

Adam has turned back and is watching me. "I try to keep fresh flowers here for her," he says. "I remember how she always loved picking the first wild flowers each spring, how you and she . . ."

He blinks rapidly, looks away, and clears his throat before facing me again. "I miss going places with the two of you. I always felt it was nice of you to put up with me," he adds with a slight smile. "Though sometimes I felt like a fifth wheel."

"You hated it when we shopped for clothes," I remind him lightly to soften the moment. "You thought we didn't know, but Beth used to poke me in the ribs and say, 'Look at Dad. He's so bored.'

"I wasn't bored," he protests. "I loved watching the two of you. It didn't matter what you did."

There is a small silence as we each, separately, acknowledge our pain. I stick my trembling hands into my pockets and feel the left one close around Beth's gold necklace—the other reason I came here today.

"Adam . . . what did Beth and Susan argue about that last day? Do you know?"

He waves a hand dismissively. "Argue? I don't think they did, not really. Oh, Beth had been wanting to stay here rather than go to school in the East. You knew about that."

"Yes."

"Well, I do remember that on the day of the storm, Susan and Beth got into it on the phone. Susan was in Seattle, and she called between classes to check in with Beth. Apparently, Beth was upset about something, and she chose that moment to talk to Susan again about wanting to stay at home. She didn't want to go to college at all, she said."

"And what did Susan say to that?"

"I don't know . . . I don't recall her mentioning anything more, except that Beth hung up on her."

Adam looks away, and I know what he is thinking: *I never saw her again after that.*

"If only—" He turns back to me. "If only I'd known why she was so determined to stay home, I might have argued more for her side of it. But she wouldn't talk to me, and I thought it'd be good for her to go away, given the condition her mother was in. Naomi . . ."

I look up at him.

"Did you know? Did she talk to you about it?"

"A bit," I say carefully after a moment. "There was a boy, you know."

"The Lawrence kid? But surely that was just a crush, not the sort of thing an intelligent young woman like Beth would allow to get in the way of her future."

I can't help my sardonic response. "Perhaps Beth wasn't thinking like an intelligent young woman. Perhaps she was thinking like a woman in love. You remember love, don't you, Adam? That thing that makes people do things they wouldn't otherwise dream of?"

He flushes, but doesn't respond directly. "Are you saying Beth told you this boy was the reason she didn't want to go away?"

"Not precisely. I do think he was a large part of it."

"But if this kid meant so much to her, why didn't she simply tell us about it? Why didn't she at least tell me?"

I laugh softly. "And you would have done what? Told her she was absolutely right, that she must throw everything over and follow her heart?"

I see my point is made.

"And Susan," I press. "How might she have responded? 'Oh, my, yes, dear Beth. Love has made me deliriously happy, as you can see, so of course I'll support you while you toss aside college and marry the boy of your dreams.' "

Adam looks at me sharply. "Beth wanted to *marry* this boy? For God's sake, I hardly ever saw him around the house. They can't have been that close."

"They were madly in love," I tell him flatly.

"Beth told you that?"

"No, she didn't have to. All the signs were there. They were meeting in the woods every day after school. Beth had a special place, and she's the one who set it up to meet him there."

Adam pales. "I don't understand. Why didn't you tell me about this?"

"Oh please. If I'd run to you about everything I knew regarding Beth, she never would have come to me at all."

"But about something as important as this?"

"It's only important in retrospect, Adam. At the time, you wouldn't have seen it that way. You'd have brushed it off as a crush, the way you did just now."

"Not if I'd known how she really felt."

"You couldn't know. You were too busy, remember, snapping up my ancestors' lands, telling me how sorry you were but that we'd have to break it off, that you couldn't live with your conscience, couldn't go to Confession, couldn't attend Mass, couldn't receive Communion . . ."

I am out of breath, and amazed at the anger I still have, to be able to say all this.

Again, I see I've hit my mark. Yet there is little satisfaction in it now. I sigh. "Oh, Adam. Let's not do this. It's my own guilt talking, that's all."

He frowns. "Your guilt? But why? You never did anything but love Beth. You did everything you could to help her."

"Not everything."

Because the tragedy of it is, I never did tell Adam about my mother's warnings regarding Beth. I was so caught up in my pain that last week, in Adam's talk of ending things, I could barely function at all. When I did try to reach him about the vision of Beth in the ravine, he never returned my call. And I, confused and hurt, hid in my pain. I rejected my mother, her visions, Adam . . . and yes, God and the Great Spirit forgive me, even Beth. I simply ceased to care.

And now, suddenly, as if a door of information has opened, I am remembering Beth in my garden last spring, remembering how tired she was, how pale, and I am putting it all together now . . . first the tiredness, then the vision, with Beth clutching the butterfly pendant. And I am realizing what she meant when she said, or I thought her to say, "Black feet."

I open my mouth to tell Adam what I have only now discovered, and then close it. Would it help him to know? Or hurt him?

Since I know so little of Adam these days, I cannot decide, and therefore I choose silence. It is best, I think, to at least cause no harm.

I take up the little Italian purse that seems so silly now. I cannot wait to get home home to Crow Cottage, where everything from clothes to spirits are so much simpler than here in this office with its echoes of the past. And there is something I must do.

"Adam, I have to go. Will you at least see if you can put a bit of a muzzle on Travis Hartmann? Not for my sake, but Pete's? He doesn't deserve to be dragged through this craziness of Susan's. He's up for re-election. This could hurt him badly."

"I'll talk to Travis, of course. I already have, for that matter. But, Naomi, I can't force him to listen."

"I still don't understand. Hartmann's your personal attorney. He takes orders from you."

"Not any longer, I'm afraid. He started out that way, but last year he was hired on as corporate attorney. He works for my board of directors now, and takes his orders from them."

I can see from the distasteful grimace that he doesn't like this state of affairs, and I remember how upset he was at having to go public with the company and losing control.

"I still don't understand. If Hartmann's not your personal attorney anymore, why is he running errands, looking into police records for you?"

"He didn't actually do it for me. He did it for Susan, to help her get over all this. Susan and Travis have become friends."

"Good God. That's a surprising and rather frightening mix. How did that come about?"

"Last year, after all that happened, with Beth . . . I just wasn't there for Susan. I tried. I swear to God, I tried. But she was too far gone in grief and depression. And the truth is, I couldn't get my mind off Beth, either. Or you."

That startles me, as all this past year I've had images of him holding Susan, consoling her, the two of them coming together as husband and wife in a way they never had before. Bonding over the loss of a daughter.

"I did call you, finally, several times," Adam says. "I thought about you all the time, and I knew how you must be hurting. You never returned my calls."

I look down at my hands, and the emotion that grips me is all too familiar. I remember those calls. They came not in the summer when I needed them, or even in the fall, but the winter. They came far too late.

"Why would I do that?" I say. "For what earthly purpose?"

A flicker of sadness crosses his face. "You felt betrayed, I know that. And you had every right to feel that way, to tell me to go to hell."

"No. It wasn't like that. I thought if I talked to you, you'd just tell me again how terribly sorry you were, but that you really had to be with Susan. And that's the last thing I needed to hear just then. In fact—" I walk away a bit, folding my arms as I turn back, in an offensive courtroom posture that rushes in by habit. "I'm not so sure what you're saying now is true. Adam, isn't it just possible that you're memory is a trifle colored by the passage of time? Maybe you think now that you wanted to be with me again, but if you'd really wanted to, you'd have found a way. You're not the kind of man to be put off just because someone doesn't return a phone call."

He is looking at me with an odd mixture of remorse ... and something else. "My dear Naomi," he says, smiling and surprising me. "I'd nearly forgotten how tough you can be. And how clear-headed."

I almost laugh. "Clear-headed? Is that what you think? Well, if I am, now, then maybe I've learned a few things this past year."

I am feeling very tired suddenly. "Adam, it's just that none of this seems to matter very much anymore. I can't work up enough anger, or even caring for it. So what do you say we drop this. I've got to get home."

I turn to the door again, then pause as he speaks my name quietly.

"Naomi?"

The smooth bronze knob feels cold and heavy, like my heart. "Yes?"

"I wish you could forgive me."

A bitter sound escapes my lips; I can't help it. "If you want forgiveness, go to your priest," I say.

*   *   *

I am on my way back across the central atrium when I see Travis Hartmann himself coming toward me. He carries a briefcase and walks with an important swagger. He is blond, in his mid-thirties, and built like someone who spends his weekends in a gym. Rather handsome, one might think, till one looks into the eyes. They are the color of slate, and I remember thinking when I first met Travis Hartmann in law school that those eyes seemed harbingers of trouble, much like the storm clouds that overhang Puget Sound on any given day.

"Well, well," he says. "Imagine finding you here . . . and after all this time. What are you up to these days, Ms. Wing?"

"Hello, Travis. I might ask you the same."

The rather lop-sided smile he gives me is an odd mixture of distaste and seduction. I've always thought Travis Hartmann couldn't help coming on to women; it is part of the victory if he gets us to not only fall for him but, because of his machinations, fall apart as well. In court, he must always get an opposing female attorney to like him, to flirt back, to give an inch or two, even when she's losing.

For me, he's never held that kind of charm.

"Actually, I'm glad you came along," I say. "Travis, what the hell is all this fuss about missing files?"

"Fuss? I'd call it a demand for Pete Shelton to clean up his act, or he could be out on his ear. That entire office is in disarray. When something as important as an autopsy report turns up missing . . ." He shakes his head sadly, as if actually distraught over this state of affairs. Though if I know Travis, he'll find a way to twist it to his benefit.

"The reports aren't missing, they're misplaced," I say. "Those things happen when offices are moved."

He clucks his tongue. "My, my. Defensive, aren't we? Your sheriff friend can't stick up for himself?"

"Travis, you and I both know you had another agenda when you went through that little act on the courthouse steps. Maybe Adam believes you did it to help Susan, but my money says you're aiding and abetting old Willie Putch. He wants Pete's job, doesn't he?"

Hartmann raises a brow. "And if he does, why should that concern me?"

"Oh please. You handle a significant number of cases in Island County, thanks to Adam Lambert and the connections you've made through him. You'd love having the local law in your pocket, as well." I pause. "Or is it more than that? Do you and Putch have bigger plans? You put him in office and he backs you for . . . what? Congress? The Senate? Putch has even more connections than you, come to think of it."

"Precisely why he wouldn't settle for Pete Shelton's job." Travis smiles. "Governor, perhaps?"

"No chance. Willie Putch is an old horse. He's way past retirement age, and he hasn't the stamina to run with the big boys anymore. The one thing he's wanted for years, though, is Pete's job. He lives on Whidbey, and he likes the idea of having a position of power on a small island like that. Not a whole lot to do, plenty of time to wheel and deal behind the scenes."

"You seem to know a lot about our former colleague."

"I've opposed him in court a few times."

"When you were a lawyer, you mean."

His tone implies that those were the old days, and they're gone.

"I'm still a lawyer, Travis. And if you defend Susan Lambert in her accusations against me, you'll find I still make a formidable foe."

His smiles widens. "Surely you wouldn't defend yourself. 'A fool for a client,' and so on?"

"The only fools I know are the ones who hire you."

Travis Hartmann shakes his head and laughs. "I'd forgotten what a sharp tongue you had. A lovely tongue, nevertheless. And a lovely woman, Naomi Wing. A sheer delight. I've missed you."

"Save the charm for Susan Lambert. I understand you and she have become friends. Come to think of it, Travis, I've known you since law school, and I've never known you to do anything that's completely self-less. What are you getting out of this relationship with Susan Lambert?"

He sends me a smile that says he should be offended but will let it pass. "The truth is I like Susan. And while Adam is my friend as well, I can't help thinking she got a raw deal the past couple of years."

"A raw deal."

"Sure. Look at it this way. The woman gave her first thirteen years of marriage to being the perfect wife, perfect mother. Then you came along and in a few short weeks the whole thing was shot to hell. Sorry—nothing personal, just an observation."

"Well, observe this. Adam and Susan's marriage was over long before I came along. But I'm sure you know that. You've been Adam's lawyer for years."

"Still, they might have worked things out."

I don't point out that Susan was on a downhill slide for years before I turned up, that the pills, melancholy, and constant anger were apparent from the first week I met Beth. One had only to look at Beth, at her tentative reactions when she thought I might be angry at something quite innocent she did, such as dropping a pan in the kitchen or spilling a beverage. Her frightened eyes would flick my way, and she'd hold herself very still until she saw it was safe to breathe again.

"If you care so much for Susan," I say, "if you and she are so close, then you must have some influence over her. Talk her out of pursuing this crazy notion that I had something to do with the way Beth died. And that's what it is, you know. Crazy."

Hartmann narrows his eyes. "Do I detect just a trace of fear, Naomi Wing? Is there something you know that you've never told anyone?"

He has struck a nerve, and I steel myself not to glance away, but to meet his gaze. "I don't think so," I say sweetly. "I've told everyone I know what a jerk you are, Travis."

I turn on my heel and walk without apparent hurry to the elevator, which is half full and just about to close. Once inside I lean weakly against the brass rail that rims the interior. I am drenched, exhausted. I cannot wait to leave Seattle behind.

CHAPTER 7

I see I am on the ferry heading back to Whidbey Island. I don't know how I got here. Habit, I guess. I am sitting in my car, staring at the trunk of the car ahead: a BMW, its finish coated with mud. No espresso in the lounge this trip; I have only the energy, now, to sit and stare . . . at the car, the mud, the rain coming down alongside the boat in desolate sheets.

The winter before Beth died, it rained without ceasing. Between the green of daylight hills the rain was thick and white, like fog, and at night in the beam of a flashlight it resembled droplets of snow. The boats that hadn't been moored properly for the winter tossed in the marinas, and the rain beat down on my roof as Adam and I lay close together in my bed.

When Adam said he loved me, a full five years ago, I understood that this did not mean eventual marriage. I knew he would not leave Susan and take up residence with me. Adam and Susan were both staunchly Catholic. There would never be a divorce, not even annulment. Adam was clear on that from the first: Susan was his wife, they had married in the Church. Besides, he couldn't hurt her that way.

So no, I did not see us married. Cocooned in the romantic glow of early love, however, I did see us before the fire in my little cottage night after night—not just once a week or so. I saw Adam kicking off his slippers as the logs spit and fumed, laughing gently at something he'd read in the *Seattle Times*. I would be painting or perhaps showing him something Beth had drawn that day. I would not, I told him firmly, be a now-and-again mistress, sitting alone on holidays or during one of Susan's many frantic, Valium-inspired crises.

Aside from the fact that we met only in the city—never in my cottage—it happened much that way. We had our idyllic times, and though unwitting, Beth was a part of them all. She was a joy we shared, and I was content with that for awhile.

But love expands the muscle of the heart, and with its newly bloated strength it seems to shout, "Look what I can do!"—much like a kid on a new bike, reckless of any danger in the road ahead.

And so it happened that after some time I began to think that if I could only have Adam's child—Beth's brother or sister—that would somehow bind them both to me. Instead of being simply a mistress, I would be Beth's sibling's mother, and by virtue of this tenuous blood tie (for again, I never imagined it would become a legal one) she might be inspired to turn even more to me.

In my own defense—and that is my training, is it not, to defend?—I must tell you that I saw this at least partly as a means of protecting the child. I longed to reassure Beth that even though Susan might not love her enough, she would always have me.

How I would manage letting Beth know of her sibling's birth and parentage without wrecking the Lambert family—the Sunday outings, the annual picnics and fireworks they held on the island each summer for long-entrenched friends, the yearly vacations in Hawaii, London, and New York—I did not know. In those days it mattered less, somehow, that I work things out ahead. I simply believed, with the faith of the beloved, that things would turn out all right.

It is growing late, perhaps only an hour and a half left until dusk as I pass the Lambert mansion. A dim glow emanates from the front windows, but I pass so quickly I am not sure if the workmen have left on a light, or if it is merely a reflection from the setting sun. I wonder how close the workmen are to being finished inside. I wonder if Adam will come back here to live when they are.

Arriving back at my cottage, I am anxious to get them all out of my mind: Adam, Susan, Hartmann. But there is something I must do first. I wonder if, once I've done it, I will ever again be able to walk in the woods and listen with joy to the elusive owl, thrill to a red-tailed hawk, and share a few peaceful moments with the deer. Or will my guilt over the day Beth died be forever a weight on my soul?

So many sins of omission, and commission. Things

I can never tell anyone about. Travis Hartmann was uncannily right about that.

But first the little ceremonies: the changing of clothes, the fixing of a pot of tea. I must lead up to my task, for I am certain now that the thing I suspected while talking with Travis Hartmann was correct. I know what I will find in a particular little book in my mother's old room. If I had been more Indian, growing up, more interested in the myths and culture of the native tribes, I might have remembered this book sooner. I might then have known immediately why Beth wore the gold butterfly. Perhaps I might have helped her. I might even have saved her life.

That thought is enough to make me stall for time. As I change into jeans from the uncomfortable suit, I think of anything else but what I know is coming. I think of my mother, for instance, who used to say that women's "success" suits aren't all that much different from warpaint. She looked upon makeup much the same way. "Too many women are in disguise," she said often, "one way or another."

Crossing to the French doors that open onto the patio, I snap the outside lights on, including the floodlight at the dock. It illuminates the water's edge, reaching up to include an old bare oak that was struck by lightning years ago. There is movement among the twisted limbs, and I know the crows must be settling in for the night. Feeling chilled, though the night is warm, I lay paper and kindling in the potbelly stove, add small logs, and hold a lighted match to the paper, opening the damper all the way. In the kitchen I put the electric teapot on to boil. In a cupboard to the left of the sink are all my herbs for tea. I choose chamomile and passionflower that I've blended myself to help me relax.

My mother tried to teach me about herbs when I was young, but I didn't believe in them then. Therefore (at least this is what my mother said) they did not work for me. Her recipes for tinctures are in a box over my kitchen sink now. Often I take that box to the table and leaf through it, seeking to discover a new salve for a burn, or a headache balm. I wish, sometimes, my mother were here to argue with me. "But nettles sting like crazy," I remember complaining. "How can you possibly eat them? Don't they tear you up inside?"

"Not if you boil them, Naomi. Don't you ever listen? *Iyeeee!*"

It was true, I never listened. I had my own way of doing things. I was so much like her it was scary.

It is as the tea is boiling that I think I hear a sound somewhere in the house. I cannot be sure, because of the bubbling water. But the hairs on the back of my neck prickle.

It was only a squirrel, I think, *running along the roof.* I have never had an intruder in all the years I've lived here. Still, I am nervous as I turn the tea kettle off and tiptoe quietly into the living room. There is no one there. Entering the hallway, however, fear slices through me. There is a light on in my mother's old bedroom. I know I did not put it on.

"Who's there?" I call out.

There is no answer, and I tiptoe forward. My knee hits something and it tumbles over and falls at my feet with a loud rattle and hiss. My heart leaps into my throat. My gaze jerks down.

It is only the rainstick Beth and I made on one of our weekends together. I reach down to pick it up— a long hollow stick three inches in diameter, filled with beans and rice. It feels strangely hot. I turn it over and over, wondering where the heat could be coming from, but am baffled. My palm begins to burn. Just as I am about to drop the stick it comes to life in my hand. Wriggling and hissing, it becomes a snake. I scream and drop it, jumping away.

The snake slithers away into a corner, and laughter emanates from my bedroom. Shaking, I stare at the door, the light beneath it. Then I run forward, throwing the door open so hard it bangs against the wall.

"Damn you!"

Katherine Wing sits on the window seat, holding a Kachina doll and smiling.

"Now is that any way to talk to your mother?" she says.

She is dressed in jeans and a shirt; her skin is clear and smooth. Sitting here cross-legged, tiny as she is, she looks about ten.

"Mother, you scared me to death! I *hate* this. You can't just keep turning up in my house."

She arches a brow. "*Your* house?"

"Oh for heaven's sake. Ours, then. I'm sorry. But, Mother, you shouldn't do this now, my nerves are all on edge."

I am sorry I swore at her. But then, she is not like any ordinary interfering mother, to whom I could deny a key and insist she call before making a visit.

Wearily, I sink to the edge of the bed. "What manner of trouble are you bringing me today? I warn you, I'm not in a very good mood."

"I suspected as much. You've remembered, haven't you?"

I look at her silently.

"You remembered about the book," she insists slyly.

"Yes."

She throws up her hands. "I must say, it took you long enough. And you were right, daughter. If you'd been more Indian, you might have known what Beth was trying to tell you. You might even have been able to help her before it was too late."

"Are you trying to hurt me, Mother?"

"No. I am simply pointing out that we all make mistakes. Mothers are not perfect people—not even surrogate mothers."

"I would never turn a stick into a snake, however." I cast her an angry look.

"It got your attention, didn't it?"

"Oh, Mother . . ." I sigh. "How long will it take you to learn that you needn't go to such extremes?"

Her shoulders slump. "My dear daughter, life can be boring on this side. I long sometimes for another cause . . . one last great march."

She seems so innocently frustrated, I cannot find it in my heart to seriously fault her for her little trick. After a moment, we both smile.

"So . . ." my mother says, reaching behind her for a book she's stuck behind the pillow at her back. "You'll find what you want, I think, on page twenty-four."

The book's cover has a blue background, and on it is a single white feather. My memory is clear now:

Beth sitting here this same way, legs crossed, poring through these pages. She was thirteen at the time. I'd known her only a month or so, and on this particular day I was just coming in from the garden. She had begged off from helping, as she had her period and was suffering from cramps. I'd told her, only half in jest, that she might find a remedy in one of my mother's books.

"What are you reading?" I asked curiously, as she seemed quite engrossed.

"*Blackfoot Myths and Legends.*" She held the book out so I could see the cover. "Some of them are pretty weird, Naomi."

"I can't argue with you on that."

"There's one that says the Blackfoot girls used butterflies and snakes to ward off pregnancy!" She laughed.

"Real ones? You mean they wore snakes around their necks and live butterflies in their hair?" I am only teasing. "Well, all I can say is *yuck.*"

She laughed, and I did too. "You're right. Yuck. But I suppose if I got pregnant and I wasn't married, I'd try anything." She gave a delicate shiver. "I wouldn't wear *real* ones though! Maybe a pin."

I agreed that a symbol might be best, and never gave our conversation another conscious thought until today. It was just one of those talks one has with a teenaged girl: only half listened to and soon forgotten.

"I was so blind, Mother," I say now. "The butterfly pendant . . . I never once considered that it might be more than a simple gift, the kind of token a boy gives a girl when they're dating."

"But how could you know?" my mother asks, her tone surprisingly sympathetic. "Beth wasn't the kind of child to believe in myths, was she? At least not to the point she'd depend on them?"

"No. But she was open to ideas. And curious. I remember her saying once when I had a sore throat, 'You don't really know what might work. Give it a try, Naomi. Cover all the bases.' Then she went out to the kitchen and boiled me up a terrible tasting tea from one of your recipes."

My mother looks at me sharply. "Did it work?"

"Maybe. I guess so."

She nods wisely. Smugly.

"And if I hadn't been so wrapped up in pressing Adam for some kind of commitment last summer, I might have seen more clearly what was going on with Beth. Instead, when she didn't look well I thought it was just that she was tired—first from graduation, then from getting ready to go away to school. Not to mention the usual problems with Susan."

"But if the child wasn't candid with you, Naomi . . ."

"And that's the other thing. Why wasn't she? Why couldn't she come to me when she found she was pregnant? We were so close. At least up to those final weeks."

"Daughter, you of all people should know that when a man and woman, or a boy and girl, first fall in love, they shut everyone else out. They think they are all-sufficient. And they certainly don't think they need their mothers anymore."

She gives me a huffy look, and I know she is reaching into the past and talking about me and Pete now.

"I didn't want to talk to you about Pete," I say, "because I knew you were trying to take him away."

"Child, listen to yourself! He was a boy! I was old enough to be his mother."

"I am no longer a child, Mother. And I never thought there was anything sexual or romantic about it. You wanted Pete because he was young and strong and you were getting tired. You wanted him to fight your battles for you."

My mother's eyes narrow dangerously. "Pete Shelton was a young man looking for adventure, a mission, something to raise his life above the ordinary. I saw this and I used it, I'll grant you that, to entice him into working for the Movement. But people cannot be taken away from us, Naomi. They never in the first place belong to us, only to themselves. Furthermore, daughter—no one has ever had to fight my battles!"

"And Pete found that out after a while. Once you got your second wind, he left, didn't he? He came home to Whidbey. But by then it was too late for us."

"Ah . . . so you're still blaming me for all this, are you?"

"No. I haven't the energy for blame anymore. Things just are, and all we can do is live with them."

"With our *perceptions* of them, you mean. There is always more than one version of the truth, Naomi. We each have our own stories, we mothers and daughters."

I glance down at the book in my hands. "Enough, Mother. What was Beth's truth? Do you know?"

She looks at me sadly. "It's up to the child to tell you, Naomi. I can't interfere."

I can't help it; I laugh out loud. "*You?* Not *interfere?*"

Her expression becomes reprimanding. "Not while she is still on this side, Naomi. First she must cross the River of Ghosts."

I feel a jolt, like a kick to my stomach. "What do you mean? Beth is still on this side? I don't believe it!"

"It's true, daughter. Night after night I see her kneeling on the bank of the River of Ghosts, weeping."

I am on my feet. "Weeping? You see Beth, and she's still on this side, and she's weeping? Mother, is this another of your tricks?" I would grab her and shake her, but I know there is nothing there.

"Naomi, please! I told you the truth about Beth last year and you did not believe me. Now she is dead, and our land is gone . . ."

I throw my hands up angrily. "Stop it! I've lived with that guilt for a year. What are you trying to do to me?"

"Nothing to *you*, Naomi. Only for the child. You could help her."

"How? What can I do?"

"Uncover the truth. Set her free."

"But what truth? *Was* there foul play? Or do you mean about the baby?"

And then it strikes me. "Mother, there was nothing in the coroner's testimony at the inquest about a fetus."

My mother nods wisely. "And why do you think he didn't mention that little fact?"

"I don't know. Incompetence? It was a bad time on the island just after the storm. Between that and his drinking, Gray Steen might have actually forgotten by the time he got to court."

"Did he have the autopsy records with him in court?"

I strain my memory to think back. "I'm not sure. I wasn't in very good shape myself, and I don't think it occurred to any of us to question his testimony. We had no reason to think it was anything but an accident. Mother . . . are you saying Beth wants this to come out? Did someone hurt her? Was it Curt Lawrence? Was he the father?"

"Naomi, please . . . why not ask her yourself?"

I follow my mother's eyes across my lawn to the bank of the Sound. It is raining again, and in the circle of light from the dock I see a bright red raincoat, a flash of blond hair. My heart almost stops. How many times over the years did I see that red coat—that same wheat-blond hair?

"Beth—?"

I turn back to my mother, but she is gone. I look again at the edge of the water, disbelieving. Never in the year since she's died have I had a vision of Beth.

Then I am running, running through the cottage, out into the rain, and it is cold on my face, but my heart is warm. Tears stream down, hot on my cheeks. "Beth!" I cry again.

The figure straightens, turns, looks into my face.

It is not Beth, but Susan.

CHAPTER 8

She is shivering, half frozen. I cast a look about, wondering if she's alone. "My God, what are you doing here?" I say.

Tears stream down her blue eyes. Mascara runs, the finely molded lips twist. Susan's hands run distractedly through her hair. "I thought I saw her! I thought I saw Beth."

We both look around now, and I shiver as well. There is no one here. No Beth. Yet I wonder if this is where my mother sees her . . . here on this bank—my bank—weeping. Did Susan somehow sense her daughter's presence here?

I turn back, and cannot help but feel sympathy for this woman who has suffered such a terrible loss, and who stands before me this way, pale and weak. "She isn't here now," I say gently. "Susan, are you out here at the mansion alone?"

She is staring into the water and doesn't seem to hear me.

"Susan?"

Her blank gaze turns my way. "What? Oh, yes. I'm alone."

"What are you doing here?"

"I don't know . . . looking into things."

A cold wind comes up and she hugs herself. She's lost weight, it seems, and the once-soft planes of her face are now far too lean. There is so little in her to be angry at, in this moment, or afraid of.

"Come inside," I say. "I'll make you a cup of hot tea."

Her eyes clear. For a moment they narrow, and I see something that startles me, that I can only interpret as pure hatred. I fully expect her to hit me in the face. But in the next moment she says with an odd formal courtesy, "Thank you, Naomi. I would like a cup of tea."

CHAPTER 9

I've hung the red coat inside my door, and Susan now sits with a tea cup poised on her lap, knees together, finishing-school style. We have been talking about the weather, the state of my garden and if the zucchini is good this year. I feel as if I have fallen out of reality and into some strange Fellini film.

"I have a wonderful recipe for stuffed zucchini," Susan says brightly. "I'd be happy to share it with you. I have it at home. For the most part it's lots of garlic, a touch of nutmeg, and nearly a whole stick of butter. Of course, the cholesterol count is high. You absolutely must use real butter or it's not the same. Then you pour a nice tomato sauce over it and put it under the broiler a few seconds. Pure heaven."

I try to respond as an ordinary friend or neighbor would, though my mind is frantically casting about for what to do about Susan. Now and then she flicks me a look that gives me a chill. It is gone so quickly, however, that I'm left wondering if I actually saw it or imagined it.

It is in one of these moments that she says abruptly, "Are you and Adam seeing each other again?"

I am caught so off-balance from that, I cannot answer at first. "I . . . no."

She nods as if it's as she expected. "It couldn't last. Nothing ever does with Adam." A shadow crosses her face.

"Susan, I don't think we should talk about this."

That flicker in her eyes again, cold and hard. "You must have quite a deal of guilt about all that, Naomi. Loving another woman's husband . . . stealing her child."

"Susan, I'm sorry. I truly am very, very sorry that I hurt you. If I could go back and do things over, there are many things I would change."

"Oh really?" Her tone is angry now. "And what exactly would you do differently, Naomi?"

"I . . . for one thing, I would try harder to bring you and Beth together. She loved you so much, Susan. I never took your place as her mother. You've got to believe that."

She jumps to her feet. The tea cup rattles to the floor, spilling its contents. "Don't tell me what I've got to believe! You and Adam, you think you've got me fooled again, don't you? I know you were there at his office today. I know you're plotting together behind my back. It's just as it always was."

I set my tea down and stand, facing her. "No, it's not. I swear to you. There's nothing going on now between Adam and me. It's over."

"You think so?" She laughs bitterly. "It's never over

with Adam. He holds on. He'll squeeze the very breath out of you, if you let him."

"You're wrong. He's not that way."

Again she laughs. "You think you know him better than me? You think because I was taking pills and drinking, I didn't know what was going on?"

"No. No, that's not what I think at all. But I may have seen a different side to him."

She makes a scornful sound. "Oh, he has that, all right, different sides. You'll see."

"I told you, it's over, Susan. It's been over a long while."

"He'll be back."

"No. It ended when Beth died. You know that." I don't say, *You made sure of that*, but it's what I'm thinking.

Red spots rise in her cheeks. "Don't you dare talk about Beth!"

She turns away abruptly and stumbles, reaching for my desk to steady herself. Her gaze rests on my mother's Tsimshian soul-catcher. She takes it up in a trembling white hand and studies it. After a moment she says more calmly, "What is this?"

I am grateful for her change in mood, and try to match it. "It's called a soul-catcher," I say quietly. "The Tsimshians used to put it in a person's mouth when they were ill. It was my mother's."

She nods. "Beth told me about it once. She told me about you and your mother too. You didn't get along, did you?"

"Beth said that?" I cannot hide my surprise.

Her chin juts out, and there is a glint of triumph in her gaze as it swings to mine. "Of course. You think she didn't tell me about you? At times it was all I heard. 'Naomi this, Naomi that.' I got so sick of hearing your name. *Sweet Naomi. The one who did everything right.* Never lost your temper with her, never ignored her, never wished she wasn't around."

"I enjoyed her company, Susan, that's all. It had nothing to do with being *sweet.*"

She laughs again, though there is no humor in it. "Oh, I know that, believe me. I guessed it the moment we met five years ago, when Beth brought me to meet you. I knew you were after more than my daughter."

"Susan, please. Let's not do this again."

But her eyes have gone vague again, and it's as if she is talking to someone else, not me. "I knew it for certain, of course, at the Christmas party. Beth's last birthday, her . . . her last party. And I tried so much harder with both of them that night. Beth and her father. I'd bought a new dress, you know, that white one, the one that clung to every curve, and I'd been on a diet for weeks so I'd fit into it by Christmas. Every morning I'd get up and try it on, just to see if it fit." Her mouth trembles. "As if a dress could make the difference. Make Adam love me again, instead of . . ." She looks directly at me now, clenching her fists. "Instead of you."

My own mouth trembles under the weight of her pain. "I never wanted to hurt you, Susan. I swear I didn't. And I am so terribly sorry."

She looks at the soul-catcher, then at me, her voice breaking. "I wonder about Beth's soul. I wonder if she's all right. I know you Indians see things. You have some sort of psychic powers, don't you? Do you ever see Beth? Do you talk to my little girl?"

"No. No, she doesn't come to me."

Susan scans my face as if searching for truth. She sighs and looks away, back to the soul-catcher, a thumb stroking the polished wood.

"She did love you, Susan," I offer again. "It's always difficult . . . they tell me . . . with teenagers."

Her back is rigid, though her shoulders heave. She turns to me, tears now streaming down her pale face. She still clutches the little wooden soul catcher, and her arms are folded across her chest in an "X," much like the statues of saints one sees on cathedral walls. I have always wondered if they are beseeching God in prayer or merely protecting themselves from His wrath.

"If Beth ever . . . if sh-she ever comes to you," Susan stutters, "will you tell her something for me?"

I want to tell her that Beth will never come to me, that my mother is the only one she comes to now and with good reason. I am almost tempted to tell her why—and what actually happened the night Beth died.

Another part of me only wants to be rid of her, doesn't trust her, remembers that this woman has talked of charging me with her daughter's death.

I can only nod. "What would you like me to tell her?"

"That I'm sorry," she says softly, her face twisting horribly. "Just tell her I'm sorry . . . please!"

Spinning on her heel, she runs across the room and dashes out my door. I grab Beth's raincoat and run after her, calling. But she runs as if the devil himself were at her heels, and I have not even left my stoop before she disappears in the mist, her thin white blouse a ghostly flicker as she passes through the nearest stand of firs.

The rain is coming down now in torrents. In the naked oak tree a dozen or more crows cling to thin branches that sway and crackle in the wind.

CHAPTER 10

Though I would rather cut out my heart than speak with Adam again today, I go back inside, lift the phone, and call him at his office, on the private line. Though the secretaries and receptionists will have left by now, I take a chance that he will be there, working late as he so often did. He is.

"I thought you should know," I say without preamble, "Susan's out here at the house. She doesn't seem well."

"She's there on the island? But there's nothing on. No phone, no heat, and the place is only half boarded up, it's a mess . . ." He pauses, clearly worried. "You talked to her?"

"Yes. She was down at the water's edge, in Beth's red raincoat. She said she was looking for Beth."

"Damn! It's even worse than I thought, then."

"It does seem that way."

"I'll have to . . ." He falls silent. "Naomi . . . I know this is a terrible imposition. But it will take me over an hour to get there. Would you . . . ?"

"Baby-sit?" I cannot hold back the sarcasm. "No problem."

"It's just that if she were to do something to herself . . ."

I sigh. "I know. We've already got more guilt than we need. Okay, I'll keep an eye on her till you get here."

There is evident relief in his voice. "Thank you. Naomi . . . ?"

I lay the phone down softly, hugging myself against a sudden chill.

Pulling on Wellies and a raincoat, I head out and into the woods. Fallen needles from the tall Douglas firs make a soggy carpet beneath my feet, and I've got to watch where I walk. There are roots from thick shrubbery sticking up as well, laid bare by the recent heavy rains. It is a root such as this that Beth is assumed to have tripped on before falling into the ravine. Personally, I have never believed it. She knew these woods too well. But I've never wanted to think much about it, either, as thinking about it will do no one any good, least of all Beth.

Still, I can't help what runs through my mind as I follow the well-worn trail from Crow Cottage to the Lambert mansion. There was no real trail before Beth; it was she who blazed it that first year when she was thirteen. She played in the woods often when the weather was nice. She'd lie in a clearing on her stomach, talking to grasshoppers, praying mantises, caterpillars . . . building little hills in the dirt for them to climb on or burrow into. There is one such clearing on the other side of the Lambert grounds, quite near the fatal ravine, and I am possibly the only person who ever knew that Beth spent hours there in the summer sunshine, reading, daydreaming, hiding out from Susan's wrath. She told me about it long ago and swore me to secrecy.

"It's warm and sunny there, Naomi, and the grass is so soft and green. I'm the only one who knows about it, I think, except for the deer. Sometimes I go there early in the morning when the grass is still all dewy, and it's so beautiful! Everything glistens like diamonds, and lately there's been a little fawn just lying there in the middle of the clearing. He lets me come and sit near him, but sooner or later his mommy shows up and shooes him away."

With that she had looked uncommonly sad, and I couldn't help wondering if she was thinking more of her own mother than the deer. It seemed sometimes that Susan's mission in life was to spoil Beth's every small joy.

Of course, I was undoubtedly prejudiced, looking at it as I did from the viewpoint of a mistress. The wife is always so faulty, the husband so fine.

Drawing near the Lambert house I see the same lights on as earlier. They fan out from the living room and kitchen across the now-ragged lawn. The rest of the house is dark. I shiver, for it does not seem a friendly house, nor has it ever, even at its best, to me. There has been too much pillaging of the land. Though a new lawn was trucked in, the original trees, majestic old fir and cedar, were razed for the reconstruction. Adam always talked about replanting, but it somehow never happened. To my admittedly prejudiced imagination, therefore, the Lambert mansion seems a sore thumb, crying out by day and night. It does not surprise me that no good came from the building of this house, no happy hearts or joyful times.

That I myself have had some responsibility in that is something I readily admit, though I do not wish to ponder it at the moment.

I go up the steps to the colonnade porch and ring the brass bell. It tolls mournfully inside, echoing through empty halls. I listen, but there are no other sounds, no footsteps nearing the door.

Twisting the knob, I find it gives. Wiping my Wellies on a fiber mat, I open the door and step inside. "Susan? It's Naomi. Are you here?"

My voice resounds mournfully, too, it seems. There is still no answer.

"Susan?"

I have been here only once before, at Beth's seventeenth birthday party, the Christmas before she died. I went under duress, as Beth had insisted on inviting me and there seemed no way out. It was a terrible night, fraught with guilt and paranoia over every seemingly "knowing" look or word from Susan, and I left as quickly as possible. I do, however, remember the basic layout: a large, mirror-lined "ballroom" for entertaining on the left, an even larger, luxurious living room on the right. Bedrooms upstairs. Formal dining room and gourmet kitchen at the back. I poke my head into the living room and see no one, though a light is on. Furniture is draped with white sheets, and a torn, ivory-colored satin drape flaps at a broken window. Rain streams in. The floor beneath the window looks soaked; an odor of mildew pervades everything.

My nose twitches. I fight back a sneeze as well as depression. I cannot even imagine Beth here in this house. There is no sense of her soul lingering here, no sign that she ever made a dent on the spirit of this house. The house, in fact, with its heavily frescoed ceilings, its pink marble floors and pillars, seems to wrap itself around me, choking me, and I stand here fighting for breath.

Reaching out a hand I grab for the molding around the wide doorway, for balance. "Susan?" I call up the curving stairway in a louder voice. I must find her and get us both out of here. I'll insist she come back to Crow Cottage with me; it is not good for people, I sense, to be inside these walls.

Little needles of tension stab at the back of my neck, an instinct my mother claimed I inherited from my warrior ancestors; an actual physical sensation that warns of impending doom. Cautiously, I move toward the stairs, looking up to the long gallery above. "Susan? Are you up there? Adam's coming from the city. He asked me to look in on you."

I am at the bottom step, my foot on it, when I feel something behind me. My heart nearly stops. Wheeling about, I half expect to see knives flashing down. Instead, not inches from my face, is Susan's. She has made herself up heavily. Her eyebrows are black and in a high arch, her lips scarlet and garishly large. There are bright spots of red on her cheeks, and she is wearing a sheer black negligee that is trimmed in black sequins. Beneath it she is quite naked. She stands back from me and makes a pirouette.

"*Now* which one of us do you think he'll want?" she asks in a voice that is hysterical rather than sultry. She rubs her hands over her breasts and juts them out, as if to show me how proud she is that they are still firm, that she is still able to entice.

I remove my coat and hold it out to her with a shaking hand. "You look lovely, Susan. But it's cold in here. Put this on, why don't you?"

She throws back her head and laughs, ignoring the coat. "The two of you . . . you thought I was just the quiet, mousy little wife, didn't you? Did he tell you we never made love—not once in the past ten years? Did he tell you I couldn't stand him anymore? *Do this, Susan, do that. Plan a party, Susan. for all my dear, sweet business friends. Be here, Susan. Watch Beth. Don't go to work, don't do anything but what I want you to do . . .*"

She takes a few steps back into the ballroom. I follow, an unwilling yet captive audience as she does a bizarre light dance step across the room, as if waltzing. This is all the more bizarre for the strangeness of the ballroom itself. Crystal chandeliers are reflected over and over in the mirrors lining two walls, and holding court at the far end of the room—odd in these surroundings—is a statue of the baby Jesus, one I know to be called *The Infant of Prague*. He holds a miter and is decked out in velvet, ruby-studded robes. Beneath the statue is a tiered wrought-iron rack holding scores of red votive candles, every one lit. As Susan dances near the statue, they flicker wildly.

"I fooled Adam, though," she continues. "All those nights he thought I was staying over in Seattle to study? I had my own friend!"

My mouth drops, and she laughs smugly, whirling about to face me with her hands on her hips. The black negligee swirls; folds of chiffon and sequins glitter. "Surprised, are we?" she taunts in a singsong voice. "You thought you were hiding something from me, and all the while it was me hiding something from you! And you . . . poor little Naomi, so guilty, thinking you were taking Adam away from me. Well I didn't *want* him, do you hear? I *never* wanted him . . . not since the day we married! So you see, you were doing me a favor."

I can hardly think with this grotesque scene playing out before me. Yet in my gut I feel a knife, as through my head whirl the months, the years, of hiding all that love, of being alone on holidays, weekends . . . the lies, the shattered hopes.

"Why didn't you just tell him?" I muster at last. "Why didn't you set him free?"

"*Adam?* Free? He'll never be free, that's the joke," she cries. "Because it isn't me who's holding him, you know—it's the goddamned Catholic Church!"

Her words echo through the near-empty ballroom. The statue of *The Infant of Prague* seems to tremble at the blasphemy. But through the lunacy Susan adds softly, "You knew that, didn't you, Naomi? You knew he'd never divorce me because of the Church, didn't you? I would have had to die." She pauses dramatically, then tosses back her hair and smiles. "That's why he tried to kill me."

"*Kill* you! What in the name of God are you talking about?"

"Not much in the name of God, my dear Naomi. Adam was hoping I'd do myself in with all those pills.

He never even tried to stop me."

"That's not true! He's been after you for years to get help, to see someone. You refused."

She smiles. "That's what he told you, is it?"

I hesitate for only a second before answering firmly, "Yes. That's what he told me. And I believe him."

"Then you're a fool."

"Are you saying you *do* want to get well? You'll go with me now to someone who can help you?"

The blue eyes flicker.

"Well, Susan?" I have not been trained as a lawyer for nothing. If there's one thing I know, it's how to lead the unsuspecting witness into a trap. "I know the director at The Pines. It's a good place, more like a spa than a hospital. Will you check yourself in?"

Her gaze slides away from me, and she jumps, as if startled. From the doorway comes a shocked voice. "What the hell's going on here?"

"Adam!" Susan displays surprise, then breaks into a too-bright smile. "Darling! Your lover wants to put me away!"

Adam looks from her to me, a question in his eyes. "Naomi?"

"Adam," I say carefully, "Susan thinks you never wanted her to get well. I told her that if she really does want to get well, I know someone who can help."

He takes a step toward his wife, stretching out a hand. "Susan. . . ."

"Don't touch me!" she cries, jerking back. "And get out of my house, you and your oh-so-loving mistress! Just get out and leave me alone!"

"I'm not leaving you here, not like this. You're not—"

"What? Sane? In my right mind? And just what would that be, Adam? Believing every word you say? Believing you when you said you were in Seattle nights, working? Sleeping in your office, wasn't that what you said? Or, no—I remember. You said you were staying at a hotel—alone. Oh, I was insane all right, insane to believe you. But I'm in my right mind now. And it's all quite clear. First she steals my child, then my husband. Or was it the other way around? Well, never mind. Just don't think you fooled anyone. Beth knew, too."

The knife that Susan has already so skillfully placed in my gut now twists.

"What are you talking about?" Adam says, paling. "Beth never knew!"

"You think not? Then why did she die?"

"Susan, stop this!"

"It was because of you, both of you, that Beth didn't want to live anymore!"

"That really is crazy," Adam hurls back. "You've got to stop. You can't go on like this."

"And therefore I should let you put me away? Oh, I don't think so, my dear, thoughtful husband. Besides, you're bluffing. You've never really wanted me talking to people about what went on here. You're afraid I might slip and tell something you'd rather people didn't know."

"Adam," I say quietly, "What is she talking about?"

He doesn't answer. Instead, he takes a step toward Susan, his face dark with anger. She stumbles back.

"Lay one hand on me, and I'll tell everyone what your little lover here did to Beth the night she died."

Adam's fists clench. "Naomi did *nothing*. *Nothing*, do you hear?"

"And you, Adam. What if I tell them about you? You told the police you were in Mukilteo that night, trying to get home, but the ferry was down. Well, damn you, Adam Lambert—*I* was at the ferry! I didn't see you, and I didn't see the Mercedes. Where the hell were you, really? Where were you when our daughter died? And when I was standing on that ferry dock screaming at the harbor master to get me a boat, get me home no matter what it took? Oh, it made a great story for the papers, the worried father racing home to his daughter. But you and I both know that you were not there. So where the hell were you, my faithless husband? And how did you get to the sheriff's office on the island so soon after the storm ended? I was on the first boat going over the next morning, but you were already there, weren't you? There with your lover—"

Raising a hand to her forehead, she pales and looks suddenly faint. The rage seems to leaves her in a rush, and Adam reaches out a hand, but Susan whirls away. The too-sweet perfume hits my nostrils as she runs to the end of the ballroom and throws herself at the foot of the statue of *The Infant of Prague*. There she kneels and covers her face with her hands, weeping. "I didn't mean it, I didn't mean to do it. Oh God, please forgive me!"

Instinctively, I move to follow her, thinking to somehow help. But Adam grabs my arm. "Wait. Leave her alone. She'll be all right."

"But—"

"Believe me, it would only make her worse."

Together we stand helplessly and watch as Susan, her shoulders heaving, tumbles words from her mouth like a litany. "Sweet Jesus, I didn't mean it, I didn't mean it, I did everything I could. Please forgive me, forgive me, oh, sweet Jesus . . ." She sinks to the floor, face down, arms outstretched.

"Adam, we've got to—"

"Wait." There is a sound at the door. We both turn. "It's Annie Lowell," he says, softly, so that only he and I can hear. "Susan's therapist. I asked her to meet me here."

The woman is shaking out a black umbrella and placing it, closed, inside the ballroom door. Her pale blue trenchcoat seems to be soaked clear through. As she removes it I note that she is tall and quite thin. She removes a matching rain hat and shakes it and the coat, then her hair, which is short and dark. Adam starts toward her and she puts out a hand in a delaying gesture. Dropping the coat and hat, she approaches, her large, dark eyes resting not on us, but Susan.

"How long has she been like this?"

"I've only been here a few minutes," Adam answers. "Naomi?"

Annie Lowell's troubled gaze swings to me.

"She came to my cottage over an hour ago. Actually, she was down at the water's edge, and we talked there, then she came inside. She was upset when she left, and I followed her here."

The psychiatrist gives me a sharp look.

"I was worried," I feel compelled to explain. "I wanted to see if she was all right."

"I asked her to come," Adam adds.

There is something akin to contempt in Annie Lowell's eyes before they drift again to Susan. She starts toward her.

I turn to Adam, and he shrugs. But he looks as awkward as I feel; it is as if we've been both reprimanded and excluded.

The psychiatrist slips off her shoes and walks lightly across the bare oak floor. As she reaches Susan she stoops down beside her. Placing a hand lightly on her shoulder, she speaks softly. I hear the murmur of her voice, but can't make out the words. Susan shakes her head, making a low, distressed sound in her throat. Then she gives a great shudder and crumples. The psychiatrist catches her and, sitting on the floor, holds her in her lap, letting her cry. "That's right," she says in a soft voice, "get it out, get it all out."

Susan continues to cry in loud, heartbreaking sobs. Adam takes a step as if to go to her, but Annie Lowell spots it and shakes her head. He stops.

"I should be with her," he says.

"Could you help her?"

He looks at me, and there is sorrow in his eyes. "Probably not. She listens to Annie now better than me."

I understand his pain. Having looked after Susan all the years of their marriage, it must be difficult to let go. Even more difficult to know that one is no longer needed.

Annie Lowell and Susan are standing. They walk toward us, the therapist supporting Susan with an arm around her waist. The black negligee is ripped above Susan's breast, as if she's been tearing at it. One thin white hand holds the shredded remnants together to cover her skin. On her face is a look of embarrassment now, and she does not look up to meet our eyes.

"I'm taking her home," Annie Lowell says. "I'll keep an eye on her. She'll be all right."

Adam looks doubtful. "Shouldn't she be in the hospital? I can arrange—"

Again there is that look of scorn as her gaze slides from Adam to me. "Haven't you both done enough damage for one day? No. What Susan needs right now is a good night's sleep, not to be locked up in a strange place. My patient and I can decide together, in the morning, what steps to take then."

"With all due respect," Adam says, "I don't think Susan is capable of making decisions about the kind of care she needs."

Annie Lowell's eyes flash with anger. "With all due respect, Mr. Lambert, you and Susan are no longer together. You are not her legal guardian, and she has every right to decide for herself the kind of care she needs."

"But she's not getting better—in fact, if anything, she seems much worse."

At this Susan's head snaps up. Her eyes narrow. "Stay out of it, Adam! Leave me alone, get out of my life. Annie is right. Maybe *you* don't think I'm getting better, but you don't know me. You don't know what's inside my head. You never have."

"Susan—"

"No, don't touch me! Don't ever come near me again. Don't you get it, Adam? I don't love you anymore. I don't want you around me. It's over."

Strangely, Susan seems more lucid now. And stronger. Adam blanches and steps back as if struck.

His shoulders hunch in that self-protective posture I saw in his office earlier.

My heart goes out to him. He truly is helpless in the face of Susan's wrath. At the same time I see her in a new light, and I cannot help but believe she means every word.

I see all this, of course, from outside the circle. Standing back in the shadows I know as I have always known that I am not part of this picture, nothing but an observer. I realize, too, that the same might be said for Adam now.

I only wonder how long it will take him to know this.

He turns to me. "I'll see them to the ferry." There is a question in his eyes, which are dark with pain.

"Yes," I say after a moment, and nod.

I am in my cottage, alone, lying beneath the eaves in my loft bedroom. Below, tips of the old cedar by the kitchen window brush softly against the glass. The last shards of a fire crackle in the pot belly stove, and a scent of leftover smoke and ash is bitter in my nostrils and on my tongue. Across the screen of my mind flash images of Susan in that black negligee, Susan flaunting herself before me, then before Adam . . . Susan here in my cottage earlier, tears streaming down her face, crying for Beth.

What is my responsibility to her now? I wonder. Is she my sister—are we one, as all people are said to be one? And did my actions over the years affect her, even when she was not aware of them?

When it comes to that, would she be hurt by my actions now? I see her damning Adam, telling him not to touch her, that she does not love him any longer. Was this true? Or only the ravings of a madwoman?

I don't know. And that is the hell of it. I simply don't know.

There is a soft rustle at my door, below. I lie rigid, staring at the ceiling, holding my breath. Footsteps cross my living room floor and pause at the bottom of the loft steps. "Naomi?"

"Yes."

The steps move upward and draw near. Closing my eyes, I wait. Moments later Adam sits beside me on the bed, touching my eyelids softly with his lips. "It's been so long," he says huskily. "So long."

With my eyes still closed I take his hand and place it on my breast. "Yes," I say. "Too long."

He lies down beside me, holding me close, stroking my face then my breast. My cheek is against his chest and I can hear his heart. It is racing. His breath displaces strands of my hair. That small movement makes me reach for him, crying out softly, and my hands are all over his skin, and his on mine. It is as if I've been starved for a year, and here before me has been placed the banquet at last.

Briefly, I remember Susan again. And then she is gone.

CHAPTER 11

Pale morning sunshine slides through my stained glass window. I sit on the window seat, while in my bed, his head on my pillow, Adam sleeps. He snores lightly, a sound that has always been music to me. Yet this music . . . does it, in some small way, now resemble a dirge to my most precious, dying ideas of myself . . . the person I thought myself to be?

He wakes and turns. I watch him stretch and then I cross the room in bare feet to sit beside him. "Good morning." I stroke his hair back from his forehead, then run a finger along the deep furrow in his brow. It is almost like old times. My heart turns over—a poetic idea, but I would swear I can feel it move. It is good to have him back, good to be able to help him, to ease his pain.

"Good morning, sweetheart," he says, taking my hand and kissing the palm. "Have I told you lately that I love waking up with you?"

"Not lately."

He smiles. "No. Well, we'll have to amend that."

"It seems we just did."

He draws me down to his chest. I stretch out, one leg thrown over his, and nestle in the old familiar pattern. Together we listen to the cedar dripping early morning dew on the roof. I remember that we have never been together here in my bed before.

"They caught the ferry all right?" I ask.

"Yes. I talked to Susan again about the hospital. I told her I'd pay for the best." He gives a sigh. "She laughed at me."

I am silent.

"Naomi, it's not that I think money can fix things. I just want her to know that I care about her and want to help."

"You could have just said that, Adam." It has always been difficult for him to understand this. Faced with overwhelming problems in his marriage, Adam has more often than not reached for a financial, rather than an emotional, solution.

"Believe it or not, I did try," he says. "She nearly spit in my eye."

Despite myself, I can't hold back a smile. He tilts my chin up. "What's so funny?"

"I'm just seeing a whole new picture of Susan. She may have fallen apart last night, but I think she's getting stronger overall, don't you?"

"Stronger? Is that what you'd call it?"

"Well, I think that when people are trying to pull away from a relationship they may do crazy things, but it's all part of feeling their way through new emotions, learning new strengths."

He strokes my back. "Are you speaking from personal experience?"

"Partly. In those first few weeks after Beth died and we parted last year, I spent entire nights in the woods communing with my ancestors, burning smoke, and screaming inside. I wore my mother's beads and feathers, and I didn't wash for days on end. Anyone who came upon me would almost certainly have thought I deserved to be locked up."

Adam holds me closer. "I'm sorry you had to go through that."

"I'm not, at least not anymore. It helped me get through it, in some strange way."

He shakes his head. "I'm sorry, but I don't see that happening with Susan. After last night I'm more inclined to worry about what she'll do next. I'm particularly worried about you."

I push myself up and sit cross-legged, facing him. "Do you think that possibly your worry about Susan might be something you need to start dealing with?"

"What do you mean?"

"Only that you always saw her as your mission. It must be hard to let go."

"Mission?" He frowns.

"Isn't that what she's been, since long before we knew each other? Weren't you always there making sure Susan was all right, that she hadn't fallen asleep and left the stove on, hadn't tripped and was lying unconscious in the tub or at the bottom of the stairs?"

He moves irritably. "I guess I never saw it as a mission. It was my responsibility as her husband."

"Hmmm." I slip from the bed and, with my back to him, pull on my terrycloth robe.

" 'Hmmm?' What does that mean?"

"Nothing. Just hmmm."

"Boy, I wish you wouldn't do that. Where are you going?"

"Shower."

"Now? Why don't you come back here and lie with me a while."

"Not right now. I'm . . . I need to wake up."

My words, of course, have a double meaning. For I am remembering what Susan said at one point last night. *"He'll be back. You'll see."*

What does she know of Adam that I don't? How did she know this—last night, and Adam coming here—would happen, when I honestly believed that it would not, not in a million years?

I feel in danger of falling once more into that deep, dreamless sleep of futile love. This time, I must keep my eyes wide open. I dare not lose myself again.

Adam is gone . . . into the city, a meeting, and I sit on my dock huddled into a lumberman's red-and-black jacket for warmth. The air is cold, as it is early still. A thick curl of steam rises from my coffee as I scan the first pages of the *Journal*. And yes, here it is, the article Pete warned me about. The interview with Willie Putch. My name isn't mentioned, but there are questions raised regarding Pete, and the way he runs his department—hints that the missing files might not be lost but were purposely removed: ". . . to the benefit of person or persons as yet unknown."

The effect is one of an opening sally, with the promise of more to come. Details follow, repeated from yesterday's paper.

Yesterday. Has it been only twenty-four hours since so much happened? It seems impossible.

"See you this evening?" Adam said as he was leaving, his lips at my ear. And I, who had been so determined not to simply fall into the old pattern again, drew his mouth down to mine and whispered against it, "Yes. Hurry back."

Setting the paper down I sip my good strong cup of Seattle's Best and stare across this little inlet to the woods that encircle the Lambert property. Beyond my sight, but clear in my mind, is an old fir tree whose trunk splits in two a third of the way up. Another third and the two trunks come together again, becoming one. There's not much healthy greenery above them, however. Only a few scraggly branches.

There is an old story that says the roots on either side of this tree were nourished differently, and therefore a trunk that should have been as one was forced to split and become two. Each went their separate ways. Later, when they were both weathered and strong, they came together again.

I once believed that could happen with people.

Now, sitting here with Adam's scent still fresh in my memory, I'm not so sure. One can link hands and hearts, even bodies, in all good will. One can hope for a return of the old passion. But often it simply isn't there. Perhaps you limp along, pretending for awhile. Yet sooner or later, what you end up with isn't much more than that undernourished tree.

Will this happen to Adam, I wonder, and me?

CHAPTER 12

It is just after nine, and I am making use of the soft morning light to toy with an idea for a painting. It began as a scene in the country with a small boy and girl playing by a brook, nothing very original or exciting, as my heart isn't in it. But the more I put brush to canvas, the more the girl child looks like Beth. The boy child has no face. I stare at that blank face, wondering, and then, in one swift motion, lift my rag and smudge the boy out completely.

It is just then that Pete calls.

"Hi," he says. "Are you riding this morning?"

"I hadn't planned to. Why?"

"I'd like to meet you . . . say, down at that beach where we used to ride?"

"Oh? What's up?"

"I'll tell you when I see you. Ten too soon? I need to be back in the office by eleven-thirty."

There is urgency in his tone, and I am thinking there must be something new about Beth's missing files. Or Susan's accusations.

Is he going to arrest me? No. If that were the case, he'd have me come to Coupeville. Or he'd be at my front door with handcuffs.

It comes to me, suddenly, how long it's been since Pete came to Crow Cottage.

I agree, finally, to meet him. Hanging up, I sigh and clean up my paints. With one last wondering look at the smudged boy on my canvas, I head upstairs for a change of clothes.

The sun is high and warm when I arrive at the beach. I am riding a roan, Calypso, borrowed from the McCoy's farm down the road. I've thought of buying another mare, but there are cash constraints since I haven't been working. Now and then I tutor someone from the university, and that keeps me in food, paints, and canvases, but I have to be careful. I struck a bargain with Pat McCoy, paying him back by mucking out his stalls once a week.

Briefly I wonder what will happen to Calypso if Susan has her way and I'm dragged off to jail. Will he get enough exercise? Pat McCoy is getting on a bit; he doesn't ride as much as he used to. Then I remember my mother saying, "The Great Spirit watches over us all, Naomi. Why do you worry so much? Maybe it's because you don't know the Great Spirit anymore."

Well, in recent times I've spoken quite often to the Great Spirit, and though I'm not entirely convinced there's no need to worry, and that I still must fiddle away at things to fix them on my own, I do understand that letting go now and then isn't all bad.

With determination, then, I let go, putting Susan and my shaky future at the back of my mind and giving Calypso his head. He tears across the sand and rock the way Allegra did in the old days—face a bit sideways to the wind, the heavy muscles bunching with each lift of hoof, black tail flying. I know if I don't rein him in soon he'll have us all the way to Langley. When we ran out of beach we'd be up hill and dale, through rivers, creeks and woods. I laugh and yell, "Whoa, boy, easy," slowing him down to a trot. For the first time in two days, I begin to feel almost good.

Checking my watch, I see that it's a few minutes after ten, and Pete's late. I shade my eyes and cast a long look over the rim of hill, remembering that he used to come from that direction, on a trail just above the Snohomish ceremonial rock. The rock is still there, but there are houses on the hill now, private wooded lots, and I don't know if Pete's managed to find access through those woods. For that matter, I don't know if he even rides here anymore.

I am remembering, of course, the romantic, long-haired young man of twenty years before. So it comes as a jolt when I hear the roar of a motor approaching from behind me and see the present-day Pete, black hair clipped to just below his collar, tearing across the sand in his shiny red Jeep.

The Jeep draws near and hurtles to a stop, spraying sand and startling Calypso. The horse shies, whinnies, rolls his eyes. I speak to him quietly, "Easy, boy, easy now," and flick an irritated look at Pete. "I thought you were riding with me."

"*You're* riding with *me*," he says, grinning. "Hop in."

"You may have noticed I'm on a horse, Pete. You expect me to strap him to the fender like a deer?"

133

"Tie him up behind. I'll drive slow."

I shake my head, still annoyed, but I'm curious to hear what Pete has to say. Finally I dismount, reassure Calypso with soft words, and tie his reins to the extra wheel mounting on the back of the Jeep. "Good boy. Good boy. It's okay."

I climb in beside Pete, take another look at Calypso, and as Pete throws the Jeep into gear, I say, "Easy, easy," but to my driver this time. The Jeep begins to move at a snail's pace. Calypso digs in his heels, snorts and tosses his head, but then has a change of mind. As we pick up speed to five miles per hour, he follows quietly enough behind.

"You look nice today," Pete says with a sideways glance my way.

"Nice, is it?" I give him a look. "But how can that possibly be, when I'm wearing pants? Of course, I suppose I could have worn a dirndl skirt and ridden side saddle like a proper lady, flashing a wink of bare knee."

He has the grace to flush. "Sorry. I didn't mean that the way it came out yesterday. I'm just worried about you, Naomi."

"Worried? Why?"

"You've been out at that cottage too long alone. It can't be good."

I laugh. "Living in the country, no stress, no time pressure, nothing but vegetables, trees, and an owl to hoo me to sleep at night? That's bad?"

"You know what I mean. You've got all that education and experience, you should be putting it to use. Your mother—"

My voice softens dangerously. "I didn't agree to meet you to talk about my mother."

"Dammit, this isn't about her, it's about you. Katherine pulled a lot of strings to send you to Harvard. It seems like you might—"

"My mother did not pull strings," I remind him angrily. "I got in on a quota."

"She worked her butt off to keep your tuition paid."

"I worked my own butt off waiting tables."

"To pay for books," he argues, "and incidentals. Katherine—"

I reach for the door handle, my voice shaking. "Stop. Let me out. If I'd known you wanted to drag all this out again, I never would have come."

I am remembering now why I've seen so little of Pete in the past ten years. And I wonder: Why do men do this? Why do they feel they have to teach us, instruct us, look after us? The corollary to Adam and Susan, of course, does not escape me.

Pete throws out a hand and grabs my arm, then pulls the Jeep to a stop. "Sorry. I didn't mean to get into any of that. Forget it, okay? The truth is . . . I have a favor to ask."

"A favor." I am still tired from last night's events, and not precisely thrilled. "What do you need?"

He looks around, scanning the beach, which is empty aside from us. "Why don't we take a walk? I was up all night, and I need to work some kinks out."

He does look tired, now that I think of it. And worried. "All right, But no more talk about my mother, or I'm leaving."

He smiles. "Deal."

Sliding from the Jeep, I walk around to check on Calypso and give him a reassuring pat, then follow Pete down to the water's edge. From behind him I have time to note that his shoulders are slumped as if they carry a great burden, and I am reminded of his troubles with Sally Ann and their marriage. I have been so caught up in my life and its latest developments, I haven't thought about Pete. At best I've assumed his problems must be temporary, the sort of thing married people go through time and again. Now I wonder if things are far more serious than I'd thought.

"Pete . . ." I have caught up and stand with him, looking down at the small waves that lap at our feet. "How's it going today? With Sally Ann, I mean."

He shoves his hands into the pockets of his leather jacket and kicks at a rock in the sand. "I'm pretty sure she's leaving me. She's talking about taking the kids to her mother's in South Dakota."

"But she's done that before. Last summer, in fact. Doesn't she visit her family every summer?"

"This is different. She won't be back."

"Oh, I can't believe that! Sally Ann wouldn't actually leave you, no matter how bad things get. She's crazy about you."

"Not anymore."

"Pete, I just don't get it. Is there something you haven't told me? Is there someone else?"

He begins to walk. His stride is fast, his legs so much longer than mine, it's hard to keep up. "Hey. What is it? What's going on?"

He stops, turns, and we stand face-to-face, me puffing, and him angrier than I've ever seen him. "Tell me about you and Adam Lambert."

"Adam?" I struggle to hide my surprise. "Pete, that's really off the wall. We were talking about you."

"I don't want to talk about me. I want to know if you're starting up with Lambert again. And if you are . . . is it serious?"

Now I'm angry. "I don't really think that's any of your business. And I don't understand why you're even asking me. What's it got to do with anything?"

He shrugs.

"And what makes you think . . ."

"One of my deputies saw him driving in on the highway last night. He followed him to the Lambert house. Then he followed him to Crow Cottage. After that, he didn't need to follow him anywhere at all . . . not till seven this morning."

My face grows hot. "You were *spying* on me?"

"Not you. Lambert. You were just part of the package. A surprise package, I might even say."

"Well, if you already knew this, why didn't you just say so? What were you trying to do, trap me?" Then it hits me. "For God's sake, Pete . . . why are you having Adam followed?"

The wind has come up, and it lifts Pete's dark hair from his brow. The skin of his forehead is taut, the eyes red and strained; there are circles I've seldom seen before.

"Dammit, Pete, you said you need my help. But this is no way to go about getting it. Spying on me, having Adam followed—"

He grabs my shoulders. "Naomi, don't you get it? It's got to be you being involved with him that's driving Susan Lambert crazy. If it wasn't for that, you think she'd be raking up all this old stuff, calling you a killer, demanding we press charges? This all adds up like a classic case of revenge. And you want to know what I think? I think Hartmann himself took the damned reports. I think he stole them the other day while I was out at lunch. And I think he did it for Susan Lambert."

"You think . . . For Susan? That's crazy. Why would he?"

"Figure it out. He steals the files and hides them so nobody can prove you're innocent. Maybe you'll never be proved guilty, either, but your reputation will never be the same. With this hanging over you, try getting another job in a law firm, ever. Wouldn't Susan Lambert just love that? She loses a child, you lose a future. Tooth for a tooth. Least, that's the way she'd see it."

"But even Travis Hartmann wouldn't get involved in something like that! If the truth ever came out, it'd devastate his own career."

Pete shakes his head irritably. "Naomi, you're talking like an innocent, like you didn't go to Harvard and practice the profession for years before you quit. Look, think of all the angles Hartmann could play with this one. First, he's hand in glove with Putch, who'd kill to make me look bad so I'll lose the coming election. There's motive number one. Then Susan Lambert comes along with this idea to discredit you, and he not only sees the opportunity to help Putch, but he's got to do it anyway, to keep Adam Lambert happy. The guy pays Hartmann one hefty salary for having just this sort of slick move in his repertoire, I'll bet. And so far as any risk is concerned, tell me Hartmann's not smart enough to know precisely how to cover his ass."

I pull away angrily. "Just one moment. How did Adam get into this? Are you saying you think Hartmann not only stole the files, but Adam *paid* him to do it, to keep Susan happy? You can't really believe that."

He looks at me sadly, as if facing an incompetent child. "If you were married to a loon like Susan Lambert, wouldn't you do almost anything you had to, to keep her happy?"

"But not *this*. Adam wouldn't do this. Not hurt me, to help Susan . . ." My voice trails off uncertainly as I remember that Adam left me last year for precisely that reason—to help Susan.

"You see what I mean," Pete says.

"And will you stop reading my mind!" It's as if I have no thoughts that are my own around him. Yet his are closed off to me, and have been since he fell into file behind my mother, leaving me and running off to fight, with her, some Indian battle or other.

Of course, I think with compunction, I have only myself to blame. I deliberately turned off the connection, refusing to read Pete any longer, not wanting to know what he thought, who he thought about, or, in particular, who he loved. Every time he left me to go on the road with my mother, I was afraid he'd meet someone—terrified that when he came home I'd see another woman in his heart. Better not to know, I reasoned, not to imagine, but to simply close up and say good-bye.

I am immediately surprised and ashamed that I still feel so much emotion over this. It seems that every time I think I've come a long way something hits me between the eyes to show me I've mistaken an inch for a mile. *Hello*, the child Naomi calls from behind the wave of a tiny, vulnerable hand. *It's me — still here.*

"I'm sorry," Pete apologizes. "I didn't mean to upset you."

"It's all right. I'm sorry too. I just didn't realize you knew so much. Dear God, Pete, has the whole town been talking?"

"About you and Lambert? Not that I know of. I just couldn't help . . . well, you know. Noticing."

"But we were so careful. We never saw each other on the island. Never once."

"So how did Susan Lambert find out?"

"I don't know. I've always supposed she just divined it, the way wives will."

Which isn't quite true, as I think I do know the moment Susan discovered her husband and I were lovers. "Actually, it may have happened last Christmas," I say. "There was a party at the Lambert mansion . . ."

"I know," Pete inserts dryly. "I was there."

I look at him, embarrassed. "Of course you were. Sorry, I forgot."

"Maybe that's because you didn't have eyes that night for anyone but Adam Lambert."

"You noticed? That's how you knew?"

"Let's say I wondered if there might be someone, even before then. But I never saw you with anyone, and I also thought you might just be so caught up with Beth, you didn't have time for a man in your life. I guess it should have occurred to me. I mean, there you were, the three of you going places together, the wife out of it half the time on pills and booze. Talk about opportunity."

"You don't have to say it like that! We never did anything around Beth. She never knew . . ."

He raises a skeptical brow.

"She didn't," I insist.

"Not ever? Even at the end?"

At this I hesitate. But then I move on, impatiently. "We didn't plan to love each other. We didn't plan to hurt Susan. It just . . ." I search for the way to explain it, something that will help him understand. Perhaps even help me understand.

But Pete says softly, "Just *happened*?" There is a flicker of anger in those dark eyes.

"Damn you, Pete Shelton. If I didn't know better I'd think you were jealous."

"It's not that. I care about you as a friend, and I don't want to see you get hurt again. If Adam Lambert is involved in the theft of those reports—"

"You don't even know if they're stolen. This is just some wild theory you've concocted. Besides, it wouldn't really help anyone to steal them. All we've got to do is get Gray Steen to reconstruct his medical report, write it up, and that's that."

Pete shakes his head. "I've already talked to Steen. Our redoubtable Island County coroner says he can't remember everything."

My mouth falls open. "Can't *remember*? Details about the death of a seventeen-year-old girl who was well-known and loved on the island? Whose father is a millionaire businessman in Seattle?"

He shrugs. "Well, after all, it's been a year, and his examination of the body took place right after that killer storm. We lost seven lives in Island County in twenty-four hours. Gray was overworked. I can see where he'd forget details.''

My disbelief is clear. "That's not it. He's been hitting the bottle again, hasn't he?''

No answer.

"Dammit, Pete. Why on earth doesn't someone do something about him?''

"I can't answer that, Naomi. You know politics. The man's got friends. Look, I've got to ask you some questions.''

"Questions. That's why we're meeting here today?''

A look of discomfort crosses his face. "It's part of it. Naomi, the way I see it, the one way we can get Susan Lambert to drop all this is to satisfy her about the way Beth died. Now, what's she's claiming is that you were the last to see Beth alive. She said she talked to her daughter on the phone that afternoon, and Beth said she was on her way over to see you. Now, look . . . I know you've answered this before, and you've always denied seeing Beth that day. Frankly, I don't think you've been straight with me. You did see her that night, didn't you?''

I walk a few feet away, shove my hands in my pockets, and wonder how much to tell him. Enough . . . but not too much? Give him an inch, he'll take . . .

Looking back at the hills, I can't help thinking wearily of all the secrets they must hold. So many thousands of centuries of history, so many people who thought their own particular problems were of paramount importance, only to be dust now. Dust to dust, as the Christians would say. And who would be shocked by any of their secrets now, who would even care?

I turn back to Pete and say carefully, "I guess it doesn't matter now. Yes, I saw Beth that night."

His face darkens. He frowns. "Why the hell didn't you tell anyone? Especially at the inquest. Why didn't you just say you'd seen her?"

"Well, for one thing, I didn't want to hurt Adam and Susan. Pete, Beth called me in tears. She'd just talked to her mother on the phone, and she said she'd begged to be allowed to stay here and go to school at U-Dub. Susan apparently said absolutely not, she was going East. They had a bad argument, Beth threatened to leave home, and somewhere along the way, Su-san—according to Beth—told her to 'just go ahead and run to her precious Naomi.' Beth did. She came to Crow Cottage nearly hysterical. She told me she hated her mother, that Susan was cruel and had hit her more than once in the past few weeks. That was the first time I'd heard that, and it shook me. Beth said she wanted to come live with me. She said she'd rather die than stay at home."

"For God's sake, Naomi!" Pete says angrily. "What did you say?"

"Well, what Beth didn't know was that immediately after she phoned me, and before she got to my house, Susan called. She sounded calm and quite reasonable. She told me Beth was upset with her, and asked me if I'd back off if Beth came running to me, as she put it. She said that if I wasn't always there, Beth would have to turn to her instead of me. I told her I wasn't trying to come between them, that I'd never wanted that. I told her I'd see what I could do."

I am tired, suddenly, and sigh, sitting on a rock at the edge of the water. Folding my arms around my legs, I continue with my recital, which is true so far as it goes. "When Beth came I told her I'd never been a mother, but it had to be the toughest job in the world. I told her that Susan did love her, and that if she yelled at her, or hit her, it had to be only because she'd reached a breaking point, and that she'd reacted the way she did on the phone because she was jealous and hurt. I told her to go home and call Susan, to try to work it out."

I look at Pete. "Beth was an exceptionally good child, I think. But children, no matter how good they are, know how to push their parents' buttons. Beth wasn't beyond that. She'd probably said something to Susan like, 'If Naomi was my mother, she'd let me stay here and go to school.' And Susan, already hurting, responded the way she did out of anger and jealousy. It may not have been the best response, but it was all, at that moment, she could do."

"You sound like you've been giving this a lot of thought," Pete says. His tone is less angry, but there is still an edge.

I shrug. "I've had a year to live with it. And if nothing else, it's helped me to understand my own mother better. If I'd been on her side more often, instead of always challenging what she did and the way she believed, maybe we'd have gotten on better."

"You're not blaming yourself for that, are you? Katherine had that tough shell. It wasn't always easy to get through."

It's not often, over the years, I've heard him say a word in my defense rather than my mother's, and I flash him a grateful look. "I'm not really blaming either one of us. I just wish we'd both taken the time to understand each other better, while there still was time."

"Well, you know, it's easier to see that from hindsight. There's a lot of kids on this island that I talk to about things like that, just hoping to smooth things out at home for them when there's trouble. But kids don't like to listen."

I smile. "Why should they? They already know it all. *We* did."

He laughs. "Who was it that said he was amazed, between the time he was eighteen and twenty-six, how much his parents had learned?" Then he sobers. "So what else happened that night, Naomi?"

I look away. "What makes you think anything else happened?"

"It had to, for Beth to have been so upset."

I get up from the rock and begin to pace, thinking, *Well, I've given him his inch, and he's after that mile. That would be Pete.*

Another inch, then? But no more.

"While Beth and I were talking," I say, "Adam called. Things hadn't been going so well between us, in fact we were in the midst of breaking it off. I hadn't actually seen or heard from him in two weeks, and I wasn't expecting to. Well, Adam's call was intercepted by my answering machine, and I didn't pick up, as Beth and I were in the midst of all that *Sturm und Drang.* What I forgot was that I hadn't turned the volume down on the machine, and her father's voice came through loud and clear. 'Naomi, darling,' he said. I remember the words as if they're engraved on my heart. 'I know I said we shouldn't see each other anymore, but I'm worried about you. This storm looks like it's getting bad. Listen, I'm coming out there. I'll check on Beth first, and then I'd like to see you. Please be there. I . . . I do love you.' "

I am shaking at the memory, and cannot meet Pete's eyes. But I feel them on me. Are they judging? Surely no more harshly than I. "In that moment, Beth learned everything—all the things we'd tried so hard to keep from her for four years. She learned it all. Her face . . . it was so terrible. So pale. I tried to talk to her, to explain somehow, though what in the world could I say? She had just had that argument with Susan. And I had turned her away. I'd told her to go back home and make up with her mother, for God's sake. Then to hear her father . . ." My voice breaks. "Pete . . . she ran out into the storm. And I've always wondered if she ran from me directly into that ravine . . . if that's what killed her."

He grabs me by the shoulders. "How much guilt do you need to carry around in life, woman? And you're not even looking at the facts. The burn marks on her face, for one. They had to have come from the kerosene lamp in her own living room, when it tipped over. That means she didn't go directly from Crow Cottage to the ravine. She went home."

"I know. I've thought about that. It's the only thing that's saved me, in fact. But even so, she would still have been feeling betrayed when she got home. She might even . . . Pete, I've never said this to anyone else. But what if she was so hurt and angry she picked up that lamp and threw it? What if Beth started the fire, then had to run from it? Don't you see? The guilt would still be mine."

"No," he says staunchly, firmly. "The most you might do is share it."

My smile is shaky. "Oh, Pete. You're standing up for me again. Reminds me of the old days when you marched with my mother, and she was angry because I didn't come too."

He drops his hands. "Shoot, Naomi. You had better things to do. I knew that. Katherine did too even if she'd never admit it."

"But were they better things? Going to Harvard, learning the law? What have I done with all that since?"

"You'll get back into it. You've still got it, it hasn't gone anywhere."

"But my zest for it has. No, I don't know if I'll ever go back. Especially if . . . Pete, what am I going to do about Susan? I can't tell her what happened between me and Beth that night. To tell her what Beth said about her now would be terrible. And for Adam to learn that Beth heard what he said on my machine, that she knew—and that this may have led, even partly, to her death? I just can't do it."

Pete sighs and is silent for several moments. Finally he says, "How bad off do you think Susan really is these days?"

"I don't know. One moment she sounds almost reasonable, the way she did that night on the phone. The next? I tell you, Pete, she seems a madwoman. I think there's more to it than depression. She goes into these moods, and she acts truly deranged."

"Naomi, you think maybe Susan—and for that matter, Adam Lambert—are covering something up?"

"Covering up? I can't think what."

"Well, we always have to look at the family when there's a suspicious death. Stranger things have happened. And if one of them did something, that might explain why all this is going on. Especially now, when the anniversary of the, uh . . . you know, the death . . . is coming up."

"Pete, that's crazy! I can't believe you're even saying it. Besides, Adam and Susan weren't even on the island when it happened. And they're both devastated over losing Beth."

He looks at me skeptically. "You used to think like a lawyer."

"Well, in the last year I've discovered I like thinking like a human being."

"That doesn't mean you have to let yourself be taken in by people. If I were you I'd ask myself what Adam Lambert is really up to."

"Pete, the man's daughter is dead! You said it yourself, we're coming up on the anniversary of that death, and it's bringing everything back. Besides that, he's wracked with guilt because he thinks he wasn't a good enough parent. So is Susan."

I cannot talk to him any longer about this. There are too many ghosts being raised, too many memories I simply can't deal with. Aside from that, I can't risk Pete ferreting out more facts, things I haven't yet told him. And never will.

"Is that all?" I say a trifle coldly. "Are you finished with your third degree?"

"Yes," he says. "I'm finished with that."

"Then I'm out of here." I turn back toward Calypso and the Jeep.

"But I also had a favor to ask," he adds. "I don't suppose this is the time for it now."

"Hardly." But then I relent, turning back. "All right, what is it?"

"It's not for me. For some people I know, over in Mason County."

"Mason County. You mean the Hood Canal?"

"You got it. They need someone like you on the Coordinating Council, someone who'll look after their legal interests in meetings with county officials."

"Pete, they've got all kinds of native groups working on that. Have had, for years. They don't need me."

"On the contrary, they need all the help they can get. The waters are so contaminated now, they can't support enough fish for both the Indians and non-Indians in Mason County. Plus, there are all those Asian immigrants competing to harvest mushrooms and basket-making materials. Naomi, this is about survival. They'll have to come to some sort of compromise."

"It won't help. It's too late to reverse most of the damage."

"But not too late to stem the tide."

I sigh. "How did you get involved in this?"

"There are a lot of us involved. Naomi, some of our own people are responsible for abusing the land in recent years. But a lot of us care about bringing a healing about. You know environmental law. We could use your help."

I look at him standing there so earnestly, pleading his cause, and see in my mind's eye my mother, urging him on. Urging *me* on. "Get involved, Naomi," she is saying. "Maybe you'll win, maybe you'll lose. If nothing else, it will take your mind off things."

In truth, those are words I've been hearing from her for the past year now. But I don't feel ready. Not yet.

"Sorry, Pete. I can't do it. Not now."

"When, then?" he says stubbornly. "When are you going to start living again?"

"I am living," I answer just as stubbornly. "It may not be your way, Pete, but it's mine."

Turning on my heel I stride back toward the Jeep, and when I reach Calypso I put my arms around him and hug him. He nuzzles my neck, and I try to lose myself in the moment. But Pete comes up behind me and says, "Naomi, one thing. Be careful, will you? Don't be walking into dark corners."

I swing back to him. "What do you mean?"

"Just that you need to keep your eyes open now. Don't just accept everything Adam Lambert says."

Angrily, I untie Calypso and mount him, taking the reins. "You know, I keep forgetting what a suspicious mind you have. Sometimes I *almost* forget you're a cop. You always see to it I remember, though, don't you?"

I urge Calypso into a trot, then a gallop, leaving my old friend and his cynical warnings behind. Yet despite myself, I cannot help hearing Susan's words to Adam last night. "You don't want people to know what really went on around here."

What on earth did she mean?

Though an even more important question might be: Why do I let people who have their own ax to grind, make me—even for a minute—doubt my own mind?

CHAPTER 13

"I had a call today from your friend the sheriff," Adam says that evening at Crow Cottage. We are sitting side by side on my dock, on chaise lounges, and the air is warm, the sun just sliding down beyond the tips of the firs. Across the sky stretch fluffy white clouds that are tinged with deep rose and aqua. It is a perfect summer's night, or would be, if the anniversary of so much pain for both of us was not drawing near. I also cannot help realizing that this is the first time we have sat here this way, openly, without fear of being caught by either Susan or Beth. It is a bittersweet moment, as I would give it and a thousand others to have Beth here with us tonight.

I look over at Adam and he sets down the *Seattle Times* he has been leafing idly through and reaches for my hand. "Pete Shelton wants to talk to me about the missing files. And about Susan."

"I thought he might. I saw him today."

"Did you? What did he want?"

"I'm not precisely sure. He knows you were here last night. One of his deputies saw you. Adam . . ." I glance over at him, watching his reaction. "Do you think Travis Hartmann might have taken those autopsy records and only pretended he found them missing?"

He gives a start and drops my hand. "Travis? Why on earth would he do that?"

"Oh, I don't know. For Susan? To give her something to use against me?"

He swings his legs off the chaise lounge and sits sideways, facing me. "You don't honestly believe Susan would do that? Or that Travis would go along with her? Is this what Pete Shelton is thinking?"

"Well, you know cops. They have to consider every angle."

"Even so . . . It sounds more like he's trying to whitewash any responsibility his staff may have in losing those files."

I draw up my legs and hook my arms around them. "Actually, I've considered that, but it isn't the way Pete does things. He's always been good about owning up to responsibility. Look at the way he's stuck with Sally Ann."

"Sally Ann?"

"His wife. I like Sally a lot, always have. But they're having some problems, and I think I see why. She's a typical Gemini, flighty as a butterfly." I can't help smiling. "One minute she wants to be an actress, another a dancer. I can imagine that one moment she wants to be Pete's wife, and the next she's got it in her head to leave him and set up housekeeping in a fifth-floor walkup in New York. She'd see that as highly romantic and adventurous. You know, I kind of envy her that free-spirit quality. But it must be tough for someone like Pete to live with."

"And just exactly what is 'someone like Pete'?"

"Well, since he stopped rabble-rousing with my mother, he seems to prefer being settled down."

Adam smiles. "Are you saying he's become a stick-in-the-mud?"

"Not exactly. But again, he's got that strong sense of responsibility."

"Do they have children?"

"Two. A boy and a girl, six and nine."

"Having children does give one an added sense of responsibility."

"Yes. Adam . . . Pete also suggested that you might have sent Travis to steal those records."

His eyes widen. "Now that really is reaching."

"That's what I told him."

But there is a question in my voice; I cannot keep it out.

"You don't think I could have done that?" he asks.

"No. I don't think you'd have Travis steal the files to help Susan in her attempt to hurt me. But I did wonder if . . ." I let it hang.

"If I'd had Travis take them and hide them." Adam guesses, "so that Susan couldn't get to them and hurt you?"

"The thought crossed my mind."

"But, sweetheart, that presupposes that I believed Susan's accusations that you had some hand in what happened to Beth, and that the autopsy records would prove it. I'd never in a million years believe that."

I don't answer, and he takes my hand once more and says, "I would do almost anything to protect you, Naomi. Truly, almost anything. But I didn't do *that*. Do you believe me?"

"I . . . yes. I do."

He smiles. "Good. Now I have a question for you. I'm going out to the cabin tomorrow morning. Would you like to go?"

When he says "cabin," I know he means to visit Beth, as that is where she is buried, on the grounds of another home Adam owns, on the far side of the island.

"What about Pete? When are you supposed to see him?"

"I told him I had business meetings tomorrow but that I'd get back to him. Suddenly, I feel like playing hooky. How about you?"

I have a moment of unease that I cannot explain. Perhaps a sense of impending doom. Then I shrug it off and take his hand. "Yes," I say. "I would like to go to the cabin with you."

CHAPTER 14

A couple of years ago Adam built his "cabin," as he calls it, on the west side of the island, overlooking the beautiful San Juan de Fuca strait and the vast Olympic mountain range. The setting is lovely and rustic, in the trees, on the side of a hill. Beth loved it there, and now she's buried on that hill, in a plot surrounded by roses and azaleas in all shades of white and pink. At the head of Beth's grave is a tall white angel, its wings spread and tilted slightly forward, as if to envelope and protect.

"I'm glad you chose that spot for her," I say to Adam now. We are in the Mercedes with the top down, and he is driving. The day is sunny and warm, but as we near the cabin I begin to feel the cloud of sadness that always envelopes me here. I wonder if Adam knows how many times I've come here alone; it is the first time we've made this journey together.

"You know," I say, "when you first suggested this last night, I wasn't sure it felt right. I'm still not certain. What if Susan picks today to come out here? I'd hate running into her."

"She never comes here anymore," Adam says definitely.

"Never?"

"So far as I know, not once since the day Beth was buried. To tell you the truth, I've always thought it a bit strange."

"Well, people experience grief differently. It must be too hard for her."

He looks over at me briefly. "And what about you, Naomi? You've been out here, haven't you?"

"I . . . yes. How did you know?"

"I've seen the fresh wildflowers you leave every week. And in the winter, the little bunch of herbs from your window box, tied with a ribbon. A blue ribbon, Beth's favorite color. Sometimes you've left a feather or a shell."

I am surprised. "But I always tucked them away, so they wouldn't be too obvious. I meant them only as a little message to Beth, and I didn't want Susan finding them and being upset. You found them? You knew they were from me?"

"Of course. Who else?"

We are at the gate now, the rustic wooden gate that is always locked, though I'd found my own way in through the woods.

"Do you mind that I've come here?" I ask.

He stops the car and puts an arm around me, pulling me close. "Mind? Those little gifts kept me going. I'd pick them up and hold them, and somehow I'd feel connected to you again. I'd see us together again, all three of us, doing the things Beth liked so much to do . . . the museums, the art galleries, and those awful old movies she was so crazy about at that little theater near the Market. *Creature from the Black Lagoon, The Monster That Ate Tokyo . . .*"

He pulls back, and we both laugh, though I see his eyes are tearing as mine are. I reach up to wipe his tears away, and he grabs my fingers and holds them to his lips. "Oh God, Naomi," he whispers. "I miss her so much."

"I know," I say, holding him tight. "I know."

We are standing over Beth's grave. Each of us has said our private prayers for her, shared our thoughts with her, and in my case, at least, asked for forgiveness, as I always do. There is so much to be forgiven for.

It feels odd to be here with Adam. I wasn't present for the funeral, as Susan had Travis Hartmann call to inform me that I would not be welcome. Then there was the final call from Adam, saying he could no longer see me or take my calls.

Now, nearly one year later, we stand here hand in hand. And as I look up to the tips of the fir trees blowing gently in a soft wind, the sun peeking through and all things seeming normal and as they should be, I wonder if this is testament to the undying quality of love—or to the inexhaustibility of foolishness? All those months of struggle to find my balance again, all the nights alone believing he was with Susan, and being torn with utmost sadness over losing them both in one fell swoop: Beth, who was like my child, and Adam.

What do I do with them now, those hapless resolutions founded in loneliness and pain? How do I "sit with them," as my mother might say?

"After the first few times, we nearly always came here alone," Adam says, breaking into my thoughts. "Beth and I, that is . . . to the cabin."

He leans forward to rearrange a glossy green vine that has trailed its way up the white angel these past few months. Lovingly, he tucks a tendril around one arm. "Susan almost never came. And that seemed best. I'm not saying it was always her fault that we didn't get along, Naomi. There's a lot I've accepted responsibility for this past year. But when Beth and I were here alone, there was so much less tension."

"I understand." Just as I understood that this was one place the three of us could not visit together, as there was always the chance that Susan might show up. For that matter, Beth might innocently mention that I'd been here, thus raising questions in her mother's mind.

I nod in the direction of the cabin, which stands on a cliff beyond our sight, through the trees. "Have things been closed up?"

"No. I stay here overnight now and then."

"Adam, are you sure it's all right for us to be here tonight?"

"I can't think why not."

"But Susan isn't exactly predictable these days, it seems. What if she takes it into her head to come out here, after all?"

He shakes his head. "I just don't see that happening. We should be safe for tonight."

Safe. It seemed a rather strong word. But I didn't question, at the time, his use of it.

I ask myself now: Was I already beginning to lose my "self" again?

"I can't believe you call this a cabin," I say as we enter through double pine doors with stained-glass insets. "It's more like a fancy lodge."

"Only the living room. I had to make it large for Beth's piano. And it's not really that fancy. You'll see."

A slightly musty odor reaches my nostrils, and together we go around opening windows. There are several across the front looking out to the water, the casement type that roll out when one turns a crank. While I take those, Adam opens windows in the back. The sudden cross-ventilation brings a stiff breeze to the living room, toppling photos on Beth's black grand piano.

I glance around, getting my bearings. Aside from the piano, there is only a simple white sofa in a wide U-shape facing the windows and the view, bookcases along an inside wall, two upholstered white rocking chairs, and two glass end tables. I know it was Beth's idea to furnish the cabin this way, as I recall her telling me about it. "I told Dad, let's make it light and airy. Not too much clutter. I really don't like places that are all loaded down with dark heavy furniture and knick-knacks all over the place, do you, Naomi?"

Though I have quite a lot of furniture in my cottage, not to mention "knickknacks," I didn't take this personally. None of my things are heavy and dark. And too, I knew she was merely trying to create the exact opposite of the elegant Lambert mansion, where she'd never felt truly at ease.

I cross to the piano to straighten the picture frames, and feel a knife in my heart as I pick the first one up and glance at it. Beth's thirteen-year-old face smiles at me the way it did then, open and bright, her sense of adventure written all over it—sticking, in fact, right out of her eyes. I remember how she loved to do the unconventional, the unexpected thing, and how her friends at school followed her lead. She was always initiating little schemes, harmless fun that would somehow land her in the principal's office. Susan and Adam would be called, and generally it would be Adam who would drive back from Seattle to bail her out. Often Susan was not available, and though I'd have gone myself, those times when I was on the island, I never had the right or authority to do so.

Adam comes up behind me.

"You know," I say, blinking back tears and running a finger through a light film of dust on the piano, "I seldom got to hear Beth play. There was that one time when she invited me to her recital, because Susan couldn't come. And another at her school, when she played for that musical the kids put on."

"I wish you could have been there. Her mother was . . . indisposed," Adam says.

"Yes. I realized that must have been the case, later, though I don't think I knew it at the time. And I kept meaning to rent a small piano so Beth could play it when she was at the cottage, but I kept putting it off. Oh, Adam! So many things put off."

"You were good to her, Naomi. You gave her countless moments of love and . . ." He breaks off, then says slowly, "I was going to say peace. But it was more than that. You gave her safety. You haven't anything to regret."

Together we finish straightening the photos, many of which are of Adam, Susan, and Beth together. They are of those things that families do, and I can imagine Susan with copies of these on a mantel at the mansion, showing them off to party guests and friends. *"See, this is Adam trying out the new NordicTrak. And this is us digging a hole in the front yard for that new tree. Oh, look! Here we are getting on the plane for Hawaii, and this is us at Haleakala, the volcano. Lord, it was cold up there. Remember, darling?"* And Adam would smile and lay an arm about her shoulders, giving her a squeeze.

As in most family photographs, of course, there is often someone making a goofy face. Here it is Beth one time. Adam another. I set the silver frames upright on the piano, trying not to think, and reach for a photo framed in ornate gold, only to have Adam take it from my hands. "I'll put this away," he says quietly.

"No, let me see it."

He would rather I didn't, but my fingers are already turning it over. In the background are tall snow-capped mountains that might be the Alps. In the foreground stand Susan and Adam. They are on skis, and they are kissing. They look very young. And happy.

"Our honeymoon," he explains. "Beth insisted on having this photo here. I think it helped her to believe that if things were good once, they could be again. I'm sorry, Naomi."

"Don't be. She was your wife." I turn away. "For that matter, she still is."

"Only in name," he hastens to assure me, placing his hands on my shoulders. "You saw how it was. There's nothing left now."

"Except for pity," I say. "And pity can be a powerful force." It can, I am thinking, keep us apart as surely as love.

"I won't abandon you again," he says fiercely, turning me to face him. "That's what you're afraid of, isn't it? I promise you, I won't abandon you again."

I let him hold me, but part of me is at a distance. While my hands and heart are with him, my head goes off somewhere. There it sits in judgment and fear. *Be careful, Naomi*, it warns. *Look out.*

I get the formal tour next, and I note that the master bedroom is indeed not fancy, but rather Spartan. A dark pine bureau with a framed mirror stands against a white wall. On the king-size bed is a blue-and-white quilt in a handmade, Early American-style. On either side are pine night tables, and above the bed is a crucifix.

I have always wondered how anyone makes love beneath a dying Jesus. I don't know how *I'll* manage it—if that's the plan—much less sleep in Susan's bed, however infrequently she's used it.

"What's that door to?" I ask.

Adam crosses to it, a door with a window, on the far wall. He opens it, and I see that it leads out to a rather large landing with a patio table and four chairs. From there, stairs go down to a garden. Beyond the garden are woods.

"I like to sit out here in the early morning," Adam says. "I can watch the deer from here."

"Are there a lot of deer?"

He grins. "A kajillion, as Beth used to say."

Her room across the hall is more amply furnished. My heart tilts at sight of the fluffy pink coverlet and canopy. Lacy curtains at the windows waft gently in a warm breeze. On shelves are some of the stuffed animals Beth collected and never outgrew. I spot one that I gave her on her birthday two years ago . . . a little pink pig, which she named Wiz, after the pigs that fly in the tornado scene in *The Wizard of Oz*.

I swallow the lump in my throat and see that there are tears in Adam's eyes. He wipes them away with a finger and says, "I never get over it. No matter how many times I come here, the wound is always fresh and new. Naomi . . . do you think that no matter how twisted she might be with the facts, Susan might be on the right track? Do you think it might not have been an accident? Could someone—anyone—have hurt Beth?"

"I don't know, Adam. I don't think so. But—"

It is time, I think, to tell him about Beth's pregnancy. I've been waiting for the right moment, and here in Beth's room where I can almost feel her presence, I seem to hear her saying, "Now, Naomi. Tell him. Tell him everything."

But I don't know everything, I say. *You didn't confide enough.*

"Tell him," she insists, her young voice strong in my ear, though I cannot actually see her. "Tell him what you know. I'll take care of the rest."

I feel a light pressure on my shoulder and turn, but there is no one there. Adam is by the shelf of animals, picking one up and then the other, studying each as if they might jump to life and bring Beth with them.

"All right," I say softly. "I will."

Adam turns, a question in his eyes. "What was that?"

I shake my head. "I've just made a decision. Adam, please sit down. Here." I pat the bed. "We need to talk."

Adam is livid, on his feet. His hands clench and unclench. "What are you saying? Beth, *pregnant*? That's impossible!"

"She was seventeen years old," I say gently. "Nothing is impossible."

"But who? Not that Lawrence kid!"

"I thought you liked Curt Lawrence."

"He's an idiot. He thinks his family can buy him a place in the world. His highest goal, in fact, is to take over his father's business."

I cannot help smiling. "You did that."

"And you know I didn't want to. It was the worst mistake I ever made, and I'd never make it again."

"You don't have to. You're not a kid anymore, just getting out of school. Curt Lawrence is. And times are tough."

He flashes me a suspicious look. "Are you defending him? Exactly how much do you know, Naomi? Is it true? Beth really was pregnant? Was he the father?"

"Stop! Slow down. I just found out myself. And I don't know if he was the father or not. Beth never talked to me about him."

"Then how do you know—"

I explain to him about the Blackfoot legend, the butterfly, and Beth's state of health in the few months before she died. I don't mention that my mother as much as confirmed my suspicions, though I'm sure he would understand. "I'm certain of it, Adam. She was pregnant."

He sits suddenly, his shoulders slumping. The nearly invisible lines in his face droop and deepen; he seems to age before me. "She was too young for that! Too damned young! She shouldn't have had to go through that alone. Why didn't she talk to us? If not to Susan and me, why not you?"

I have no answer for him.

"How well did you really know Curt Lawrence?" I ask after a moment.

"Not as well as I should have, it seems. I knew his father, long before Curt and Beth started dating. The kid seemed nice enough at first, at least on the surface. Good manners, a good student. But there was something . . ." He shakes his head. "I never really understood what Beth saw in him. He seemed rather cold to me."

"I agree. I only saw them together that once, at Beth's party last Christmas, but he wasn't the sort of boy I'd have expected her to like. Still, she seemed happy enough. Remember how she came running in from the summer room, her face all flushed and happy?"

"Yes, I remember. In fact, Susan and I both asked her what was going on. She acted shy, and said she was out there having a birthday dance with a friend."

"She told me that too. Did she mention who the friend was?"

"No. We were both certain it was Curt Lawrence, but come to think of it, why didn't she just tell us that?

We were never openly disapproving of him."

"And when she began wearing the butterfly pendant. Did she ever tell you Curt had given it to her?"

"No, only that she'd bought it for herself, because she liked it."

"Adam, I don't think she wanted us to place too much importance on it. She might even have been afraid that I, in particular, would connect it to the Blackfoot legend and know why she was wearing it. I only wish now I had."

He sighs. "That wasn't your fault. Beth kept so many things to herself. Little things when she was little ... obviously, larger ones as she grew up."

"But, Adam, there were signs. I realize that now. They were all there, laid out before me, and I just never saw them."

"Still, how could you think ... Naomi, Beth wasn't a backward young woman. I'm sure she knew about birth control. Why in the name of God would she trust in some ancient superstition to protect her?"

"I don't imagine she did. She was probably just covering all the bases, as she put it. But while we're on the subject ... are you sure she knew about birth control?"

"Well, of course. Don't most kids these days?"

"But did you talk to her about it?"

He turns pink. "I ... no. It didn't seem my place."

"Oh for heaven's sake. Then what about Susan? You think she talked with Beth?"

"Well, I just assumed ..."

I can see it in his face as he understands that his assumption may well be wrong, given Susan's condition these past years.

"Other kids, then," he insists. "Don't they exchange information about this sort of thing?"

"Not kids like Beth. You know how private she could be."

His eyes close briefly. "And that, of course, is my fault. I always asked her not to talk to people about what went on at home."

He stands and begins to pace. "Damn! To think she went through all that alone. And what about Curt Lawrence? Did he know?"

"I've no idea."

"Well, I want to talk to him. I've half a mind to go over there right now."

"But Beth may not even have told him—this could come as a shock to him as well. At least wait till you've calmed down."

"I don't give a damn how much of a shock it is. If he . . . if he slept with Beth and didn't protect her . . ."

In his tone is a mixture of anger, pain, and frustration. It is clear he is blaming himself for Beth's plight, as much as Curt Lawrence.

"In the morning," I say quietly. "We'll go together. All right?"

He rubs a hand over his eyes, and I put my arms around him. "We'll work it all out. I want to talk to Curt anyway. I keep wondering if he saw or at least talked to Beth that night of the storm. He might be able to tell Susan something, even some small thing, that will help her."

He places his hands on my face. "I love you, Naomi Wing. Have I told you that?"

"Not lately," I can't help answering.

"Well, I do. I don't know how I got through this last year without you."

"Just remember that," I say.

We leave it that we will talk to Curt Lawrence in the morning, and though Adam has still not regained his balance completely since learning of Beth's pregnancy, this has given him something to hang onto, a sense that he's taking some sort of action. I've learned in the past that this is essential for him. Meanwhile, I try to take his mind off Beth, and mine as well. There have been so many hours spent in grief since this time last year, and there are moments when the soul cries out, "Enough." It is then, I've discovered, that something kicks in, some protective force to keep one from going mad.

"What would you like for dinner?" I ask, scrounging through the fridge. "There are some nice vegetables here. I could fix pasta and veggies with that creamy garlic sauce you always liked. Would that do?"

"More than," he says, kissing me on the neck. "And while you do that I'll be a real he-man and go chop some wood. It does get damp here at night, even in the summer."

"That sounds good." I look around. "Is there any wine?"

"Right there in the—" He breaks off. "I forgot, you don't know." Going to a cupboard above the sink, he reaches up and opens it. There are only three bottles. Two are red, and he brings one down and sets it on the counter. "The other is champagne, but it's never been chilled. It's Susan's favorite, the only thing she ever drank. I think this bottle's been sitting here now for a couple of years—at least, since she stopped coming here. Would you like some?" He holds the bottle up, and I recognize the expensive California label, but shake my head. He closes the cupboard door and leans his forehead against it momentarily. I know he realizes he's said too much. It was so much easier not to think about Susan when Adam and I were in my apartment in Seattle.

"The red's fine for me," I say. Then, sticking my head back in the fridge, I add brightly, "My oh my. Coffee, eggs, bacon... There's certainly plenty of food."

"Well, I stop at the little market down the road and buy things. Most of the time, I'm afraid, I forget to eat them."

I pull out parmesan cheese and a small carton of half-and-half, sniffing it. It seems fine. "You know," I say as I hunt through pots and pans under the counter, "I've been thinking. Why don't you call Annie Lowell and see if she knows how Susan is doing? I'm sure you'd like to know if she's all right."

He sounds surprised. "You wouldn't mind?"

"Not at all. You can't help worrying about her, I know that. Just call, get it over with."

"Actually, I would if I could, but the phone here isn't connected."

"Not connected?" I flick a wry glance at him. "You, without a working phone to keep track of business?"

"Believe it or not, I haven't wanted to be disturbed this past year when I'm out here. The surest way to prevent that was to cut the thing off."

I smile. "Well, you're right about one thing. It's hard to believe." This is a new Adam, one I haven't known before.

"Sometimes I meditate," he adds. "Sometimes I simply remember."

I pause with my hand on the water faucet. "Does it help?"

"It seems to." He doesn't sound sure.

"You have doubts?"

His face clouds over. "I don't know . . . sometimes I think I've become too ingrown this year. I have strange thoughts and find myself doing things I'd never have done before. It frightens me a bit, to be honest."

"Frightens you? How?"

He shakes his head and reaches into a large bottom drawer for work gloves. "I don't know. Look, don't mind me, I'm probably just exaggerating things. And it's getting late. I'd better go out and start on that wood. Meanwhile, woman"—he deepens his voice and assumes a drawl—"you rustle us up some grub, you hear?"

"Yes, sir!"

I laugh and kiss his cheek. If I feel a trifle uneasy as my gaze follows his back to the door, I tell myself it is only natural, this thing he is going through. Over and over again when practicing as a lawyer, I saw that when terrible things happen to people, such as losing someone they love, they change. They begin to reach inside and pull out whatever's there—even the dark patches, the shadows that in ordinary, everyday life, are so easy to elude.

* * *

There is pasta bubbling in a big pot when Adam comes back in, his face, hair, and arms damp with sweat. He carries a big load of wood and says, "I somehow don't think we'll use this tonight after all. It's warmer than usual."

"Really? I thought it was just me, all this heat from the stove." He passes by me on the way to the living room. "Adam? I can't find any nutmeg. I can't make my secret sauce without nutmeg."

I hear his loud "huffff" as he drops the logs to the stone hearth. "What was that? I didn't hear you."

"I can't find nutmeg."

He comes back into the kitchen, pulling off his gloves and setting them down on the counter. "I doubt we have any. I don't remember ever needing it for anything."

"Oh."

If I sound crestfallen, I am. There is nothing worse than putting effort into a great sauce and then not having the one ingredient that makes it different from all the rest. At least there's nothing worse for a vain chef, which I am.

"Is it that important?" he asks.

"Well . . . we won't starve." I smile.

"It's that important," he says firmly. "I'll just run down to the market. It's not more than ten minutes down the road." He lifts the lid and peers into the steaming pasta. "Can you stall for twenty minutes?"

"I can stall. I'll put this in cold water."

"Right, then. I'm off. Anything else?"

"No, that's it."

He grabs his car keys from the breakfast bar and heads out the door, whistling. His color is better now, and so are his spirits. I am thinking that chopping wood is good for a man's soul.

I pour the pasta into a pan of cold water, and while I wait for Adam to return, I decide to step outside and walk for a few minutes in the cool air. Going down the driveway I stop to appreciate the tall rhododendrons that line it, their lush pink flowers a nice change from the usual green and gray of evergreens that proliferate on the island. Taking a short, narrow path from there, I come out on a slight hillock above the water's edge. The land curves in here, and looking to the right and then left I see shoreline for miles, rimmed with fir and cedar. Most of the property on this shoreline is now owned by people like Adam, with money. Some have moved here from other states to avoid the crowding there. I can't help wondering where they will go next, as the services they demand cause similar crowded conditions here.

I think of my mother, and how she would have hated to see the way things have grown here just in the past six years. The ancestors of these cedars once provided housing for Skagit, Snohomish, Snoqualmish. The Snohomish on the other side of the island surrounded their villages with palisades of cedar, fourteen feet high. The walls had bolted doors, and openings for shooting arrows. Thus barricaded, they believed themselves safe from attack. In the long run it mattered not; the white man came with bullets and higher palisades. There are, I've discovered, always those with higher palisades. One is never quite safe from attack.

I think of Pete Shelton's ancestors walking this land, and how different things were then. The Snohomish raised dogs for wool, tying their forelegs together and shearing their fur with a stone knife. When the salmon began to run in summer, they had ceremonies, called potlatches. The potlatches were rich with dancing and singing, with spirit guides and gifts of property, fish, and shell money. It was custom for the men to show off their power, and one, it is said, even proved his by swallowing hot bullets and making them come out at his side. When I first heard that story I was five, and even then I understood that men will do just about anything to prove they are strong.

As for all of my mother's talk about the innocence of the natives here, it is historical fact that the Snohomish had slaves, and that their warriors cut off their enemies' heads, bringing them proudly back to the village to prove their worth. Often, when my mother would go on one of her frequent angry jags about Indian rights, and the inequities—when she would don the mental warpaint—I would remind her of this. She would rant about the beauty of the old traditions, the old ways, ever scornful of my school friends and their new suburban houses "with their ugly chrome furniture, their stereos and large screen TVs." I would argue, "At least their fathers are watching Seahawk games on those TVs, not out lopping off a neighbor's head!"

Of course my own father never lopped off anyone's head, and neither did Pete's, for that matter. But like my mother, I was not above using any argument.

Once she went on and on about the Indian reverence for the land, and I—who had carefully done my

homework to prepare myself for every potential po-
lemic—argued, "What about women? They traded
them like shells! And when a wife was abused she had
to apply to the chiefs for a divorce. If they didn't think
she should have it, she didn't get it." I was twenty
when this particular argument came up, home from
Harvard pre-law for the summer. My closest friends
in the East, the women I allied myself with, were
marching—but for themselves. For women's, rather
than Indian, rights.

"Naomi," my poor mother complained more than
once, "I have not worked all my life to put you
through law school, only to suffer this betrayal."

Come fall, I would relate these stories of verbal
sparring to my friend and dorm mate, Rose Goldman.
She was the first to compare my mother to her own.
"They live with guilt, and they can't stand it if we
don't too," she had said. I remember we were standing before the dresser mirror in our room, in our underwear. Our legs had gone three weeks without a
shave, and we had talked about liking them that way.
Rose, whose hair was coal black, said she felt like a
sleek, sinuous panther, and loved to stroke her thighs.
I, while nearly as dark as she, had always wanted to
be blonde. I said that I sometimes closed my eyes
when touching my legs and felt like a tawny cat. That
we talked about these things at all was an indication
of the self-conscious consciousness-raising we were so
determinedly involved in.

Rose had cut her hair short that summer, and with
her skinny figure she looked like a boy. She ran a
brush through it, taking all of three seconds, then
donned jeans and a work shirt. I remember I laughed

at her comments about our mothers. Then, still standing beside her in the mirror—wanting to dress as much like her as possible, wanting to assimilate rather than be shunned as in high school—I had pulled on a work shirt of my own. Unlike Rose, however, I took an extra few seconds to inspect myself, the lay of my now-long hair, the white-pink gloss of lipstick.

"C'mon, Naomi," she had said, irritated. "Let's go get 'em." She grabbed up two placards on sticks that stood in a corner. One read: EQUAL PAY FOR WOMEN. The other: DAY CARE FOR ALL. She handed me the day care one. I took it—though I'd sworn at that time never to have children, never to become trapped that way. Fighting for day care for single mothers gave me a certain virtuous glow: my cause was unselfish, not directed to any need of my own.

I thought, as I left the dorm that day with my twentieth century totem, *If Mom could see me now*.

It was easy enough to laugh about my mother and the battle she waged back then, a battle to force the government to return the tormented, toxic lands to their original owners, to those who would, presumably, hold it in reverence and awe. It was a battle I saw as old and tired, never to be won. Easy then not to see through her eyes, natural to want eyes of my own. My young mind was as yet not partitioned into soft little pockets here and there, the way the mind eventually becomes with experience, with the passage of sorrow and time.

I scan those trees again and remember something Adam told me two nights ago, when we first came together again. "Naomi . . . about that Wintu land deal."

"I don't want to talk about that," I answered, reluctant to let anything disturb my newly resurrected feelings of love. "It's done. There's nothing more to say."

"No, you don't understand. I want you to know that I wasn't aware of what Travis was doing. I never authorized him to go ahead with that purchase last year."

I sat up, pulling the sheets to my breast. "He forced the owner to sell that land, Adam! Oh, it was all legal, but unethical as hell. And he did it when I wasn't thinking straight."

He took my hands. "I know. I know, and I'm sorry. But you've got to believe me, I didn't want it that way. I wasn't thinking clearly either, or I would have tried to stop him somehow. Up till then it had at least been a fair fight, you and Travis going at it tooth and nail, and the truth is, I fully expected you to win. No, amend that. I wanted you to win."

"Oh, Adam."

"Please believe me. I mean that. I tried to tell you last winter, but you wouldn't return my calls."

I waved my hand irritably. "Let's forget it. It's all water under the bridge now."

"No. It's not. Naomi, you've got to at least believe that I never wanted those timber lands, not after you told me what they meant to you and your mother. But when Beth . . . when she died, when I wasn't there half the time to keep an eye on things, the board insisted Travis go all out to finalize the purchase. I didn't know what he was doing until it was done."

Strange, I think now, how little all that seems to matter. My mother is gone, and the land is gone. What little of it wasn't flooded by dams has been clear-cut by now, I would think, for timber to boost the Lambert Enterprises till. I want to care about that. And intellectually, I do. If I could live last year over and file that injunction in time, if I could prevent Travis Hartmann from playing his dirty little tricks, I would. But in my heart the only loss that matters, the only one I truly weep for, is Beth.

I remember something else Adam said two nights ago: "I never really knew my daughter till I came to know her through you. Before that she was simply 'my child,' a beautiful but distant little creature I didn't understand at all. Susan and I . . . we gave her as much as we could. We tried to raise her to be thoughtful of others and not just herself. But it was you who taught me who my daughter was."

"Well," I answered, "maybe it was easier for me. All I had to be was a friend."

I suppose that's something I'd learned by then. Not how to be a daughter—or even a mother—but a friend.

It is getting late, and in a few more minutes the sun will be down. Adam has been gone now for nearly an hour. I've not yet reached the point of great concern, but I am fretting around the edges of it. The thing that bothers me most is that if something has happened— a flat tire, perhaps (I don't want to think the word *accident*, yet it flashes into my mind)—I would never know, with the phone disconnected as it is.

Of course, someone would notify me, wouldn't they? They'd arrive at the door—

No. How could anyone possibly guess I'm here? It's Susan they would call.

The pasta has gone cold and rubbery; the sauce I'd so carefully tended to keep it from curdling is now a thick, gluey mess. I don't care about that. I just want Adam back. I want to know he is safe.

Of course he's safe. He simply got caught up in conversation with someone at the market. He may have simply forgotten the time. People always worry this way when someone doesn't show up. They think the worst. Then the "missing" person turns up and gets yelled at for causing so much worry.

This is my train of thought, and it is not much, but something. A possibility to cling to as the rain comes down and I stand at the window, waiting.

Waiting. I did so much of it in those four years of being Adam's mistress, his lover. How is this different? *Is* it different?

It occurs to me that there must be a phone at the market, and Adam probably called Annie Lowell from there, to see if Susan was all right.

And what if he learned that she wasn't? Did he drive off in a panic for Seattle, leaving me here?

No. He wouldn't do that. Even in the old days, he never just went off and stranded me anywhere. He was always careful to tell me what was happening, careful to let me down easy.

Wait. There is something wrong with that last statement. What is it? Ah yes . . . there is nothing easy about being let down.

A light rain begins. I glance at the hearth, and wonder if I should make a fire. When Adam gets back, he may be cold, even drenched.

I am becoming seriously worried when it is after nine o'clock and the rain worsens. I am just about to go out on foot and look for him when I hear a sound outside the cabin, near the drive. Looking out, I don't see the Mercedes, or Adam. Yet I am certain I heard something. I run to the back and look through the kitchen window. It's too dim back there to see anything, and the trees too thick. I squint into the darkness, and for a moment I think I see something move in the trees, then it is gone. A deer? Perhaps only a possum or a skunk. Though I stand motionless watching for several seconds, I see nothing move again.

I go back to pacing and worrying. Then I hear another sound. This time it is overhead, upstairs. "Ad—?" I start to call out. But I realize that's impossible. He couldn't have come in without my seeing him. Not unless he'd entered from the outside stairs, and why would he do that? The thought sends a jolt of fear through me. Who is up there?

I strain my ears to listen, wanting to believe I made a mistake. It was probably only the house creaking, the wood contracting in the cool of the night. Yes, that's it.

But there it is again. A step. And then another.

Frightened now, I try to remember the layout up there. Aside from the two bedrooms, there's a bath in the hall, and one in the master bedroom. A linen closet, too. That's all I can remember.

The floor creaks again. "Hello?" I call out, gathering my courage. "Who's up there? Adam, is that you?' "

A door closes softly. The creaking stops.

I run back to the fireplace and reach for a poker. Holding it in front of me I tiptoe to the foot of the stairs. "Hello?" I call again, more firmly now, though my legs are trembling. I have never been one to hide when I'm afraid. If I think there are spooks in my closet at night, I must get up and throw open the door.

I start up the stairs. As I reach the first landing I hear footsteps run across the master bedroom floor in the direction of the outer stairs. The door up there opens and closes, then someone runs down the steps and alongside the house, toward the front. The sounds fade into silence.

I lean weakly against the balustrade catching my breath. But in the next moment there's a click at the front door.

Slowly, I start back down the stairs, hugging the wall. A figure appears outside the front door, clearly outlined against the stained-glass window. A man. The knob turns slowly.

Adam?

His name nearly leaves my lips before I realize there is something stealthy and too quiet about this figure. I crouch on the steps, still holding the poker, though my palms are so sweaty it nearly slides from my grip. The knob catches, turns again. I hold my breath, wondering if I locked the door after Adam left. I can't remember.

It opens. The man who stands there in faint relief is not Adam. He is much too broad in the shoulders, his head too large. I step out, the poker held in front of me. "Hold it! Who are you? What do you want?"

A flashlight blinds me.

"What the hell?" I hear in an old, far too familiar voice.

Travis Hartmann.

*   *   *

"And to think I honestly believed it was over with the two of you," he says. "My dear Ms. Wing ... now what would you be doing here?"

I lean against an arm of the sofa. My legs are shaking so bad I can no longer stand without support. "You scared me half to death, Travis. What the devil are you doing prowling around here?"

"I'd hardly call it prowling around. I came through the front door."

"I noticed. And I'm quite sure I didn't hear you knock."

"Of course not. I expected Adam to be here alone. He's never required that I knock."

I see now that he is wearing a business suit and carries a briefcase. Both are wet from the rain. "What do you want here? It can't be business. Adam doesn't do business out here."

"I'm aware of that. Actually, I have news about Susan." He swings his head around toward the kitchen. "Where is the master of the house, anyway?"

I won't be put off by his nonchalance. There is something wrong with this picture. "Travis ... were you upstairs just now?"

He smiles. "Still answering a question with a question, I see. Still playing the lawyer, in word if not in fact. But, no, I was not upstairs. As you saw for yourself, I just got here."

"I saw you come in. I did not hear you park."

"That's because I parked at the bottom of the hill," he says in an exaggeratedly patient tone. "I was afraid I'd get stuck up here, if the rain got worse."

"So you walked straight up the hill to the cabin?" I glance down at his black shoes, which are covered in mud and evergreen needles.

"Yes, Ms. Prosecuting Attorney, I walked straight up the hill." He smiles that supposedly winning smile. "Why?"

I don't answer, and Hartmann glances round again. "My turn now? Where's Adam? Will you tell him I'm here? I'm in a bit of a hurry."

"He went to the market, down the road. He'll be back any minute. You said you had news about Susan?"

He sets his briefcase down. "I'm afraid so. She's gone."

"Gone? What do you mean?"

"Annie called her twice today and got no answer. She went to Susan's apartment, and she wasn't there."

I shrug. "So she went out for a walk or something."

"No, you don't get it. Susan and Annie have an agreement. Susan checks in with her before she goes anywhere—and I mean *anywhere*."

"Sounds more like a warden than a psychiatrist, to me," I can't help commenting.

Travis grunts an agreement. "Talk to Adam about that. It was his idea."

I try not to show my surprise, but it's impossible.

"Didn't tell you that, did he?" Hartmann all but gloats. "Well, it's true. He keeps tabs on her that way."

"I don't believe it. Why would Susan go along with a thing like that? Or Annie Lowell, for that matter?"

"Because Adam declared an ultimatum: either Susan does what he says, or he has her committed."

I fold my arms. "Now I know you're lying. Adam can't have her committed. They aren't married anymore."

"Is that what he told you?"

My confusion must show, for he smiles again. "They're not legally separated. There have never been any papers signed. You didn't know that?"

I stare him down, though this shakes me. I had assumed things were further along. "Why would I need to know that?" I say with an air of casual disinterest. "It's none of my business. Is it yours? I don't recall that you practice divorce law. And the last I heard, you aren't even Adam's personal lawyer anymore."

"No ... as a matter of fact, I'm representing Susan now."

"I see. Cozy little arrangement. But that being the case, tell me more about this 'agreement with Annie Lowell.' Has Susan been so bad that Adam can actually enforce such a thing? Make her check in all the time?"

"Now, you know I can't answer that, Ms. Wing. In fact, I've already said far too much." He glances at his watch. "I wonder what's keeping Adam."

"I'm sure he'll be here any moment."

There is a flicker in the cold gray eyes. "Maybe. But you look worried. What is it? What's wrong?"

I shrug. "Nothing, so far as I know. But why don't you have a seat while you wait? I'd really like to know more about Susan. What exactly might she do— turned loose, so to speak?"

"Ms. Wing, you never give up, do you?" His tone is admiring, yet at the same time cool. "Of course, that's not precisely true. There was that one time, after Beth Lambert died ..."

My voice takes on a hard edge. "Don't go there, Hartmann. Don't take me on, not now. I'm not as distracted as I was a year ago."

The eyes narrow. "No . . . it doesn't seem so."

He becomes all business. "About Susan. Since she's disappeared, and Adam has apparently gone off as well, I suppose it's my responsibility to tell you. Susan can be . . . erratic. I won't say dangerous, but perhaps somewhat harmful to herself and others. Without *meaning* to be," he hastens to add. "It's simply that she has, shall we say, episodes, in which she isn't herself. One can't predict, under conditions of stress, what she might say or do."

"I was witness to one of those episodes a couple of nights ago," I say. "As a matter of fact, have you looked for her at the mansion? She was there that day."

"That's the first place we looked. After her apartment in Seattle, of course. No luck. I actually hoped I might find her here."

"No. According to Adam, she never comes here. Unless . . ." Without conscious volition, my gaze drifts to the stairs. Hartmann's eyes follow. Then he fixes them on me.

"Is she here?" he asks softly.

I shake my head.

"She *was* here, then?"

I don't answer, and he heads in long swift strides for the stairs.

"There's no one there," I say. "Whoever was up there is gone."

He doesn't seem to hear me. "Susan? Suze?" he calls, with what appears to be genuine concern.

"I'm telling you, Travis, if it was her, she's long gone."

He starts up the stairs. I follow, but cannot keep up with his anxious pace. He is at the master bedroom before me, standing stock-still just inside the door, when I reach the upper landing.

"Holy shit," he breathes, his jaw dropping.

"What is it?" I push past him.

On the mirror over the dresser, in bright carmine lipstick, has been scrawled the word MURDERER. On the bed, both white pillowcases have been marked with large red "X's". Above the bed, the crucifix has been hung upside down.

I draw closer to the crucifix, thinking that there is something else wrong with it, though I don't at first know what it is. Then I see it: On the figure of Jesus, over the white "cloth" that drapes his lower torso, has been painted a bright red penis.

CHAPTER 15

"She's been here," Travis says softly. "It was her."

I am feeling ill. "I can't believe she'd do such a terrible thing."

"But she did. Susan has this thing about religion."

"Travis, what's wrong with her? Really?"

He is still staring at the crucifix. "You don't want to know."

"But you do know? How? Just how close *are* you and Susan?"

He looks at me. "Like family," he says. "Now leave it alone."

I would press for more, but this room is giving me a real bad feeling. "Let's get out of here," I say with one last glance at the bed, the marked pillows, the word MURDERER. It does look like the same vibrant red lipstick Susan wore two nights ago at the mansion.

"You say Adam's been gone a couple of hours?" Travis asks.

We are back downstairs in the living room, and it is clear he is feeling just as shaken as I. There seems no reason now to keep my worry from him.

"Nearly. And the store's only ten minutes down the road."

"Dammit, Naomi, if you'd told me this in the first place—"

"I don't have to explain myself to you," I snap. "And it's your client that's the problem here, not me."

We are arguing like kids on a school playground, working our tensions out on each other. "All right," I say, standing and reaching for my purse. "Enough. I'm going to walk down the hill and call the police."

"Give it a few more minutes," Hartmann argues. "When Adam gets back, we'll ask him what he wants to do. He may not want the police in on this."

I stop at the door, looking out, then back at Travis. "And what if he doesn't get back? What if something's happened to him? For God's sake, you saw that mess upstairs. If Susan did that, what else might she have done? Run him off the road? He could be lying in a ditch somewhere."

"We don't know for *certain* she did it," he says now, a note of caution entering his voice.

"No, it could have been the lipstick fairy."

He flashes me an angry look. "I don't need your sarcasm, Naomi."

"Oh for God's sake. Do you ever listen to yourself? You are the most arrogant, not to mention the most unethical jerk I've ever had the misfortune to meet, much less study for the bar with."

He frowns. "I never studied for the bar with you."

"Like hell you didn't. You, me, and Ron Ferguson. That night in Fellowship Hall."

"I don't remember that."

"No? Well, I do. You stole my study notes. You passed the first round of exams and I—because I didn't have my notes—failed. I had to retake the exam."

He frowns. "All I remember is a girl . . . I didn't know that was you."

"You didn't know . . . Oh, never mind. The point is, you were a liar and a cheat then, and you're a liar and a cheat now."

He turns beet red. "Now? What the hell does that mean?"

"It means you're working both sides of the fence. You've got Adam on one side and Susan on the other, and you don't want to lose either of them because there's big money in it, either way. Oh, and let's not forget the board of Lambert Enterprises, Inc. You've got to keep them happy too. How do you do it, Travis? I'll bet you don't sleep at night, you're so busy keeping all your stories and your angles straight."

"I genuinely like both Adam and Susan," he says smoothly. "I'm doing my best for them both."

"Right. And if your client, Susan, ends up in a mental hospital and doesn't need your services anymore? How many bucks less per year will that mean to you, Travis? Don't tell me that doesn't bother you— enough, anyway, to keep you from reporting this incident to the police so that Susan could be picked up and taken care of properly."

"I've had enough of this." He grabs his briefcase. "I'm leaving. You can tell Adam for me that I've done my best."

"Your best?" I laugh. "At what?"

"Just tell him that. *I've done my best.* He'll know what I mean."

He spins on his heel and heads for the door, his shoes leaving muddy prints and tiny pieces of fir needles on the light carpet. Without consciously thinking about it, I reach down to clean them up. Holding a small handful of needles, I stare at them. Then at Travis Hartmann's shoes. He has paused at the door to shake his head as if washing his hands of me. But when he sees what I'm holding, the cold gray eyes narrow.

"Looks like you've been in the woods," I say.

"Only along the drive," he answers coolly.

"There aren't any needles along the drive, Travis. No trees. Only flowers."

In three long strides he is at me, a hand closing with an iron grip around my wrist. "Just what is that suspicious mind of yours thinking now, Naomi Wing?"

I try to wrench my arm away, but his fingers tighten. "It's thinking," I say coldly, "that whoever was upstairs ran into the woods. And it's thinking I may have jumped to too quick a conclusion about Susan. Perhaps she wasn't the one up there after all."

He laughs. "You really think I'm the type to go around writing obscenities in lipstick? And just what motive might I have to do that, my dear Ms. Wing?"

"I don't know, Travis. Maybe you'd like to frighten me? Scare me off? But off what? You tell me."

His mouth twists. "You know, you really are more trouble than you're worth, I remember that now. But maybe you won't be around causing trouble much longer. Wasn't it Shakespeare who said, 'Hell hath no fury like a woman scorned'? Susan may be at your place right now, waiting for you."

"You think so? Well, I'd probably be a lot safer there with her than here with—"

Just then I hear my name called from the drive. "Naomi?"

I swing around, and Hartmann's fingers loosen. In one swift jerk I am free of him. "Adam!"

Turning, I run out and down the front steps, straight into Adam's arms. "Thank God! I was so worried about you." My relief is so great, I plaster myself to him, my arms tight around his neck.

He holds me away a bit and laughs lightly. "I'm sorry. The road was slippery and my car went into a ditch. I had to wait for a tow truck, and I'd have called, but of course the phone's not working here—"

He breaks off, his gaze moving beyond me to Travis Hartmann, who stands on the porch observing us.

"Trav? What are you doing here?"

"It's a long story, Adam. Maybe your girlfriend would like to tell you."

Adam's eyes flick from him to me. "What's going on?" he says tightly.

"Susan's missing."

"Missing?"

"Yes. She may have been here, Adam."

Confusion flickers in his eyes. "At the cabin? I don't understand. Was she or not?"

I sigh and take his arm, leading him inside. "Come upstairs, I'll show you."

* * *

191

Adam stands in his room, looking as upset as I feel. He has taken down the crucifix and is holding it gently in his hands. Though I've never embraced a formal religion, I understand how much symbolism means to all religions, and I can't help but feel shocked with him.

"She's getting worse . . ." he says, as if to himself.

Travis Hartmann stands behind us, by the door. "I didn't know what you'd want to me to do."

He looks at Travis. "What does Annie think?"

"Well, she doesn't know about this incident yet, of course. But she was deeply worried when she learned that Susan had taken off without letting her know. Up till now, she's been pretty good about checking in."

"Yes. Up till now." Adam places the crucifix carefully on the bed.

"I don't understand," I say. "It seems like you've got Susan under some sort of house arrest. What on earth has she done to require that kind of treatment?"

He avoids my eyes. "It's too long a story for now."

"I don't care," I say. "I want to hear it."

He glances at Travis again, then at me. "I'll tell you, but later?" he asks. "I'd very much like to get out of this room."

Downstairs once more, Travis makes as if to leave, picking up the briefcase again and pulling his keys from his pocket.

"One moment," I say.

He raises a brow.

"Adam, I'm not entirely sure I believe Susan did all that upstairs."

"Not sure?" He shoots a look at Hartmann. "Naomi, who do you think it was?"

"Let's just say I'd feel better if our friend here would show us what's in his briefcase."

"Travis, you mean?" His surprised laugh is tinged with embarrassment. "You can't be serious."

"Oh, but I am."

"Surely you don't think . . ."

"I don't know what I think. I just want to be sure he doesn't have a lipstick on him."

On Adam's face is a mixture of confusion and chagrin, but Travis smiles that charming, rather sensual smile and says, "And what if I do, Naomi? How do you know I don't wear lipstick in my more private moments?"

"Just open the briefcase, Travis."

He shrugs. "As a matter of fact, you've reminded me that I do have papers for Adam to sign." He places the case on an end table and opens it. Inside are a handful of legal folders, two pens, and a cellular phone.

I pick up the phone, flip it open, and hear a dial tone. "My, my. Now, I wonder why you didn't share? All that time we sat here and I worried about Adam—not to mention that I nearly had to walk down the hill to call the police—and you had this in your back pocket, so to speak."

Travis smiles easily. "Sometimes discretion is the greater part of valor, Ms. Wing. I didn't want you going off half-cocked, calling the police and causing trouble for Adam and Susan."

I look at Adam. "And how do you feel about that?"

He directs his answer to Hartmann. "I don't like it, not at all. Just what have you been up to here, Travis?"

"Protecting your interests," he answers. "Doing what I'm paid to do."

Adam doesn't look happy. But he surprises me by saying, "Trav, I think you can go now. I'll talk to you when I'm back in the city."

"All right." He reaches for the legal folders. "If you'll just sign these—"

"No. I don't want to sign anything right now. They'll keep till later."

Hartmann looks disconcerted, but he shrugs and snaps the briefcase shut. He walks to the front door. "In the city, then. Call me."

"Wait a minute," I say. "We may not have found a lipstick in the briefcase, but search him, Adam. See if he's got it on him anywhere."

He looks at me as if I, like Susan, have lost my mind. "Really, Naomi . . ."

"Just do it, will you? Satisfy my curiosity."

Again, he casts a perplexed look at Hartmann. "Do you mind?"

Travis shrugs. He walks back, puts the briefcase on the sofa, and removes his suit jacket, showing us there is nothing in the pockets. Then he lays that over the arm of the sofa. Pulling his pants pockets inside-out, he holds out a set of keys that were in one.

"This is it," he says. "Satisfied now, Naomi? Or must I strip to my underwear?"

"Just your socks," I say.

He flushes. "Oh, really now, this is too much."

"Socks, Travis."

He sends Adam a look of conspiracy, as if it's the two of them against me. "It seems your girlfriend has a thing for men who like walking in the woods."

His gaze slides meaningfully to Adam's feet. The bottom of his jeans, and his running shoes, are both caked with needles and mud.

"Why not have Adam remove his?" he says. "That way you two can play footsy after I'm gone."

Adam's face reddens. "That'll be enough, Travis. Your bad humor lately is becoming a burden."

"Well, then, why don't I just relieve you of it for now. I'm going back to the city. And, Adam—as my last official act of this miserable day, I'll call Annie Lowell and tell her what happened here. You can take it from there."

"I don't know why you have that worm working for you," I say.

It is near sunset, and we are upstairs with a bucket of soapy water and sponges, removing the damages done to Adam's room. Adam has made a second trip to the market, where he placed a call to Annie Lowell himself. She agreed to phone the market with a message if Susan returned to her apartment or turned up elsewhere. Meanwhile, no one knows where to look for her, according to Annie, as she has already searched the mansion, and there's no sign of her there. On the theory that she may come here—or return here, if that is the case—we've decided to spend the night.

Rather, Adam has decided. I myself would prefer to leave. "I have a strong feeling about this, Naomi," he said. "I think I should be here tonight. Do you mind?"

I do, but then relationships are about compromise, are they not? And Adam's insistence about this is so unlike him, I've decided to go along with it for the time being.

"Travis doesn't work for me," he says now in answer to my comment. "He's Susan's attorney now."

"Sorry, but it didn't quite sound that way."

"What do you mean?"

"Adam, is Travis by any chance pretending to be Susan's friend but reporting back to you? Is he your spy in Susan's camp?"

"Spy? You make it sound as if she's my enemy."

"Well, is she? Or are you hers?"

He sets his sponge down and looks at me. "I can't believe you're asking me that."

"I can't help it. I feel sorry for Susan. She's lost her daughter, her husband, and now it seems she's lost her freedom. I don't see how that's supposed to help her get well."

"At this point, that isn't the issue, Naomi. If you only knew . . ."

"Knew what? Tell me, then I *will* know. What's been happening with her this past year?"

"What hasn't?" he says, working on the mirror again. Because it affects me less, I've taken charge of the crucifix. The cold soapy water does little to remove the greasy lipstick, and I see I'll have to take it into the bathroom, to the hot water tap. "I told you long ago" Adam continues, "that Susan's been . . . difficult, for want of a better word, since we first married."

"Yes. But difficult how?"

"Cold, unloving. Detached. I thought at first she was simply shy."

"Are you saying she was frigid?" This is the first time he's ever talked to me this candidly about the problem between them. Adam has always been protective of Susan that way, not wanting to say things against her, and that was always one of the things I loved about him.

He sits on the edge of the bed, and I sit beside him. "That's the hell of it," he says. "I don't know. Don't they say there are no frigid women, only bad husbands or lovers?"

"I've heard that. But from my own experience, at least, that doesn't apply to you, Adam."

He reaches for my hand. "Thank you for saying that. I swear, I tried to be a good husband to Susan. I honestly loved her in the beginning. Later on, when nothing seemed to work, I became detached myself. I think we fell into a downward spiral, and at some point there was nothing that could be done."

"You didn't love her anymore?"

"I don't think I ever thought of it that way. I was married to her. She was my wife. And there was no question of divorce."

That much I already know, and too well, but I refrain from saying it. "So you just kept going on."

"Yes. Until you."

"I've always wondered. You didn't have other affairs? Before you met me, I mean?"

"Never. I threw myself into my work and turned everything else off."

"That's how you were when I first met you. Turned off."

His hand rubs idly up and down my back in an old, comforting habit.

"But when did she get the way she is now, Adam? And what else has she done, that you've got her reporting in to Annie Lowell before she can make a move?"

"Well, for starters, she nearly set fire to the mansion."

"Set fire . . . My God, when?"

"Three months ago, and it started much the same way as tonight . . . except that then it was red paint. She splashed it on all the walls of our old bedroom, and wrote the words 'murderer' and 'liar' everywhere. When she was through, she tried to set the drapes on fire, but the construction foreman had come back for something he'd forgotten, and he caught her at it. He had my number in town and he called me. I got Annie Lowell, and we came out to the mansion together, but by then Susan was gone. We found her in the city, but it took hours. She was on the campus at the university, walking around naked and dazed. The local police had gotten there first, and it took a bit of doing to get them to let her go home with us."

"Oh, Adam. I had no idea. No wonder you wanted to stay here tonight. In case she came back and did something like that here."

"And that's only part of it. It got so I couldn't sleep at night, I was so worried about what she might do, especially to herself. I wanted her to sign herself into a hospital then, but she refused. I talked to Travis about having her committed, and he said it would be difficult since we had separated. He said they would suspect my motives, as a soon-to-be ex-husband. Finally we all three worked it out the way it is. At least, I thought we did. Susan's been pretty good about checking in with Annie every day till now."

"But why did she even agree to it? I can't believe that in her present state, she even knows what she's agreed to. And for that matter, wasn't that a huge burden for a psychiatrist to take on?" '

"Annie's different, she's more like a friend to Susan. Susan's been seeing her since before Beth died, is the thing. She wouldn't go for marital counseling, but she would see Annie alone. And she listens to her most of the time."

I shake my head. "I don't know, Adam. There's something about all this I don't like. It doesn't feel right."

His jaw hardens momentarily, then his energy seems to leave him in a *woosh*. He looks very tired. "I don't suppose you have a better idea?" he says with an edge.

"Not at the moment. But, Adam, Travis slipped and told me you haven't filed for a separation, let alone a divorce, yet. Are you going to?"

He hesitates. "Yes. I've only been waiting to see if Susan improved. I don't want to hit her with something like that when she's already down."

"Look, I'm sorry, but this sounds very much like the way you used to talk when we were together before. And nothing ever gets done."

"This is different, I promise you. I've come a long way, and as soon as Susan is better—"

"Better? You can say that after what happened here today?"

"May I remind you that just a short while ago you were accusing Travis Hartmann of doing all this?"

"That's true. I don't know how dedicated I am to that theory, though. There's something about Travis Hartmann that doesn't feel right concerning this, and I'm sure he's up to something. But as to whether he'd actually come here and desecrate your room this way . . ."

I shrug, giving a shudder as I look around. "On the other hand . . ." I am remembering those glacial eyes on me earlier, the angry grip on my wrist. What might Travis have done if Adam hadn't shown up just then?

"Naomi . . . Travis didn't hurt you?" Adam says worriedly.

"No. Somehow I think he'd have liked to, though."

"But why? I know you two have been legal opponents, but he came out on top in that battle last year. What could he possibly have against you?"

"I'm not sure. Of course, he knows I've never liked him. It may just be chemistry."

Adam shakes his head. "I think there's more to it. He and Susan have been getting close lately. Maybe it's only that he's feeling protective of her."

"Adam . . . You don't think they're in love?" I cannot quite believe it, even as I say it.

"In love? That seems a stretch. I do know he seems to genuinely care for her."

"Well, that's a new angle.—Travis Hartmann caring about someone other than himself."

Adam smiles. "I suppose stranger things have happened."

"Hardly. But one way or another, I think we've got to do something about Susan. First there was that hang-up on my phone, then the scene at Crow Cottage and the mansion, and now this. We can't just sit around and let these things happen."

He sighs. "I was thinking about that all the while I was walking back to the market and then waiting for that tow truck to show up. I think we've got to tell Susan about Beth."

"About the pregnancy?"

"Yes. Right now, she's blaming you because she doesn't know who else to blame. Not that I want her going after the Lawrence kid. But she needs to know there's a larger picture. It may give her some perspective on what happened."

"I agree with you on the one hand. But what if knowing about the pregnancy only makes her worse? She might really go off the deep end."

"I suppose. But it's a risk I think I need to take. Naomi, you said once that I protected Susan too much, that it amounted to enabling. And I know you're right. I can't be responsible for keeping her sane. Not anymore." He shrugs. "The truth is, it never worked anyway. It only gave me the feeling of doing something."

I reach a hand around his waist, giving him a squeeze, and rest my head on his shoulder.

"First thing tomorrow," he says, "I want to talk to the Lawrence boy. I'll need a few facts. Then I'll find Susan, and we'll talk."

"But if she's disappeared?"

"I think she'll have turned up by then."

"You seem rather sure."

"I hate to say this, but I think Susan does these disappearing acts for attention. Once she has that, she shows up again. Which is not to minimize the state she's in while she's gone, which can be downright frightening."

"Do you honestly think she'd come back here tonight?"

"I simply don't know. And that's the devil of it." He stands and says tiredly, "Why don't we go downstairs and try to get some sleep now. Tomorrow's another day."

I am not about to argue. I am too weary. We give up cleaning the bedroom as a bad job; this will take some major grease-cutters. "I'll bring someone in," Adam says. "Let's just leave everything as it is for now."

We sleep in the living room; I on the sofa and Adam on the floor beside me. He does not kiss me good night or hold my hand as we fall asleep, and I wonder about that. Such displays are not required, of course, but the lack of them seems strange. I would swear that some small distance has crept in between us. Finally, I put it down to exhaustion.

Sometime in the night I think I hear voices outside, but then I decide it must be the wind sighing through the trees. I look down at the way the moonlight shines through the window, onto the floor. In its light are Adam's muddy running shoes, covered with forest debris.

I give them only a moment's thought. Then I sleep.

In the morning we close up the cabin, and at the market Adam stops to call Annie Lowell. When he returns to the car he looks grim yet relieved.

"She's back," he says. "She's at Annie's apartment now, sleeping."

"Thank God. At least she's safe."

He turns the key in the ignition then looks at me.

"Even now you puzzle me, Naomi Wing. How can you still care about Susan?"

"She was Beth's mother, Adam. Regardless of anything else, we need to look after her."

CHAPTER 16

"I'm telling you, I wasn't dating Beth," the sullen young man who sits before us insists.

Curt Lawrence is much as I remember him, though decidedly tougher: short, sandy brown haircut, and eyes that don't flinch. A young Travis Hartmann, I think. Cool, self-contained. Not one to put himself out unless it will be to his benefit in some way.

Adam and I have come here together, after calling to make sure the boy was at home and not away for the summer. The Lawrence house is large and sprawling, light and airy. It sits on a hill above an older road on Whidbey that is lined with barns, some of them falling down, their wood a dank gray from decades of winter rains. From this wide expanse of windows one can also see new houses, many of them perched on bulldozed mounds and left embarrassingly naked of greenery. I squelch a sudden urge to run down there and toss a blanket over them. Mingled in with these oddities are fifties-era ranch houses with their paint and siding warped. Many have rusted cars in the yards, children's neglected toys, farm machinery that's suffered years of disuse. Recessions are not pretty.

The latest recession, however, seems not to have touched Curt Lawrence or his parents. His father, president of Trans-European Shipping Lines, is at work in Seattle, Curt has told us, and his mother is at the tennis club. He lounges casually on a black leather chair that I recognize as a designer piece. One leg is thrown over a polished chrome arm, while the connecting foot jiggles nervously, betraying the boy's attempt at disinterest.

"Beth told us you were dating," Adam says. "Are you saying she was lying?"

"I'm saying that Beth and I were friends, nothing more," he answers.

"Curt," I interject, "we aren't here to give you any trouble. It's just that if you saw Beth the night she died or even just talked to her on the phone, we'd like to know. It's not that we think you did anything wrong. We only want to know, as best we can, what happened that night."

He looks skeptical. "It was an accident, wasn't it? Isn't that what everyone said?"

"Yes, that's what was said. We just want to be sure."

"Well, I don't know anything about it. I didn't see Beth that night. In fact, I didn't see her much at all last summer."

He unwinds his tall, self-assured frame and crosses to a wet bar. Reaching into a small fridge beneath the counter, he pulls out a carton of orange juice and takes a deep swallow directly from the carton. Wiping his mouth with the back of his hand, he says, "Beth was acting strange last year. She went her way, I went mine."

I am remembering something. "You're at the University of Washington now, aren't you?"

"Yeah, I'm at U-Dub. So what?"

"It's just that we thought Beth wanted to stay here and not go to school in the East because of you."

He laughs. "Me? That's crazy. Why would she do a thing like that?"

I glance at Adam and he nods. I go for the shock value.

"Beth was pregnant, Curt. We think she was pregnant with your child."

He turns an angry red. "Pregnant? With my kid? No way! You're not pinning something like that on me. If Beth got knocked up, I didn't have anything to do with it. And anybody who says I did is a liar." He slams the orange juice back into the fridge and kicks the door closed.

Adam and I glance at each other. The kid is upset—but is he surprised? Adam makes one more try.

"The coroner took blood samples from the fetus," he bluffs. "With DNA testing, Curt, we can prove you were the father. Why don't you just tell us what happened, instead? Did you want her to get an abortion? Did the two of you argue that night?"

The Lawrence boy comes around the wet bar and faces both of us, hostility in every muscle. "You listen to me. Beth and I never slept together. *Not once.* So you go ahead and do all the fucking testing you want." He jabs out his right arm. "Here, you want my blood? Take it—any damn time you want. You're not gonna prove a thing."

When neither Adam nor I respond, he gestures with a thumb toward the front door. "No? Then get the hell out of here. Both of you. And don't come back."

Adam shrugs. He looks at me and I nod agreement. As Curt Lawrence is now standing with his back to us, arms folded, we show ourselves to the door.

Adam is ahead of me as we go down the walk to the car. Suddenly I feel a hand grab my shoulder from behind.

"Did you tell anyone about this?" Curt Lawrence says, his nose in my face. "Does anybody know besides you two?"

"That Beth was pregnant?" I say. "Or that you might have been the father?"

"Either way."

"No. We haven't told anyone yet."

"Then don't. I'm warning you, don't."

I brush his hand off my shoulder. "You're warning me?"

"That's what I said."

"And if I tell anyone, you'll do precisely what?"

"You'll regret it, that's all. I'll make you regret you ever opened your mouth."

Adam is looking back now, seeing this, and he's starting toward us, his face creased with anger. I don't want a scene here, so I shake Curt off and hurry down the walk.

"Are you all right?" Adam asks, darting a glance at the boy.

"Yes, I'm fine. Let's just get in the car and get out of here."

He hesitates.

"I'm fine, I tell you. Let's *go*."

He holds the door for me, com[e]
and reaches for his keys. "You kno[w]
dropping the keys on the floor a[nd]
reach for them. "I really want to
that kid in the face."

I look back to Curt Lawrence,
his front door watching us, a pu[zzled look]
on his face. "I don't blame you a

I cannot believe Beth would ha[ve]
But if she did, and if he found o[ut]
what would he do?

I can almost hear her saying,
and Curt Lawrence answering,
about it. Get it fixed."

But Beth would never have do[ne it, with her]
strict Catholic upbringing. She w[ould have the]
child alone, if need be.

But why—oh God, why—didn't she come to me?

We are heading toward Crow Cottage, each of us deep
in our thoughts. Finally I turn to Adam and say,
"What do you think?"

"Do I think he's the father, you mean? I don't know
anymore."

"He was rather convincing. But so far as we ever
knew, he was the only boy Beth was seeing."

Adam glances over at me. "Someone she had to
keep secret, then?"

"Could be. But who? And why?"

"Naomi . . . are you sure? What if you're wrong?
What if Beth wasn't pregnant at all?"

"Adam, she was. So many things fit together, now. Her moodiness, and the way she held her back so much, as if it ached. Don't you remember? You said it yourself once last summer, that she was acting like an old lady. She laughed it off, but if you put that together with the butterfly pendant and the Blackfoot legend . . ."

"I'll admit it makes sense. But—"

"And there's something I haven't told you. I saw Beth. My mother brought me a vision, and I saw Beth as clear as day, a week before she died. It was Beth herself who gave me the clue about the Blackfoot legend. She was holding that pendant, clutching it as if her very life depended on it, and she said to me clearly, 'Blackfeet.' I heard it as two words, and I didn't understand it at the time. It was only the other night when I remembered the book of legends about the Blackfeet that I was certain."

Adam utters an oath, swerves, and pulls the car to a stop. "For God's sake, Naomi! Why didn't you tell me about this vision a year ago, when it happened?"

"I didn't think you'd believe me. Adam, I didn't believe it myself. I thought my mother was working on me to upset you so much, you'd forget about the Wintu land deal."

"And you actually let that—your suspicions about your mother—keep you from even mentioning it to me? Something as important as that?"

"I know. I'm sorry. I regret that now more than anything I've ever—Adam, you'd have to know what it was like then. I told you how sly my mother could be, an angle for everything, always a hidden agenda. And we were hot and heavy into the court case by then. I was so tired, working days at Robinson-Leigh, then all night long on the Wintu briefs. But even so, she was at me all the time, pushing and pushing. I wasn't doing enough, she'd say, or I was letting my relationship with you get in the way. You know how much it meant to her, preserving those lands. She was angry with you, out for blood—" He is looking at me coldly, and the rush of words catches in my throat. I fall silent.

"Dammit, Naomi! You and that damned business with your mother! You never did see that relationship clearly, and now, if what you're telling me is that you let my daughter die because of old childhood grievances—"

He turns away and grips the steering wheel, his hands shaking. Tears fill my eyes.

"I'm so sorry. I can't even begin to tell you the guilt I've lived with this past year." I try to touch him, but he shakes me off.

"You've lived with guilt? My daughter hasn't lived at all! And you might have saved her."

I sink back against the seat, covering my mouth with my hands as it is trembling so much.

Adam leans his forehead against the wheel, closing his eyes. "I'm sorry. I didn't mean that."

But the words have been said, and they can't be taken back.

"No. You're right. You're absolutely right, I might have saved her. Oh God, I've told myself so many times this last year that I shouldn't blame myself, because she had pulled away from me all summer, and I wasn't seeing her as much. But I didn't question whether there might be something wrong, I just thought she was wrapped up in getting ready to leave for school and tired because of that—"

I break off, my voice shaking. "That was no excuse. There were no excuses then, and there still are none. I don't know what else I can say."

He straightens, rubs his face, and lets out a huge sigh. Starting the engine again, he pulls out onto the road. He is absolutely silent, and as he cuts a corner too sharply, I ask, "Are you all right?" though of course I know he is not.

"I need some time," he says stiffly after a moment.

"Of course," I say just as stiffly. It is as if some angry giant with a sword appeared out of the blue and severed any bond between us in one fell swoop.

No, not a giant. My own stupidity, my fear.

Damn you, Mother! I think to myself, then almost immediately call back the blame. This is not my mother's fault. It is mine, for still having been, at thirty-three, her frightened child. Adam is right. It is time to grow up, to stop letting her control me even from the grave. If I'd been more my own person, less afraid of her hidden agendas, and seeking, instead, the truth, Beth might be alive today.

The remainder of our drive is silent. As Adam pulls to a stop at Crow Cottage, I turn to him. "I . . . I have to ask you one thing."

He looks at me tiredly.

"Adam . . . do you remember seeing the butterfly pendant on Beth that night? When they . . . when they brought her in, I mean."

He reaches past me and opens my door. "I really don't want to talk about this anymore. And I've got to get to Coupeville."

"Adam, please. I found the pendant in my garden
the other day. If Beth—if she died with it on, don't
you see, it might make a difference . . . how it got
there."

His tone is cold, sarcastic. "Maybe your mother put
it there."

CHAPTER 17

My nerves are shot, and my heart actually hurts. There is pain in the area of my collarbones from tension and unshed tears. I can no longer sit around and think about all this. When I think, I am reminded that I was beginning to regain some peace only a week ago, and now—since Adam's been back in my life—that peace has fled. I'd have done better to stick to my resolutions, it seems, and remain untouched, alone.

I did not, however, and since I'm in the midst of all this again, I must see what I can do about it. Whatever monster is in this closet, it must be faced.

I change clothes, make two phone calls—one to information and another to Annie Lowell's office—and drive the ten minutes to the ferry. Parking on the first level, I get out and take the stairs up to the coffee shop level. The wind whips me about, disassembling the neat French twist I've made of my hair. I pull my suede jacket about me, one that used to be Pete's, and which he gave me to wear when we were teenagers.

I've never given it back. Sometimes, when I need to remember the old days, the beginning days with Pete when I was still young and relatively innocent, I wear it. It is small comfort but better than none.

Stepping out onto the passenger level, I find it warm here. The scent of fresh-brewed coffee is heartening. "A latte, please," I say to the woman behind the counter. It takes a few minutes, but I collect the latte, pay the cashier, and feel the ferry begin to move. Crossing over to a booth by the windows, I slide onto the yellow plastic seat, rest my bag on the table, and sigh.

There are few people on the ferry, I note as I raise the paper cup to my lips and look around. There seldom are throughout the week, though commuter hours can be bad. Beth and I made this trip together several times the year before she died. I was spending more time on the island then, closing myself off from the city in order to concentrate better on the Wintu briefs. Now and then Beth and I would both get island fever, and we'd dash in to Seattle to a museum, a movie, or the zoo. We would try to time it to get back to the ferry ahead of the crowds. I remember one day, however, when we were late, and ended up squeezed in shoulder to shoulder with other passengers on one of the rows of seats.

"I wonder if my Dad is here," Beth said, looking about hopefully at all the men in business suits, one so like the other.

"No, he's—" I began to say, catching myself just in time. "I mean, it's too early, don't you think? Doesn't he usually get home late?"

Her face fell. "That's true." She was sixteen then, the same age as I when Pete and I made love on the beach. But Curt Lawrence was not yet in her life, and so far as I knew she had no boyfriends, no one she really cared about. It was hard for Beth, so far out of town, to make friends. Her father and mother were her life. And me.

"Do you think they'll get home tonight at all?" she asked. Now and then Susan stayed overnight with friends from the university, and Adam—

"I don't know," I said carefully.

"If they don't, could I stay overnight with you?"

"I wish you could. I . . . I'm sorry. I'm kind of tired, Beth."

"That's okay. I understand."

I remember that she jumped up then and ran out to the observation deck. I started to follow, then sat back down and simply watched her as she stood at the rail, gazing moodily at the Sound and the surrounding green islands. Her hair was darker by then, a russet gold, and it was long, down to her shoulders. She was turning into a real beauty, and there were men of all ages whose heads had turned as she passed.

What am I going to do, I had thought, despairing. *Dear Beth. What can I do about you?*

That night, after I had safely deposited her back at the mansion with the housekeeper, I returned to Seattle, to my own apartment, and—as prearranged, of course—to Adam.

From the ferry I drive directly to Annie Lowell's office in the Manchester Building. A non-smiling, business-like receptionist named Dory shows me into the doctor's office and leaves me there.

"She'll be with you in just a moment."

I stand looking out windows that are wide, the city laid out at my feet. Lowell does well, it seems.

"Well, what do you think?" she startles me by asking with a smile as she enters from another door leading in from the hall. "Too formal? Informal?"

My gaze swings her way. "Sorry. I was just remembering my office at Robinson-Leigh. It was a tiny, well-furnished cubbyhole as befitted a young but rising associate's position. My walls were cluttered with books and piles of briefs in varying states of progress, and there were always people bustling in and out."

"You sound as if you miss it," she observes.

"Do I? If so, I haven't been aware of it, at least not till now."

She sits behind her desk, and I sit in the chair facing it. I take a minute to salt away details: the smooth dark hair, cut short as is the style these days. Her voice is husky, the eyes very large and dark blue. They seem to penetrate mine, searching for secrets. Or perhaps that is only my imagination, as I've always felt a bit uneasy around psychiatrists. One can't help but think they're always probing, analyzing, no matter how friendly they might appear on the surface.

"Susan tells me you live alone on the island," she says, "and that you left your job at the law firm last year."

"Really? I'm surprised she told you all that." I am surprised, in fact, that Susan knows all that.

"Yes, the other night on the ferry, coming home. I was curious. I hope you don't mind."

"No. How is Susan? Is she all right?"

"Tired. But yes, I'd say she's all right."

The psychiatrist straightens her spine and her tone becomes strictly professional. "As I told you on the phone, however, I can't divulge any medical information about Susan Lambert. Legally, if we hadn't met as we did the other night, I wouldn't be able to even confirm that she was my patient."

"Yes, I know. Doctor/client confidentiality. But since we did meet the other night . . ."

"I still can't talk to you about Susan, except in generalities."

"Is this general enough, then? You've heard about the incident at the cabin on Whidbey last night?"

"Yes. Travis Hartmann phoned me. And Adam."

"Do you know if it was Susan who did it? Has she admitted to being out there?"

"I can't answer that," she says.

"Then tell me this. Do you think someone else might have done it?"

"Someone else?" She arches a dark brow. "Who do you have in mind?"

"Someone who would like to make Susan look bad . . . or who, for whatever reason, would like to scare me away from Adam."

She is silent for a moment. Then, "As a point of discussion, I suppose that's possible. But who?"

"I'm not prepared to answer that. At least, not yet. But Ms. Lowell—"

"Please, call me Annie."

"Annie. As Susan's doctor and, I understand, her friend, perhaps you could talk to her for me?"

The woman tents her fingers and rests her chin on them. "Talk to Susan? About what?"

"I'd like to meet with her, and I don't know where she lives now. I tried to phone, but her number's unlisted."

"And what do you want to see Susan about?"

"There are some things I'd like to ask her. About Beth."

"I see. Well, I'm sorry. I don't know if that's a good idea."

"But surely Susan can decide that for herself?"

"I . . . yes, of course. But it is my job to advise her. Ms. Wing—"

"Naomi."

Her smile is cool. "Naomi. I can't think that having this kind of conversation with Susan would be very pleasant for either of you."

"Pleasant, no. But it may help her. And it could help me too."

"And just what benefit do you think might accrue from this for Susan?"

"I'd rather discuss that with her."

Annie Lowell looks at me as if she would like to put me on her couch and ask me questions about my childhood. It comes as almost no surprise when she actually does say, "Have you ever been in therapy?"

I cannot help it; I laugh out loud. "And did I have problems with my mother?"

She doesn't even smile. "Well? Did you?"

"Are you drumming up business?" I say.

"No. But from what I've heard . . ." At this she catches herself and looks down at her hands.

"So Susan has told you more than a few things about me." Of course she would have. But how does Susan know so much? From Beth?

Annie Lowell shakes her head. "Actually, it was Adam Lambert who first told me about you. And since Adam isn't my patient, there's no need to keep that confidential."

She sees she has scored. Heat rises to my face, and the result is a slight satisfied tug at one corner of her mouth. I decide I do not like this woman, not at all.

"I suppose it goes with the job," I say carefully, "knowing how to twist people about."

She gives a shrug. "Much like being an attorney, I would think."

The phone on her desk rings. She presses the intercom button, picks up the receiver, and listens. "Yes, Dory, I'll take it." To me she says, "Do you mind?"

I shake my head. Shoving my hands into my pockets, I stand and cross the room to stare at her bevy of diplomas, just for something to do with my energy, which is still on the angry side. *University of Michigan*, one reads. *Gates University of Medicine*, another. The list goes on. Graduate degrees in psychiatry at noted universities. Not bad.

But I can't help wondering what happens to doctors once they get out of school. I haven't run across many who thoroughly know their business ten years later. And the ones who still care about patients as people rather than profit-making diseases are even more rare.

Well, to be fair, perhaps they burn out, just like me. I can't say I've kept up with the law in the past year. On the other hand, I'm not pretending to practice it, either.

Though I'm not strictly eavesdropping, I can't help noticing that Annie Lowell's voice has lowered to a purr. "Yes, sweetheart," she is saying softly into the receiver. "I'll be home by five-thirty, latest." A brief silence. "I . . . I'm not sure . . ." And then, with a sigh and a slight smile, "Yes, all right . . . I'll stop at the market. The Scharffenberger, I remember. Brut."

She glances up and sees me looking at her. Immediately, her smile disappears. "I really must go now. I've a patient due any moment. I'll call you back in a little while, all right? Yes, dear, I won't be long."

So the tough doctor has a heart—and a friend. I suppose she can't be all bad.

She hangs up, glances at her watch, and stands. "Sorry to cut this short, but I am expecting a patient."

"That's all right. I had only one more question. Are you going to help me with Susan?"

She studies the pencil in her hands. "If I thought talking with you could actually help her, I would. As it is, I can't think of a good reason to worry her with this."

"I can find out where she lives from Adam," I say reasonably. "I can certainly see her without your permission."

"Of course you can," she says just as reasonably. "And if you upset her—if you trigger another of her episodes—you can be responsible for that as well as for the death of her daughter."

I am shocked into speechlessness. As I stand helplessly reaching for words, Annie Lowell begins to clear her desk, setting things neatly in order.

"Anything else?" she says curtly, not looking at me.

I am realizing now that Susan must have told her terrible stories about me. What other reason can there be for such a hostile attitude toward me? And even were I inspired to do so, I can hardly stand here and deny Susan's accusations. Some of them may well have been true.

"No. Nothing else."

I cross the room to let myself out, and there is a knock on the other door, from the hall. Annie Lowell waits till I've stepped out and closed the reception room door behind me. I hear her greeting someone in a hushed voice, and I hear the other voice, a man's. I cannot make out the words.

As I leave I am shaken from the confrontation, but it has not been in vain. I am remembering Annie Lowell's phone call. There was something about it that struck a chord in my memory, something I am certain is important.

And then I know.

CHAPTER 18

At a phone booth I call Pete Shelton and beg a favor: the address of the good doctor's apartment. "What are you offering in return?" he asks.

He has me over a barrel, and he knows it, so I give him what he wants: a promise to look into the Hood Canal problems and see how I can help. Pete can be a stickler sometimes about rules, but I've known him before to break them when there's something he really wants.

It takes him only a few seconds to bring up Annie Lowell's home address on the department's computer, through Motor Vehicle records. "That big highrise at Sutton and Pike," he says, sounding thoroughly exhausted. "A pretty snazzy address. Look, I don't know what you want this for, and I don't think I want to know. But why didn't you just go to her office?"

"I did. Now I'm on the track of bigger fish."

"Hmmm. Sounds to me like you're coming back to life at last. I think I approve. By the way, Susan Lambert phoned me this morning first thing."

"Really? How did she sound?"

"Strung out, shaky. Actually, she sounded drunk. She went on and on, crying about Beth and how it was all your fault Beth died, and she wanted you charged."

"What did you tell her?"

"I told her I was very, very sorry about Beth, and I understood her pain, but that there wasn't any evidence against you. I also told her that since last night, there might not ever be."

"Since last night? What do you mean?"

He makes a whuffing sound, and I hear a squeak that tells me he's sitting heavily in his office chair. "It seems our renowned coroner, Gray Steen, drove off a cliff sometime last night—right into Deception Pass."

"My God! Is he dead?"

"His car fell several hundred feet. What do you think?"

"Was he drunk?"

"I'm still waiting to hear on that and an approximate time of death. We dragged him up from there around four this morning, and the body's being examined now."

"Pete? Doesn't it seem odd this happened just now?"

"You mean just when Susan Lambert needed Steen to remember the condition of her daughter's body last year, since all the official files are missing? Nah, not at all," he says sarcastically. "I figure it's a mere coincidence. That, and the fact that there were tire tracks from another car leading to the point where Steen went off the road. By the way . . . just where was your boyfriend last night?"

I don't answer, though I am remembering, suddenly, Adam's words last night: "I would do almost anything to protect you." I am also remembering the muddy, needle-covered shoes, and the fact that he was gone so long at the store. "My car went into a ditch," he said.

It comes to me now that for some reason I didn't believe that story, even then.

But Travis Hartmann's shoes were in bad shape, as well. And where was he just before and after he came to the cabin?

"What do you think Steen was doing out that way?" I ask Pete. "Doesn't he live in Langley?"

"He did," Pete says. "Doesn't live anywhere now. Naomi? You want to answer my question?"

"Sure. Adam was with me last night. We were together at the cabin."

"You mean the Lambert cabin? The one on the other side of the island?"

"Yes."

He sighs heavily. "As I remember, that's not so far from Deception Pass."

"I told you, Pete. We were together all night."

"I hope you're not lying for him, friend. This whole thing is starting to smell real bad."

"Adam did not run Gray Steen off the road, Pete. He couldn't do something like that. I know he couldn't."

Travis Hartmann might have it in him, though. But why? And what about Susan, I am wondering? She was missing from the city all night. She was also, quite probably, at the cabin.

The only question is, what would be her motive? She apparently believed that Gray Steen could be a help to her by remembering . . .

On the other hand, what if he did remember and wasn't able to help her in her vendetta against me? What if he told her, in fact, that Beth was pregnant—thereby pointing a finger of possible guilt at the baby's father and away from me?

Would Susan be that desperate to hide this news? Enough to kill Steen and silence him?

I thank Pete for his help and field his final question, which is, "All right, I give. What do you want with Annie Lowell's address?"

"Oh, I don't know. Maybe I'll take her a bottle of wine," I say.

He makes a scornful sound. "I've met that lady. A screwdriver might be more like it."

"Meaning what?"

"Only that she's a loose wheel if I've ever seen one. One of those types that's just waiting to come off the track. If I were you, Naomi, I'd stay as far away from her—and Susan Lambert—as possible."

"Pete? About Susan. Do you think she would actually harm anyone?"

"I think she's a walking time bomb. As for Annie Lowell? If Susan were my wife, I wouldn't let her near the woman, much less trust her as a doctor. And, Naomi, don't you find it just a bit strange that your otherwise intelligent pal, Adam Lambert, does?"

* * *

With Pete's last words running through my brain, I drive directly to Sutton and Pike, parking alongside the curb a half block away. Going around to the trunk, I search through an overnight bag of clothing that I haven't seen in months, but that I've always kept here in case I needed a change of clothes while in the city. At the bottom of the bag I find a black cashmere blazer that cost a mint at a Seattle boutique a couple of years ago. I pull it out, and it's wrinkled, but should do. I remove Pete's old suede jacket and pull on the blazer, smoothing out the wrinkles as best I can.

With it, plus the French twist that I take pains to smoothe, and the fairly decent jeans and boots I've worn, I have no problem getting past the two clerks in the lobby, who are deep in conversation. I smile, wave, and sail by as if I belong here—which, I've found, is about all it takes in any high-priced establishment. They would rather not ask than risk offending a valued guest, someone they should have recognized.

I take one of two elevators up to the third floor and knock on 303, which is the apartment number Pete gave me. After a few moments it is opened—no surprise—by Susan.

She gives a start. "Naomi! What are you doing here? How did you know I was here?"

"We need to talk," I say. "May I come in?"

CHAPTER 19

Susan holds a flute glass in her right hand. It is half empty, as is a bottle of Scharffenberger champagne on the breakfast bar.

"How did you know I was here?" she says, turning away from me and stumbling a bit, slopping the champagne over the edge of her glass. It splatters on the white rug, but she seems not to notice.

"I overheard Annie on the phone with you," I say.

"You heard—" she looks disconcerted.

"I know about you and Annie, Susan. I put it together—the way she talked to you, and the Scharffenberg. There was a bottle of it at the cabin, and Adam said it was all you ever drank."

"The cabin—"

She looks dumbstruck. I still don't see—"

"It wasn't just that. There were little things, since the other night when I saw you and Annie together. It may have been something I sensed between the two of you."

"We were . . . that obvious?"

"Not at all. I'm just accustomed to putting little things together and coming up with big ones."

She holds the glass against her forehead as if cooling it, and closes her eyes briefly. I step inside and close the door.

Susan looks horribly tired. Her blond hair doesn't have its usual gloss; it has been pulled back into a ponytail but on either side hangs limply. She wears a gray sweatsuit that is too long for her, and I assume it belongs to Annie Lowell. Her face today is completely devoid of makeup.

"I suppose you can't wait to run to Adam with this," she says. Walking over to a breakfast bar, she leans against it with one palm, as if for support.

"No. I'm not concerned with telling Adam. I'm just confused, Susan. If you and Annie are together . . . why have you been so jealous of Adam and me? And what was all that about the other night? The negligee, and all those things you said about Adam, and him wanting you that way?"

She gives me a contemptuous look. "I'm not a lesbian, Naomi. I just like being with a woman sometimes. And sometimes, for some stupid reason, I still care about whether I can attract a man. Even a man like Adam."

"I see."

"*You see*," she says in that same tone of contempt. "You've never seen. It was never about you and Adam, you could have had him on a platter. I just wasn't about to let you have them both."

"Adam and Beth, you mean."

"Of course Adam and Beth! You steal my daughter and you want my husband too?" Her lips tremble, and I see before me, suddenly, a woman who is incredibly sad. Not a monster, not a crazy-woman, nor even a threat. Just a woman who's been hurt.

The glass begins to slip from her fingers, and I cross the room quickly as she sways and starts to fall. "Here, let me help you," I say.

With an arm around her waist, I lead her over to an armchair in the living room, and though her weight is mostly on me, I am surprised at how light she feels. "I don't need your help," she protests, but she really cannot stand alone. As soon as I have her in the chair she leans forward from the waist and buries her face in her hands. Her shoulders heave, and from deep in her throat come sounds of weeping.

"I need Annie," she says, the words muffled in her hands. "Please get Annie."

I hesitate, wondering if Annie Lowell is the right person to help Susan now. But then it isn't my decision to make. Glancing around, I see a phone on a cherrywood sideboard at a right angle to the breakfast bar. Crossing over to it, I reach inside my pocket for the crumpled piece of paper I wrote Annie Lowell's office number on earlier, back at Crow Cottage. Dialing, I listen to the ring. There is no answer, and I glance at my watch. An hour and a half have passed since I left Annie's office.

"Susan, I think she must be on her way home by now. She should be here soon."

I hang up and go back to her. Kneeling beside her, I search for a Kleenex in my other pocket and find one that is still clean. "Here," I say, urging her to lift her head. She does, giving a huge, heavy shudder. I dry her eyes and beneath her nose. She accepts this like a child.

"I can't get along without her anymore, you know," she says, sniffing and dabbing her nose with a finger. "If I didn't have Annie, I don't know what I'd do."

"Do you love this woman, Susan?" I ask gently. "Is she good to you?" I have my doubts, for I'm remembering how easily Annie agreed to stop at a store on the way home for more champagne. What are her motives? I wonder.

Susan looks at me, and her mouth twists into a sad smile. "Sometimes I think there isn't any such thing as love. Just people who want to control other people and call it love." A small, hysterical laugh escapes her lips, and she pushes away from me, back to her feet. Grabbing up the champagne bottle from the breakfast bar, she drinks straight from it, then stands there, staring at the bottle.

"I went to Catholic boarding school, you know," she says. "For six years, nothing but nuns and more nuns. All those rules. 'Do this, do that, don't do this, don't do that.' Never *do*."

Her wild, hurt gaze swings to me. "It's only since I've been with Annie that I've gotten over some of what the nuns did to me. All the *shall nots*, the raps on the knuckles, having to kneel and pray all night in the chapel to make up for my 'sins.' And you know what my supposed sins were?" She laughs harshly. "Talking in the bathrooms, visiting other girls in their rooms at night after the lights were out. And the funny thing is, it was all so innocent at first. We were gossiping about boys! But the nuns, you know, they were afraid we'd fall in love with each other, since there weren't actually any boys around." She falters and takes a deep swallow from the bottle again. "As if that's the worst that could happen."

I would like to take that bottle from her, yet I know that would break her focus, and it's more important, I think, for her to get all this out.

"What did happen?" I ask softly.

She wipes the back of her hand over her mouth and leans to study her face in a mirror over the sideboard. I sense she has left me, and gone off to a world of her own. "I was a pretty little thing back then . . . all blonde curls, and my eyes . . ." She frowns. "Not dull the way they are now. 'Green and bright as new-mown grass,' that's what my father used to say. He didn't want me to be sent away. He and I were pals. But my mother insisted on it, she was the one with all the fears. 'Girls in the world are up against so much these days, Susan. All the drugs and those horrid teen-age boys . . .'"

She makes a sound of contempt. "There was a priest . . . Father William. He said Mass for us every morning, and he was old, or at least he was to me then. When I first saw him I thought he looked like someone's grandfather. He had a fringe of white hair around a bald spot and a nice smile. He would tease me, calling me by nicknames like 'Lazybones,' because I was late for Mass most of the time. My father always teased me about oversleeping in the morning, so when Father William did it too, it made me feel less homesick, and I liked him for that."

Her eyes grow even more distant. "Well, one night . . . after the nuns had all been tucked in . . . good old

Father William came to my room. I was a virgin, and he told me God had sent him to help me become a woman. He pulled my covers down and unbuttoned my pajama top. Then he began to suck on my breasts, and I remember his hair smelling so oily and old, and being so afraid, because he was reaching for me, down there . . .''

My hand goes out to Susan, as does my heart. I want to wrap her up in my arms and hold her till she knows she's safe. But as I move, she jerks away. "Don't touch me! Don't you dare touch me! If you touch me again, I'll tell!"

I step back. "It's all right. It's all right, Susan. It's just me, Naomi."

She looks at me, the green eyes wet with unshed tears. I don't think she has heard me, or even knows who I am at this moment. "He said they wouldn't believe me if I told," she says in a tiny voice. "He said they'd believe him, because he was a priest. He wasn't, though, you know. A priest is a man of God. That wicked man was the devil."

"Yes," I say. "He was evil."

"He should die," she says in a strong, lucid tone that startles me.

"I . . ."

"That's it. That's exactly it. *He should die.*"

CHAPTER 20

Susan sits now on a rattan and rose-colored sofa, slipping between lucid and half-mad moments. Her back is ramrod straight, her knees primly together. Now and then she casts a quick, nervous look toward the front door.

"She should be here any moment," I say reassuringly, though I am wondering myself what's keeping Annie Lowell. While I'm no longer at all certain about her ability as a therapist, I am even less sure that my presence here is helping.

"What?" Susan says. "Oh, yes." She bites a thumbnail. "Annie should be home any minute."

She folds her hands in her lap and seems for all the world like a little girl whose parents have told her not to let in strangers while they're gone. "I hope you understand, I didn't have to tell you any of those things at all."

"No, of course you didn't. And, Susan, don't worry.

I won't tell anyone what you told me. How are you feeling now?"

"It's just that I couldn't very well come out of Catholic boarding school," she says, ignoring my question, "and marry a woman. That sort of thing just wasn't done in our circle."

"Of course not," I say, at a loss for anything else.

"That's why I married Adam."

She looks at me coolly, and I understand that she knows exactly what she is saying now.

"I married him," she says, "and when I couldn't face the day-to-day reality of not loving him, I drank. You know the rest, I presume." She gives an elaborate shrug. "I didn't mean it to turn out that way."

"But when it did? Susan, why didn't you just give him a divorce?"

The green eyes narrow. "Because by the time he asked for one, you were in the picture. And I told you—you weren't getting him and Beth too."

"But Beth *loved* you. She wanted to be close to you, you just weren't there, Susan. That's the only reason she came to me."

Susan jumps to her feet. "Damn you! Do you think I don't know that? Do you think I don't live with it every day of my goddamned life?" She looks around frantically. "Where is that bottle? *What the hell did you do with that bottle?*"

She dashes into the kitchen, shoving newspapers aside on the breakfast bar, pushing pots aside in cupboards, then yanking open the refrigerator door. Finally she slams it shut and searches under the sink.

"It was empty," I say, watching from the door. "I put it in the trash, remember?"

Susan casts me a suspicious look and tears things out of the thin, white trashcan: empty soup cans, bread wrappers, an orange skin, and finally the heavy Scharffenberger bottle. Holding it up she peers into it, then turns it over, shaking it hard, though there is obviously nothing left. At last she gives up, slumping, the bottle dangling from her loose fingers.

"I don't know this person," she says tiredly, running a hand through her hair. "I don't know who I am anymore. I certainly cannot believe I am standing here in my female lover's kitchen, digging through garbage for one last ounce of booze—and in front of my ex-husband's mistress, no less."

I try a smile. "Ex-mistress."

She looks at me sharply. And then suddenly she laughs. Something passes between us, and for the first time since walking through this door, I relax.

"Susan, neither of us can do anything about what's happened. Maybe we both failed Beth, but you were the best mother you could be, and I swear I was the best friend I knew how to be. What if we both just decide to *let* it be? Isn't that what Beth would want?"

Her smile is shaky. "That's funny. That's what Beth used to say . . . *Let it be.* Did she get that from you?"

I shrug. "I don't know. I just remember her saying, *'cover all the bases.'* I figured she got that from you."

Susan falls silent, as if reminiscing. Finally she says, "Beth was a beautiful child, wasn't she?"

"Exceptional. And she couldn't have gotten that way without you."

Tears fills her eyes.

"You know Susan, I've been doing a lot of thinking about Beth and what happened that night."

She dabs at her eyes with her fingertips. "What about it?"

"I . . . I hate to bring this up, especially now. But I don't understand what you hoped to find in the autopsy records. Can you tell me?"

She surprises me by looking embarrassed. "Anything, I suppose. Evidence of a fight, your skin under her nails, pieces of your hair . . ." She stops and swallows hard.

"Was all that your idea?"

"Not entirely," she admits. "Trav . . ."

"Travis Hartmann came up with the idea, and you've been going along with it?"

She bristles. "I'm not his pawn, if that's what you mean."

"No, I didn't think that. I imagine you must have told him what you were thinking about that night, and he, as your lawyer, provided the legal terms. Is that it?"

She puts the champagne bottle down on the counter and says, "I suppose."

"But, Susan, why did you think Beth and I fought? You see, that's what I don't understand. I've been asking myself over and over, do you know something about that night that you haven't told anyone?"

She sighs and says wearily, "Oh, I know everything about that night."

"Everything?"

She laughs without humor. "Well, I know Beth found out about you and Adam."

I am stunned. "How—?"

"I talked to Beth, that's how. After she left you at Crow Cottage. She was crying so hard I could barely understand her. She said, 'I heard him, Mother. I heard Daddy talking to Naomi, and they—' And I said, 'Slow down, Beth, tell me what you heard.' She said, 'Mommy, they're ... well, you know.' She couldn't finish it, couldn't say the words. But I knew, by the tone of her voice."

"Oh God. I'm so sorry. What did you say?"

She bites her lower lip, then looks away. "I ... I am very sorry to say that I laughed."

A small shock goes through me. "You *laughed?*"

She swings back to face me. "Don't you judge me," she says, her voice low and harsh. "Don't you dare judge me now."

"No, no, I won't ... but, oh, Susan, why?"

She pushes her hair back from her forehead. "I was tired. Drunk, I suppose. I'd gone to bed, and I was sleeping by then. Her call took me by surprise, and I didn't know what to say."

"But ... did you comfort her at all?"

A grimace of self-disgust crosses her face. "As a matter of fact, I told her I'd known all along, and if she wanted to complain to someone, she should let her precious Naomi tell her all about it. I said, 'Let her explain what she and your father have been doing behind your back all these years.' "

"But she'd never have done that! She was too hurt."

She'd have turned to someone else, I am thinking. *But who?*

Only one person: the father of her child.

But can I say this to Susan?

241

Before I can speak she says, "Are you telling me Beth didn't come back to you that night?"

"No. She never came back that night."

"And you didn't run after her? After she heard Adam on the phone with you, I mean. You didn't follow her to the mansion and at least try to explain?"

I hesitate. "No."

"I don't understand. I thought sure . . . I mean, when she called to tell me about that, so upset, I honestly thought you'd be on her heels, calming her down, and that once she was off the phone with me, the two of you—" She runs a hand through her hair, and her voice rises. "But now you're saying she was just there in the mansion alone?"

"I . . . yes."

She shakes her head. "But that isn't like you. You were always there for her, you wouldn't have let her hurt that way without doing something about it. I was certain of that, and that's why I didn't think I was hurting her that much . . . and why I hung up on her . . ."

I am silent. There is nothing I can say to help Susan understand why I didn't look after Beth that night. For though Susan has been so brutally honest with me, I cannot bring myself to tell her my own truth about that night.

"Why do you let her drink like that?" I demand of Annie Lowell. Susan is lying down in the bedroom, the door closed, and Annie is, without ceremony, showing me to the door.

"I'm her doctor," she says, "not a prison guard. I can tell her what I think about it, but I can't stop her."

"Then why don't you at least not keep any alcohol in the house? Why are you *buying* it for her, for heaven's sake?"

"She'd find it somewhere."

"Still, to have it so readily available . . ."

"Let me know when you have your degree in psychiatry," Annie Lowell says testily and closes the door firmly in my face.

Back at Crow Cottage, I steam potatoes, carrots, and garlic cloves together and sit at my dining room table, forcing myself to eat. There are ghosts all around. It is at this table that I sat so many nights with Beth. Here too my mother sat with her AIM visitors in the seventies. It is here they talked all night about their hopes and dreams.

I wonder how many dreams have come true for them—individually, if not in regards to the Movement. I wonder how many since then have gone the way of my mother, crossing the River of Ghosts with a sack full of grief.

We are not that different, any of us, I think. We enter life with bags that are packed with hope, but then little by little, hope is lost along the way.

Poor Susan. Poor child, beautiful and wide-eyed as Beth, I feel certain, when she began. And then to have her trust so badly betrayed . . . not just as a child, but all along the way.

As if I've conjured her up, I am carrying my dishes to the sink when the phone rings. I dry my hands and lift the receiver. For a moment, there is only silence. Then, "Naomi? It's Susan."

"Yes, Susan."

"I . . . I'm over at the house, and I've been going through some things of Beth's that I'd stored away. I've been doing a lot of thinking, Naomi, and there are a few trinkets I know Beth would want you to have. Could you come over?"

"You want me to have some of Beth's things?" She sounds quite sober. Still, I'm unable to believe it.

"Yes. I realize now that I can't go on this way. I can't go on blaming everyone but myself."

"I thought we talked about that, Susan. Just let it be."

"I can't. I need to do more. I need to show you— and Beth—that I'm sorry, Naomi."

I don't know what to say.

"So, can you come over?"

I glance at the clock over the sink. It is past eleven, and I am incredibly tired. I hesitate a moment longer, but then agree. "Give me a few minutes? I'm just cleaning up."

"Of course. I'm in Beth's room on the second floor. You can let yourself in, if you don't mind?"

"Not at all."

I hang up, astounded. I have never known anyone to change so radically from moment to moment. Susan is like quicksilver.

It is not until I am halfway through the woods, twenty minutes later, that I remember how deadly quicksilver can be.

CHAPTER 21

"Susan? Are you here?"

The front door to the mansion is ajar, and I push it open and step through into the hall. All about me are those ghostly pieces of furniture, shrouded in sheets. I shiver.

It has taken me longer to get here than I'd expected, as I took the time before leaving to get the butterfly pendant from my jacket pocket in the loft. Since Susan is making an attempt at kindness, I have decided that I'll give her the pendant. I won't tell her what its meaning was for Beth. That is something Adam can tell her, if and when the right moment comes.

I have never been in Beth's room, but light shines from beneath a door on the second floor. I start up the steps and am nervous, though I don't know why. Susan sounded perfectly sane, better than she's been in a long time, I would guess. I'm wondering if our clearing the air today helped. My nervousness, I tell myself, is probably only from being here in this empty house where no one has lived for so long. Too, in the back of my mind, is that scene the other night with Susan in the ballroom.

I walk toward the crack of light, and the door slowly opens. Susan stands there. "That's right. Up here." She beckons with one hand.

At the doorway she steps back, letting me pass. I note that there is no scent of alcohol on her breath, and her face is shiny, as if recently scrubbed. She wears jeans with a white blouse tucked in at the waist.

"Most of the furniture's been moved up to the attic," she says as I enter the room and glance around. "But all of Beth's things were stored in the cupboards."

The cupboards she gestures to are built in along two walls, and though they are made to look invisible, one door is open, and I see that they are only waist high. "Pretty old-fashioned, aren't they?" she says. "I think the Hillers must have built them originally to store their little boy's toys in. We decided to keep them and let Beth use them for all those things teenagers like to collect. After she . . . after last year, we put her things away in here."

A queen-sized bed stands against a third wall; it is piled high with Beth's clothes, and stuffed toys that are older and more tattered than the ones at the cabin.

"It looks so terribly empty in here," I can't help saying sadly.

"Yes. Nothing left but the bed. And of course . . . Beth's television."

There is something in her voice, and I follow her eyes to a fourth wall, opposite the bed. Built into this wall is a television with perhaps a thirty-five-inch screen.

"Beth loved watching movies from bed. Do you like movies, Naomi?" Susan asks.

"Yes. I do."

"That's right, of course you do. You and Beth watched movies together a lot, didn't you? You, and Beth, and Adam."

"Susan—"

"Let's not talk about it? You're right. Let's just go through my daughter's things."

She walks over to the bed and sits on it, lifting a pair of jeans and holding them to her chest. "I left Annie's shortly after you did, so I've been here quite a while, just sitting here alone with all this. It started me thinking."

She pats the bed, urging me to sit beside her, and though I feel uneasy about her now, I do.

"What have you been thinking?" I ask.

"Oh, about all the years. First I sorted through the baby things, then the pre-teen toys and clothes, and then—when I got to the teen years—guess what I found? Beth's diary."

She shoves clothes aside and holds up a leather-bound book. "Did you know Beth kept a diary?"

"She mentioned it once." In truth, I bought it for her one Christmas, but there is no way I can say this.

"Funny, I never saw her write in it," Susan says.

"No, I never did either. I think she took it out into the woods and sat there to write. That special place, you know?"

"No." There is a small, weighty silence. "I don't know."

I could bite my tongue. "I'm sorry. I shouldn't have mentioned it."

"No, I don't suppose you should have. Anyway, I found it, and maybe *I* shouldn't have done *that*, but I started to read it."

"Well, I guess it can't do any harm now," I say, though there is something about Susan reading Beth's diary that makes me feel queasy.

"You think not?" Susan says brightly. "You know what she said about you?"

My mouth goes dry. "No, I can't imagine. But you know teenagers—"

"She said she wished you were her mother."

"Oh, she didn't mean that, you know she didn't! Kids say those things, especially when they're angry with their parents or in trouble over something."

Susan nods wisely. "They do, yes. I know that. You don't think she meant anything by it, then?"

I meet her eyes, which are very dark now, the pupils quite large. "No, Susan. I'm certain she was just letting out her anger of the moment."

"Well, I'm glad you knew her well enough to understand that. Because she also said she wished her father would divorce me and marry you."

Dear God. "Susan, she shouldn't have written a thing like that. I'm certain—"

"That she didn't mean that, either?"

I am truly worried now about this turn of conversation—and Susan's state of mind. "Look," I say, "I'm really tired. Why don't we leave this till morning?"

She yawns. "Actually, I'm rather sleepy too, but I'd like to finish up here. I could use some coffee." She stands and smiles. "You?"

"No, thank you. I really think I should go."

"Oh no, please don't go yet! Please. I'll just run downstairs and put the coffee on, I won't be long. You can look through Beth's diary while I'm gone."

"I don't think—"

"I'd really appreciate your help, Naomi, in going through all these things. You knew Beth so well, and I just think you'd know best what to keep and what to throw away. I'm sure there are some things that meant a lot to Beth, while others . . ."

She gives a light, winsome shrug.

"All right," I say uncertainly, as part of me doesn't want to leave her like this. "I can stay a while. But let's not go too late?"

"Of course not."

Susan goes out the door and closes it softly, leaving me in Beth's room with all these memories.

I'll give it twenty minutes, I think. *Then I'll go.*

I pick up the diary, and though I have no intention of reading anything in it, it does feel good to hold it. This past year there have been so few reminders of Beth, only what has been in my heart. I've never had access to her room or her things before. I wander over to the open cupboard, wondering what else is here and what Beth would want us to save.

Pulling out a small box of trinkets, I find on top a dream-catcher with white feathers and blue beads, wrapped with strips of sand-brown leather. It is quite similar to a dream-catcher that Pete brought home once from his travels with my mother. He had handed it to me wrapped carefully in white tissue paper and explained, "They're becoming popular as jewelry now, but there was a time when only the shamans used them, mostly for protection, in their ceremonies.

I thought you'd like one." He had grinned. "You know, to protect you from all those bad courtroom spirits."

I'd hung it on my wall for awhile, but after I graduated from Harvard and moved to the city, it ended up with my mother's things, in her room. I hadn't seen it for a long while, and I wondered, suddenly, if this was actually the same dream-catcher. Looking through the box I found a Kachina doll and some odds and ends of native jewelry. Beth, I thought, must have taken them from my mother's room. But why?

To feel closer to me, to my home, when she had to come back each night to her own. That seemed the only explanation. But she could have asked. I'd have given her anything. Anything at all.

It seems Susan has been gone a long while, much longer than it would take to make coffee; by my watch, at least fifteen minutes. I sigh and wonder what she's doing. Has she forgotten me, for that matter, and left? Anything seems possible.

I cross to the door, deciding to go downstairs and look for her. Grabbing the knob I twist, but it won't move. I shake it a bit, thinking it must be stuck. But the knob is not stuck. I'm locked in.

At this point, I do not think this is deliberate; I am more inclined to think the door warped over the winter and needs repair.

I bang on the door. "Susan? Susan, I'm stuck in here. Where are you?"

There is no answer. Not a sound comes from anywhere in the house.

And now, gradually, I become frightened. If she forgot me, and I'm locked in here, how long will it take for someone to find me?

The workmen. They'll come in the morning, won't they?

Not if it rains.

I glance around again, wondering about another door. But there is none, and though I know that some of the upstairs rooms have balconies, this one does not.

At that point I hear a sound, a slight rustling. I am reminded that this house has not been lived in for a long time, yet it's been open to the elements, and to animals.

A rat. This place may be full of rats. My skin crawls.

But then I hear laughter. I whirl around. "Susan? Is that you?"

A crackling sound. "Susan? Where are you?"

Another, slightly hysterical laugh. "I'm here, Naomi. Right here."

I look toward the television set, which has come to life, seemingly by itself. Susan's face floats on the screen.

"We had all the televisions attached to the security system," she says. "Do you know what that means Naomi?"

I lick my lips, which have gone dry with fear. "No. What does it mean?"

"That I can watch you, and talk to you, and you can watch and talk to me. Well, sometimes. And you know what's even better? You can watch movies. Isn't that nice?"

"No, Susan. I don't want to watch movies. I'd like to go home."

"Oh, but, Naomi . . . you wanted to be part of our family, didn't you? Well, I arranged that for you." Her voice turns hard. "Have a seat, Naomi. You'll be here awhile."

I watch, horrified, as home videos of Beth come on. I see Beth as a baby and Susan standing over her crib making cooing sounds. Beth smiles up at her. Then Susan says, "Here, Adam, let me take that," and she moves to take the camera, while Adam takes her place over the crib. "Isn't she beautiful?" he whispers. "Like an angel."

She moves closer with the camera. "Yes," she says softly. "An angel." And on the periphery I see Adam reach an arm around her waist and pull her close.

The movie disappears and Susan is on the screen again. "Weren't we a happy little family, Naomi?" she says. "And you can be part of it now . . . just the way you always wanted to be."

I don't respond. I'm unable to.

"What, you don't like it? My, my. Well, I didn't like it much either, those years when you and Adam were playing house with each other in the city and taking my place in Beth's life. There wasn't much I could do about it, though. And there's not much you can do about this, Naomi. Just sit back and live with it."

The movies roll on and on: Beth as a toddler, Beth starting school. I am trapped in here, and there seems no way to stop it. I search frantically for some kind of controls on the television, and then, when I don't find them, in surrounding, built-in drawers, for a remote.

"Don't bother," Susan says, coming on screen again. "I've got Beth's VCR and the only remote. Isn't that a perfect arrangement? We had all the televisions hooked into the security monitors when we moved in. So now I can see you, and you can see me. Well, when I want you to, that is. Looks like I'm in control at last, doesn't it?" She smiles—a hideous, unnatural twist of the mouth.

"Susan, this really is crazy."

"Well, I am crazy, aren't I? Isn't that what Adam is always saying?"

"I don't know what Adam is always saying. But this is crazy stuff. For God's sake, let me out of here!"

"Not on your life. You've always wanted to be a part of our lives, haven't you? Well, now you can be. You can live here at the mansion, and oh . . . I just remembered it won't be the same, will it, without Beth. Well, we'll just have to fix that."

And again the home movies come on. Now I see the three of them together, happier than I ever dreamed they were, from the little Adam or Beth told me.

Was it only in my mind, then? Wishful thinking that they were unhappy together, and I was not wrecking anything?

Beth, at about eight, runs across a green lawn. Not here on Whidbey, somewhere else. She laughs at Susan and runs into her arms. Then Adam, who is taking the picture, sets the camera down and enters the scene. He puts his arms around both of them, and while Susan sticks her tongue out at the camera, Adam laughs, and Beth copies Susan. They fall together in a football kind of huddle, laughing.

*   *   *

My head hurts, and with every passing moment, I've become more and more afraid.

It is past noon of the second day, according to my watch. Inside one of the low cupboards is a square hole approximately two by two feet. According to Susan, it had a heating vent attached to it before the remodeling. It is through this hole that she slips food to me.

"Sorry I've nothing fancier," she says. "I hear you're a good cook. Well, I never was. I'm sure Adam's told you that."

On my "lunch" plate is a mix of canned peas, canned corn, and a slice of white bread. So far, I haven't eaten. The longer I am here the more my mind runs along paranoid paths, and I fear the food may be drugged. But now reason asserts itself, and I don't think Susan would drug me. She wants me awake for her hideous revenge.

I take a bite, and then another, as I am ravenous and feeling weak. I must have strength to get out of here when the opportunity comes.

It will come. That much I must believe, or I will go mad.

Susan watches me from the television screen.

"If Beth could only see you now," I say, my voice shaking despite myself. "What would she think?"

"Well, I'm sure you'd know the answer to that better than I," Susan answers calmly. "Another flick?"

This is truly a mistress's nightmare.

Late that night I hear a car, seemingly in the driveway. I run to the window and call out, though Beth's room is so far distant from the main house, I have very little hope I'll be heard. The window, I know by now, looks out only on deep woods. For Beth, this must have been a wonderful asset. For me, it means total isolation.

The sound of the car, in fact, is quite distant. Still, I yell as loud as I can, "Help! Somebody help me!"

A few minutes later the car drives away. I hear the sound of the engine grow more and more distant, and with it, my hope.

A half hour later Susan switches on the television again. "That was Annie," she says, as if chatting with a friend. "She was worried because I've been away so long. Oh, I've been checking in with her regularly, of course. If I didn't, she and Adam would have the gendarmes here."

She pauses, then says thoughtfully, "You know, I think Annie just wants to control me, the same way Adam did. They make one feel so stifled, so guilty all the time."

"Like the nuns and Father William?" I say. There is a silence. Finally Susan answers, "Yes. Like the nuns. And Father William. You're very clever, Naomi."

But she doesn't like this at all, it is clear. And with one angry flick of the remote, she leaves me in the dark again.

It is the following morning, and I have been thinking half the night. If I can get near her at all, I may have a chance.

"Susan," I call over the sound of the current movie selection, "Turn that thing off, will you? Please. I need to get outside. I need some fresh air."

"You 'need'? *You need*?"

"You don't want me getting sick and dying on you, do you?"

"I don't think I've ever known anyone to die of too little fresh air. Nice try, though."

"Well, at least let me make one phone call. I told Pete Shelton I'd be at home, and he was supposed to come over. Susan, if he doesn't find me there he'll be worried. He may come here."

"You're right. Maybe I should put you down in the cellar. He'd never find you there."

Something in her voice tells me she is only trying to frighten me. But I can't be sure.

Sometime in the night I wake to the sound of Christmas carols. For a long moment I lie here in the dark and wonder if I have finally gone mad. Then I see a flickering light against the walls. The television is on, and the carols are coming from there.

Struggling up from my pillow on Beth's bed, I blink to clear my eyes of sleep. On the screen I see a Christmas tree. Then the camera swings to another side of the room, and there are people standing, talking, holding plates of hors d'ouvres. A party.

I see myself. I am standing there talking to people I barely know; business associates of Adam's.

"Beth's last party," I hear Susan say. There are tears in her voice. "We named her after the carol, you know . . . 'O Little Town of Bethlehem.' Not after the town, of course, that would have been silly. It's just that Adam and I were listening to carols on the stereo that night, just hours before she was born. It was a beautiful night, and we had all those books, you know, that people get, with names for the baby. We had them spread out all over the living room floor by the tree. This was in the city, of course." She pauses. "We did have a life together, once. Before we moved here."

"Susan," I say desperately, "please stop. This has got to be hurting you even more than me."

"You think I could hurt anymore than I have all year?" she asks, but doesn't stop for my answer. "There we were," she continues, "poring over those books: Abigail, Alice, Barbara. Then we came to Beth, and just at that moment, as if it was meant to be, that carol began. We jumped on it, said it was a sign from heaven, as we were getting so frustrated by then, discarding relatives one after the other and trying to come up with something original. I remember that Adam rewound the tape to the beginning, and we listened to it together, and in that moment it took on a special meaning. 'The hopes and fears of all the years are met in thee tonight.' That's the way we came to feel about Beth. She was our hope for the future."

I can hear her crying then, deep, wrenching sobs, and I wonder if she's been drinking. There is nothing I can say; I've said it all, it seems, and nothing's helped either of us. So I sit quietly on the floor before the television and watch Beth's last birthday party with her.

"Beth was so excited about this party," Susan says excitedly an hour later. She is fastforwarding through endless shots of party guests waving and making faces at the camera, raising their glasses of champagne to toast the photographer—who, it seems, is a friend, assigned this task for the evening.

"I didn't want you to be there," she says, "but I could hardly deny her that on her birthday. Before the party began, Beth and I had a wonderful time sharing my dressing room. We put our makeup on together and styled each other's hair. It was a moment of closeness that was all too rare between Beth and me. Then you arrived—and suddenly I didn't exist anymore."

"I'm sorry, Susan. I didn't know." It seems all I ever say now is, "sorry."

"Of course not. You weren't thinking of anyone but yourself, were you?"

"Myself, yes. But Beth too. I remember that she looked flushed and excited, as you said. Come to think of it, she was looking about from one side of the room to the next, and I thought at one point that she seemed jittery rather than merely excited. As if she was waiting for someone special. Then some people came in, and she—"

"I remember now," Susan says conversationally. "There were several people who arrived at once, and the first ones through the door were Travis Hartmann and the woman he'd brought as his date. A Martine something, wasn't it?" She makes a scornful sound. "A dreadful woman."

"Really? I didn't notice, I suppose. I was watching Beth, and she suddenly became almost . . . high. She began twirling in that dress and showing off."

"And then she went to the piano and began to play that silly song that she and her father did as a duet."

"And I sat down with her and pretended to join in, but I was terrible at it. Then Adam . . . I mean . . ."

"Oh, don't mince words! Adam came over and talked to you, and the two of you went off together someplace. You thought I didn't see you, but I did. Of course, I suspected long before. Men don't realize how incredibly transparent they are."

"Yet you never let on. How did you do that, I wonder?"

"Years and years of practice at dissembling, my dear." At this point she stops the tape, and I hear a long sigh. The screen goes blank.

"Susan? Are you there?"

"I can hear you," she says after a moment.

"I've had a thought. Did you see Beth with any particular boy that night? Aside from Curt Lawrence, I mean."

"Curt Lawrence? He wasn't there."

"He wasn't?" I am surprised. "Are you sure?"

"I hardly know the boy, but yes, I'm sure. Why?"

"I just thought . . . if he was Beth's boyfriend, why wasn't he at her party?"

"What makes you think he was her boyfriend?"

I remember that she doesn't know yet that Beth was pregnant. If I tell her . . . will it help her? Or make her worse?

I reach into my pocket and pull out the heart-shaped pendant, holding it up to the television screen. "Can you see this?"

After a moment, the television comes on and Susan is there, leaning forward into her camera. "What is it?"

"Beth's necklace, her butterfly pendant. I found it in my garden the other day. I'm almost certain she was wearing it when she died."

Susan draws a sharp breath. "When she died? But that's impossible. How could it end up in your garden?"

"I don't know."

For several moments she sits staring at the pendant. Then she says sharply, "What has this to do with Curt Lawrence?"

"It's just that so far as I know, he was the only boy she was seeing." I hesitate now, realizing I can't bring myself to tell her about Beth. It is far too risky. "I thought Curt might have given it to her."

There is a tired but smug sort of triumph in Susan's eyes. "I can't believe that you, who were supposedly so close to my daughter, could have things so wrong."

"What do you mean?"

"Beth wasn't seeing Curt Lawrence. They were friends, but they weren't dating."

"Are you sure?"

"I'd swear to it. Don't you remember how much she was pouting before Christmas? She drove Adam and me crazy."

"I knew she was unhappy about something."

"Miserable, is more like it. All she could talk about was never having a boyfriend at Christmas, someone to give her something special, the kind of gift a boy gives a girl he loves. She was at that stage of wanting a ring for Christmas, if only a friendship ring."

"What about after Christmas, then? In the spring?"

"If there was someone, Beth never mentioned him."

I wrack my brain to remember: were there any hints, any clues? How had Beth slipped so far from me in those final months that I do not know who she was seeing? The only thing I know for certain is that it was someone who never spoke up, never even admitted he knew her.

And now the autopsy records, which could prove Beth was pregnant, are gone. And the coroner who examined her body is dead at the hand of person or persons unknown.

Who would have done this?

"Susan, put that Christmas party back on, will you?"

She laughs thinly, "Don't tell me you're beginning to like my little show."

"Just do it, will you? There's something I want to see."

I don't think she'll go along with me, at first. But then she shrugs and presses the remote. "Where do you want it?" she says.

"See if you've got that scene where Beth was acting sort of high. Just before she and I went to the piano."

"I don't see . . ."

"Dammit, Susan, do it!" I soften my voice. "Please?"

She reverses the tape, searching through it. After a few minutes she comes to a shot of the front door. Beth is calling out to someone, perhaps a maid, "That's okay, I'll get it!" Her face is bright, her smile expectant. She runs for the door and flings it open.

Travis Hartmann stands there, and beside him, his date, Martine.

Beth's smile fades. She steps back. I can't hear what anyone says, as the music is closer to the camera; it drowns out their voices. Travis leans forward to plant a kiss on Beth's cheek, but she turns her head away. Travis and his date step in, and Beth turns, does a light spin, and becomes far too animated.

She's pretending. Pretending not to be hurt.

This is when she goes to the piano, and I follow. Moments later I look up and see Pete Shelton come in. I leave Beth and go to meet him at the door. After that, Beth is lost from the screen.

"Susan," I say, "roll that back, will you, to where Beth opens the door? Then pause it?"

"You know, being your projection person isn't what I had in mind," she snaps. But she does it. I suspect her curiosity is as strong as mine.

"That's it. Stop there."

The camera is on Travis and Beth—and her crest-fallen expression.

"Susan? Am I imagining things? Or do you see what I see?"

"I can well believe you're imagining things," she says drily, "but all I see is Travis and Beth at the door."

"Think, Susan. You were Beth's mother. How is she acting here?"

"Oh, I'd say definitely disappointed. Pouty, but pretending nothing bothers her."

"Precisely. And what do you think is bothering her? What is she so disappointed about?"

"Well, maybe she was expecting someone else," she says irritably. "How would I know? Or maybe she's just pouting because Travis has a date, and she hasn't. I told you how she felt about wishing she had someone for Christmas."

"Someone? Just anyone? Susan, what about Travis Hartmann? Couldn't she be specifically jealous because *he's* brought a date?"

She laughs uncertainly. "Travis? You mean you think Beth—Good lord, no."

"Why not? Travis has that kind of charm that could fool a young woman easily. He's good-looking, successful . . . and he loves to win women over, even when he doesn't really want them."

There is a long silence. I know what Susan is thinking, as surely as if she spoke the words: *He did that with me.* For, certainly, Travis did do that with her. All the signs have pointed to it.

Finally she says very carefully, "I don't understand why you are so damned sure Beth was seeing someone. Or that she cared about someone special."

But she does understand. She has figured it out; I know this deep in my gut. "You've put it together, haven't you," I say.

"I . . . no. I don't know."

But of course she does. Just as I did, finally. All the little pieces have come rushing in to make up the one big scene.

But there is nothing that can prepare me for Susan's next words. "I thought it was some boy from school. I never dreamed Travis might be the baby's father."

"I told everyone that Beth and I fought on the phone that night about her going to school in the East," Susan says miserably. She sits in that other room, before a cold, impersonal camera, and tells her story to no one but me. Tears stream down her eyes, and she keeps wiping them away, but they keep coming. Now and then she gulps and shudders, then begins again.

"It wasn't really about school. At least, that wasn't all of it. Beth called me in Seattle to tell me she was pregnant. That was why she didn't want to go away to school, she said. Would I help her? And I said,

'Why tell me? Tell your precious Naomi! She'd be thrilled to help you raise your child. Isn't that what she's good at, raising other people's children?'

She looks at me imploringly. "I was so jealous, you see. And so drunk, I couldn't think straight. Immediately after she hung up on me I saw it clearly, that she had turned to me because *I* was her mother, and that she needed me, no matter how much she loved you. I tried to call her back, but she didn't answer. So I jumped into my car and drove like a madwoman to Mukilteo, but by then the ferry was out of service because of the storm. I sat there with the windshield wipers slapping back and forth, back and forth, and I felt they were my hands, slapping Beth's face. That was what it felt like, having hurt her that way. I hated myself for what I'd done to her."

"So she ran to me . . ." I say, my voice nearly failing, ". . . but before she could tell me, she heard Adam on my answering machine, speaking about his feelings for me."

"Yes."

"But, Susan, you said you talked to her again. You said she told you about that."

"I called her from a coffee shop in Mukilteo when I couldn't get on a ferry. By then she was back at the house, and she told me what she'd heard Adam say."

"You laughed, you said."

She flinches. "I . . . I never should have called. I'd taken a bottle in the car with me, and I'd been sitting there in the coffee shop parking lot, drinking. When Beth told me about Adam's call to you, all the fine things I'd thought to say to her vanished from my head. All I could think was that despite his promises to stop seeing you and to help us become a family again, he was getting back with you . . ."

"So you took it out on Beth."

Susan hugs herself. A long sigh escapes her lips, as if some intense emotion is released at last. "I didn't mean to. I'd been sitting in that car at the coffee shop, picturing her running to your house and you flinging the door open to her, gathering her into your arms. I pictured Beth telling you what a dreadful mother I was, and you sympathizing, telling her it would be all right, that you would help her with her baby, you'd make everything all right. So when I called her, I was already angry."

"Susan . . . do you think you were the last person to talk to Beth? Since she never came back to me, that is?"

Her voice turns sharp and angry. "Are you saying it was my fault? That I'm the one who drove her out into the storm?"

"No, I'm not saying anything like that at all. What I'm wondering is if she called anyone else after she talked to you."

"Like—?"

"Like the baby's father."

"Travis Hartmann always was a son of a bitch," she says. She is pacing, and her voice floats up and down as she passes the camera and its mike.

"If you felt that way, why did you have anything to do with him?" I say.

She turns her face to me. "You know, I'm getting really tired of you. Every damn time I tell you anything, you find some way to use it against me."

"But I'm not—"

"Shut up!" She sticks her face right up against the screen and yells at me, "Just shut up! I need to think."

Quicksilver.

Several minutes pass, with only the sound of Susan's footsteps as she paces back and forth, back and forth. I glance at my watch and cannot believe so little time has passed since I first woke up to the sound of Christmas carols. I hold the watch to my ear to be sure it's working, and it is.

"What are you doing?" Susan demands, stopping in midpace. "What is that you've got?"

"My watch, Susan. That's all."

"Let me see. Hold your hands up. Both of them."

I splay them in front of the screen.

"Not there! Up! Up near the ceiling."

It is then I discover for the first time where the tiny security camera is: disguised as part of the carved molding around the ceiling. For hours I have lain in Beth's bed and scanned this room, wondering.

But what good does it do me to know?

Susan peers at my hands from her side. "Just don't try anything," she says harshly. "Don't think you can get away with anything."

"Not a chance," I say.

"And don't get smart with me. You really do think you're so damned smart, and actually, you're pretty stupid. If you only knew the half of it."

"Half of what?"

Again, she has that smug look. "Travis Hartmann, that's what. I could tell you something . . ." She shakes her head. "Never mind. Why should I help you?"

"No, tell me. If you really know something, that is."

"You think I'm bluffing?"

"I think I'm as tired of you as you are of me, so why not spice things up a bit? Tell me all you know about Travis Hartmann . . . every disgusting little detail."

Her gaze wavers. Then she shrugs. "Why not? It can't do you any good now. Remember that scam Travis pulled on you last year? That land you were trying to protect in California?"

I lean forward, near the screen. She has captured my interest. "What do you mean, scam? Everything he did was legal."

"Legal!" She laughs. "Travis doesn't know the meaning of the word. He's been working me too, you know. Keeping an eye on me for Adam, so he can get enough on me to put me away, and all the while pretending to be my friend."

"Susan . . . what about the Wintu land?"

"Well, that's the point of my little story," she says sweetly. "The sale to Lambert Enterprises *wasn't* legal. Travis didn't file the papers in a timely manner or something. I don't know all the legal jargon, but it had to do with the title not being clear. And you didn't catch it, because you were all messed up over Adam and his leaving you."

"That wasn't . . ." I start to say, but then fall silent. Can this be true? Can it possibly be true? Or is it another of Susan's delusions?

"How do you know this?" I demand.

"I know because I heard him talking to Willie Putch the other night on the phone. You know Putch and my father were old cronies before my father died? Well, our fine upstanding legal eagle said he'd taken care of you last year, and he could take care of you again. You *and* your friend Pete Shelton."

"He actually said that? Do you know what he meant?"

"Of course. Travis said he was going into court on August tenth, and all he had to do was keep you and Pete Shelton busy till then, and he'd have the land, free and clear."

"August tenth! Susan, that's tomorrow."

"Is it?" she says, her voice sugary sweet again. "My, my. And you won't be able to do a thing to stop him . . . because you'll be here."

"Dammit, you've got to let me out, now. Hasn't this gone on long enough? Let me out, so I can take care of Travis Hartmann for both of us."

"Why, how thoughtful of you, Naomi. You'd actually do this for me, as well as yourself?"

"Of course. Don't you want to get him for what he did to Beth?"

"Oh, I'll get him all right. But I can do that without your help."

"Susan, I need *your* help. If I can get to court tomorrow in time to stop Travis from getting his hands on that land, you don't know what it would mean—"

My words fall on deaf ears as she twists around suddenly and looks behind her. "What was that? Who's there?"

Someone stands in the shadows, nearly beyond the camera's reach. I can see only movement, and then I hear Susan's long, indrawn sigh. "What are you doing here? Oh, please go away. I didn't want you to know."

"My poor darling," Annie Lowell says. "What in the name of God have you done?"

"I'm just making her pay," Susan says. "I want her to know what it's like."

"Of course you do," Annie Lowell answers softly. "Of course you do. But not like this, sweetheart. Not like this."

They are both with me in Beth's room. Susan sits on the edge of the bed, looking quite small and fragile.

"I wanted her to know how it feels," she says, like a child.

Annie sits beside her and takes her hand. "How what feels?"

"To be an outsider."

The other woman shakes her head sadly. "Oh, Susan. This is all wrong."

"I didn't hurt her. I've just been keeping her here for a while."

I am leaning against the wall for support, as I feel, suddenly, quite weak. I want nothing more than to run from this place, but I haven't got the strength.

"Annie? Call Adam, will you? Ask him to take care of her? I've had about all I can take."

She looks at me coldly. "You may remember that I asked you quite clearly to leave my patient alone."

"Your *patient* needs to be in a hospital, where she won't be able to do this sort of thing."

"I'll decide what's best for Susan."

"I'm sorry, but I don't think you're qualified to do that. If you were, we wouldn't even be here."

"Susan and I understand each other. She'll listen to me now." Annie gives Susan's shoulders a squeeze. "Won't you, dear?"

"I think the worst thing in the world would be for her to listen to you now," I say.

Susan pulls away from her and jumps to her feet. "Will the two of you stop talking about me as if I'm not here? I'm not *crazy*. That's what neither of you seems to understand. I'm goddamned *angry!*"

Annie Lowell makes small "now, now," sounds and flutters a hand.

"Stop that! You aren't any better than all the rest. Everyone thinks they know what's best for me. You, Adam, Travis, and now even Naomi. For that matter, everyone I've ever known. Well, *nobody* knows what's best for me. I'm getting well, and I'm getting *even*. Do you hear?"

"Brava," I can't help saying. If nothing else, Susan's spirit now seems in fine shape.

"Oh, will you get out of here?" she says spitefully. "I've had it with you."

"Gladly." Thoroughly relieved, I head for the door.

"Wait." Annie Lowell moves ahead of me and places her hand on the door, preventing me from opening it.

"Susan, do you know what will happen now, if you let her go?"

"I . . ." Susan looks blank.

"She'll go right to the police, dear. And they'll lock you up. All the work I've done, everything I've done to help keep you out . . ."

"You really think that? They'll lock me up?"

"Of course they will."

"I . . . I guess I didn't think of that."

"I know, dear. Of course you didn't. All right, be quiet now for a minute. Let me think what to do."

"What do you mean, what to do?"

Annie sighs and says patiently, "Dear, we can't just let her go."

"But we *have* to, don't we? I mean, we can't..." Susan raises both hands to her cheeks.

"Annie?" I say "You're starting to sound as crazy as her."

"Shut up," she says.

"See, that's what I mean."

"If you don't shut up—"

"You'll what? Drug me? Knock me out?"

"Don't give me ideas."

"Of course, you could just let me go and I can promise not to say anything to anyone."

She tosses me a cynical look.

"Why not?" I press. "Susan herself said it—she didn't mean to hurt me. She was planning to let me go."

"And you would just go home and forget anything happened here?" Annie laughs, a chilling sound.

"Again, why not?"

She doesn't answer. Instead, she turns to Susan. "We'll do whatever we have to do," she says. "I'll come up with something."

"But—" Susan begins.

"Sweetheart, leave it to me. Have I ever let you down?"

CHAPTER 22

I am still locked up in Beth's room, and the only difference now is that, though the television is still on, the screen is blank. Blessedly, the movies have stopped. On the other hand, a heavy rain has begun. Wind blows against the window, and it seeps through minute cracks, causing the flimsy curtains to drift slowly in and out, in and out, like the fluttering arms of a ghost.

Susan is lying down in the next room, and Annie Lowell sits on the edge of the bed, across from me. I sit on the floor with my knees drawn up and my back against the wall, trying to figure out the best way to overtake her and make a break for it. At the moment this doesn't seem a likely scenario, as Susan has locked us both in, on Annie's orders, and she holds the only key.

Holds the key. I wonder if she does, metaphorically speaking? Can I talk my way out of this using Susan?

Annie is watching me eat. Or rather, she is waiting for me to eat. I won't touch the tray of food she's brought me, as I am certain she's drugged it with something from her doctor's little bag of tricks. She must have realized, I think, that I'm too strong for her to do anything with otherwise. I have not lived on this island and worked in my garden every day without building up a certain muscle strength. Her daily work, on the other hand, is carried out from behind a desk.

As for Susan and any help she might lend her? That could be risky, with Susan drifting in and out as she is, and Annie must know it.

"So what's your plan?" I say. "Tie me up, dump me in the Sound? I'd float ashore eventually, and who do you think they'd come after?"

"Oh, don't worry, I wouldn't do anything that clichéd."

"Then what?"

"I'm still thinking. You do, however, have a reputation, I've heard, for being a loner these days. Some say you've gotten weird, living here on the island. You've even been seen burning things and chanting in the woods."

I laugh. "Burning things? Chanting in the woods? And that's weird? Well, I suppose it must seem so, to some."

"I'll admit a certain affinity for Native American culture, myself," Annie Lowell says. "But not everyone understands these things. And if you were to seem to have gone off the deep end, finally, to have begun to imagine things . . . well, what a shame that would be. However, I don't suppose a lot of questions would be raised."

"You're kidding yourself. I've got friends. Pete Shelton, for one. The island sheriff? You may have heard of him."

"But he'd want the best for you, wouldn't he? And I'm certain I could convince him you've been through a difficult time this past year and decided to go off for a bit of a rest. Far away from all the memories here, let's say. As a matter of fact, I know a lovely, private little hospital in Minnesota. I'm quite close with the administrator." She smiles. "Well! See, now, you've helped me to work it all out."

"You are more Loony Tunes than Susan," I say. "And aren't you forgetting one very important person? What about Adam? You honestly think he'd buy all that?"

"He's trusted me with Susan," she points out quietly.

To that, I have no answer. *Why?* I keep asking myself. Why has he trusted this person with his wife? Can he have simply been blind to what's been going on?

"I don't understand." I toy with a cup of soup as if I might drink it. "You seem to be a reputable doctor with a good reputation. Why on earth would you do a thing like this?"

"I would do anything for Susan."

"Anything to control her, you mean. I don't think she's nearly as bad off as you'd like her to be."

"You can say that? After what she's done here with you?"

"I don't think Susan would have harmed me physically. As a matter of fact, I don't think I've been nearly as much frightened as sad. And worn out."

"She may be in worse condition than you think. Susan has been badly hurt, and you're part of it. You became part of it the day you set out to have an affair with Adam Lambert."

"But Susan and Adam weren't happy from the first. You must know that."

"That's not the point. Adam didn't care about her. He went waltzing off with you and didn't look back. For four years he did as he pleased, having a good life, while Susan stayed here at the mansion and suffered."

"Her suffering was partly her own doing."

"Was it? Are you saying your lover was blame-free?"

"No, I'm not saying that. But Adam tried to get her to see someone. She wouldn't agree. Not until you."

"And because of that, it was all right for him to have an affair? To create a relationship between his daughter and another woman, thereby shutting Susan out?"

"She shut herself out."

"Did she?"

"Yes. And I don't think Adam was required to just sit around and suffer with her. He deserved a life."

"I don't give a damn about you and Adam and your life," she says. "What I do care about is Susan, and the effect your affair had on her, and her relationship with her daughter."

"Beth *loved* Susan. She wanted more than anything to be close to her. Susan wouldn't let that happen, she closed her out. And I understand why, now. Susan had been hurt badly when she was young, and even though she wanted to love someone, she shut everyone out. Not just Beth but Adam. It was too frightening for her to get close to anyone. Annie, do you honestly believe that if I hadn't been in the picture, things would have been any different?"

"I think Adam and Beth would both have had to work things out with Susan somehow."

"Well, you're wrong. Things would only have gotten worse."

"Still living in a dream world?" she says scornfully. "Things would have been great if it weren't for the wife?"

"No. I've been there and back again. I know I share the responsibility for what happened between all of us—me, Adam, and Beth. And the truth is, I honestly feel for Susan. None of what happened was her fault, either. She just didn't know what to do."

The blue eyes narrow. "You 'feel' for Susan? You don't even begin to know. Have you any idea how many women come through my office who have been abused by their husbands or fathers, uncles or brothers, or some supposedly kind neighbor or friend? It's a veritable army marching through every day, and I get so damned sick of it! Susan has got to free herself of him—of all of them."

"But Adam hasn't abused Susan, not in the way you mean. She's never claimed that."

"You think it's not abuse to promise to love a woman, then leave her?"

I stare at Annie Lowell, trembling now from head to toe, and it all comes clear: the personal agenda.

"Who hurt you that way, Annie?" I say softly. "Who left you?"

"Don't you dare try to analyze me."

"You've been using Susan to fight your own battles, haven't you? Instead of helping her to get well, you've been egging her on, urging her to want revenge."

She stands and folds her arms, hiding her hands, which are shaking. "I've been much too easy with you. I'm thinking now that an accident might be a better idea. A fall down the cellar stairs? Yes, that might do it. Everyone would think you'd been looking for Susan here and gotten careless. Then we'd be rid of you, once and for all."

"Well, if you're going to kill me, Annie, you'd better do it fast. I'm sure Adam's looking for Susan by now. He should be showing up here any moment."

Her smile is complacent. "Adam's left town. Didn't you know?"

"Left town? I don't believe you."

"You're surprised? He left a message on my machine, saying he didn't expect to be back for several days."

At this, my heart sinks. "Where did he go? Do you know?"

"I'm assuming he's off on business somewhere. Certainly he's been away on business a lot over the years, hasn't he? All those overnight 'trips' he made when he was having that affair with you and actually sleeping in your apartment in Seattle? All the times he had no explanation for Susan as to where he'd been or what he'd done? Well, it looks like the tables have been turned, doesn't it? Adam won't be here to interfere. And for that, I am most definitely thankful. Have you any idea how weary I am of that man prying with things? Always worrying about her condition, wanting me to check in with him all the time, wanting a second opinion."

"A second opinion. From someone who could *really* help Susan, you mean?"

She doesn't answer, and I have been slowly getting to my feet, the cup of soup still in my right hand. "You know, we might as well get this over with. I've no desire to prolong my own agony." Carefully, I hold both arms out straight. "What do you want to do? Tie me up? Before you toss me down the stairs, that is. Well, go ahead. I'm too tired to stop you."

She looks startled. Perplexed. Her confused gaze goes from my eyes down to my arms. At that moment I fling the soup into her face and follow it with the cup. She throws her hands up to fend it off and steps back, off-balance just enough so that when I swing with my fist below her chin she stumbles backward onto the bed. I run for the door and bang on it.

"Susan, let me out! Susan!"

As I've hoped, she is already there. The door opens, and Susan stands on the threshold. Annie Lowell is behind me, so fast on my heels I can almost feel her breath on my neck.

"Get in here!" she calls to Susan. "Hurry! Help me hold her down."

Susan's wide green eyes are hard on Annie. "I heard you," she says. The eyes flicker upward, toward the tiny camera eye in the molding. "I heard everything you said. All this time . . . damn you, Annie! You betrayed me. And Naomi's right. You're crazier than me."

"Just do as I say!" Annie screams.

Susan shakes her head. "I'm not letting you hurt

her." She rushes at Annie and grabs her, holding her back. "Run, Naomi!" she cries to me.

I hesitate for only a moment. *I can be free.* I have been locked up and tormented for three days, I am exhausted and hungry, and now I can be free. I can make it to court in time to fight Travis Hartmann, and perhaps win back my ancestral lands. All I have to do is run.

And leave Beth's mother here with this horrible woman? a small voice says.

Another one responds: *Oh hell.*

I throw myself at the two of them, pushing Susan away and taking Annie Lowell down.

CHAPTER 23

"What if she comes after us?" Susan says, stopping to lean against a tree and catch her breath. I bend forward, palms on my knees, catching mine. We have left Annie Lowell only moments behind us, winded but conscious on Beth's floor.

"Well, gee, Suze, if you hadn't hidden your car keys so I wouldn't find them if I got loose, and then forgotten where you hid them . . ."

She looks at me, sees I'm not really angry, and half smiles. "We make a pretty good team, don't you think?"

"I think we're probably going to be the best of friends."

There is irony in my voice, but wouldn't it, I think, be funny if it turned out to be at least partly true?

"Where do you think we are?" Susan asks, peering into the dark. "I always get lost in these woods."

"I'm not really sure. This rain doesn't help." It is beating down, blinding us, so thick it forms that strange mist that looks like fog between the hills. There is no moon, and even the treetops seem to cling to each other for protection.

"I grew up here," I say, "but I'm all turned around with this mess. I'd guess Crow Cottage should be just a few hundred yards ahead."

Under other circumstances I'd have left lights on in the cottage to show the way. In this darkness, we could either be upon it before we know it, or we could be going the opposite way.

"Naomi . . . I can understand now how Beth must have lost her way that night. Can't you?"

"Yes. She must have been terribly confused."

But I don't want her to think about that. She's been doing well so far. I just don't know how long it will last.

"Are you ready? I think we should go."

"Yes," she agrees, wiping a hand over her brow. "Let's go."

I lead the way, forging a path through branches that are heavy and sodden with rain. Beneath my feet the ground is mushy, unstable. "Be careful," I say, holding back a branch so that it doesn't snap in her face. "Watch your footing here."

She nods and grabs the branch. I move on quickly, looking for familiar trees and rocks along the way. At times I think I know exactly where I'm going. Then I'm confused. It would help to have a moon.

We come into a clearing thirty feet in diameter. I stop dead as the skin on the back of my neck prickles.

"What? What is it?" Susan comes up behind me.

"This is Beth's place. There's something . . ."

"Her place? Where she came to write in her diary, you mean?"

"Yes."

Susan pushes ahead of me to the middle of the clearing and stands there. Her arms go up slightly, as if she is feeling a presence here, too. "Beth?" she calls softly. "Are you here?"

She is disheveled, her jeans torn by brambles, as mine are, but with her face turned up to the sky and her hair blown back, she looks like an ancient warrior, beseeching the gods for a glimpse of her child. I understand, for I have done much the same thing this last year in this very spot. But there is something about the energy here tonight that isn't good. I do not like this at all.

A sound comes from the edge of the circle, behind a rim of shrubbery and trees. The snapping of a twig underfoot. I edge closer to Susan.

"Who is it? Who's there?"

A figure steps into the clearing, but I cannot make it out in the mist and darkness. It is a blur, nothing more.

Susan cries out softly and takes a step toward the figure. "Bethy?" Her voice becomes high, excited. "Is that you?"

She whirls around to me. "It is, I know it, it's her! Didn't I tell you I saw her, before?" She turns back and takes a step toward the figure.

I grab her arm. "No, wait."

"But—"

"Susan, that's not Beth."

"Let go! Let go of my arm, I've got to go to her!"

"I'm telling you, that's not Beth."

The figure steps closer. "She's right, Susan. It's only me."

Susan's fingers bite into my arm like claws.

"Annie?"

The psychiatrist is drenched; the short black hair is plastered to her head and in her eyes. She is breathing heavily.

"Sweetheart, I'm sorry. I went a little crazy back there. You know I wouldn't have hurt Naomi. You know I'd never hurt you."

"Get away from me. I don't know that at all."

"Susan, just let me help you."

Susan backs up into me, and I continue to grip her forearm, but protectively now. "I don't want your help, Annie," she says.

"I know you think you mean that, dear, but that's only because you've been listening to her. You see how she's come between us? You've got to learn to trust me again."

Susan's laugh is harsh. "Don't you get it? You lied to me! You told me Adam didn't care. You're the last person I'd trust now."

Annie moves closer and stretches an arm out as if to touch her. Susan screams out a frightened, "No!" and yanks away from me, running across the clearing toward the woods.

"Susan, come back!" I yell, close on her heels. I am afraid for her, afraid she will hurt herself. I push through a thick stand of blackberry vines, the thorns gouging deep cuts in my legs and arms. But I can see the white blur of her shirt, now, just ahead.

"Susan, wait!"

She stops, hesitates, looks behind her, then begins running again. I am almost upon her when I realize where she is: at the ravine where Beth died. As if in slow motion I see her foot rise to take another running step, and I see the low-lying branch that sticks out from the cedar tree. "Watch out!" I yell, horrified. "Don't—"

Her foot catches, and her body is flung forward by the force of her speed. I grab for her, my hand fastening over her wrist. But she is already too far into the fall. We both go over.

I scream as I feel air all around me, and I see Susan's face inches from me, the mouth open in a wide "O," though no sound comes out. Then we slam against the side of the ravine and tumble over and over until finally we come to rest, a foot from each other.

I am scratched, bleeding, and my arm is in agony where it has been wrenched at the socket by Susan's weight. I move my legs carefully and though my left ankle is sore, nothing seems broken. Overhead I hear a cacophony of birds, protesting the interruption of their night's sleep. Footsteps in the underbrush tell me that Annie Lowell is above us somewhere.

I lean over Susan. She has landed on her stomach, her head at a strange angle, face in a deep pocket of rain water. "Oh God," I whisper, "please be all right." Thinking her spine may be injured, I dare not move her far. Carefully, no more than an inch or two, I lift her head so that her nose and mouth are just free of the water. She coughs once, twice, then groans. Briefly, her eyes open, then close.

"No, don't! Susan, stay with me!"

She remains perfectly still. I feel for a pulse at the side of her neck. At first I think there is none. But then I feel a faint thready rhythm beneath my fingertips. My relief is so great, I nearly cry.

I try to rouse her again, my lips by her ear. "Susan, we need to keep you out of this water, but I don't dare move you till we now how badly you're injured. Can you hear me? Can you tell me what hurts?"

She lies deathly still.

I raise my head and yell at the top of my lungs. "*Annie! Annie Lowell, damn you, are you up there?* Susan needs help! Call the paramedics, call Pete Shelton. Get them out here!"

I scan the top of the ravine, which is no more than thirty feet up. I could climb it, easily. But I'd have to release my hold on Susan's head, and she would surely drown.

"Annie!" I scream again to be heard above the winds. "Where the hell are you? I thought you loved Susan! You can't let her die."

There is no answer. Only the screeching of the birds, who know when something is terribly wrong.

My watch has broken, and I have no idea what time it is. Hours pass, it seems. There have been no more sounds from the top of the ravine. The good doctor has apparently run.

I change from one arm to the other, always keeping Susan free to breathe. I am reminded of the storm the night Beth died, and it does not escape me that she died very close to this spot. My mother would say there is a reason Susan and I are together here tonight.

I consider letting go of her long enough to stand and strip my clothes off, then to make a bundle of them to put beneath her head. But reaching the fingers of my free hand down through the water, I cannot touch bottom. As the rain continues to fall, the water is rising, and quickly; my bundle of jeans and shirt would not be thick enough. I dare not let go, even for a moment. I am worried now, too, about a flash flood, and the possibility that I might have to move Susan after all, thereby risking further injury.

I am certain now there's been damage, at least to the cervical spine. Her neck is at too odd an angle to her body. While her body is twisted, and partially on its side, the neck and head are more parallel to the ground.

My worst fear is that I won't be able to last. I am very tired, suddenly. The past three days are catching up with me, and I can hardly keep my eyes open. It crosses my mind that if I could only close them, just for a minute, it would feel so good . . .

I come awake with a jolt. *Where am I?* Then I know. Panicked, I look down. Susan's nose and mouth are only a fraction of an inch from the water that could kill her. I go faint with fear, then lift her head gently, one more inch, my arms feeling like lead weights. "Oh help," I breathe. "Someone help us, please. *Damn you, Mother, where are you?*" I scream. "*Where are you when I need you?*"

The words are no sooner out of my mouth than all about us, fierce winds shake the trees. There comes a wailing sound, a shriek. The winds shake me side to side, and I nearly lose my grip on Susan. Then I hear a mad half-howl, half-laugh so loud it rattles the branches. I look up and am stunned at the sight above my head.

Katherine Wing, it seems, has sent emissaries. There are a dozen or more of them, and they are leaning against tree trunks, some sitting nonchalantly and grinning, as if they've enjoyed their little trick with the wind. They are the ancestors: the cousins, the uncles, the grandfathers. Closer down, near to me, is a man whose face I remember only from old, yellowed photographs. My father, Thomas Wing. And though he surely never wore warpaint in life, he does now. There are stripes of white and black across his cheeks and one red streak down his nose. Around his head is a leather band, and in it are three feathers. My father reaches up and pulls an eagle feather out, handing it down to me. My fingers tingle as I reach for it. For a moment we touch, and his touch is like a cushion of air.

"Daddy," I say, my eyes welling as I realize for the first time in years how much I have missed him.

He turns slowly and makes a gesture to the warriors, my ancestors. They all hold their hands out. And around me I feel the same cushion of air. It envelopes me, and everything becomes light now: my body, my arms. Susan.

I look back to my father, but in that instant he is gone. They are all gone. I look to the right of me and to the back, but there is no one there. The only thing left is the eagle feather in my hand—and this new, strange lightness of my burden. It is the only way I know this has happened at all.

After that, I don't know where I go, for it seems I am here, yet not here. My body must leave me, as I feel no more pain, and though my arm is still beneath Susan's head, no weight. The rain stops and I see the moon rising, the sky clear.

Then before my eyes a vision unveils itself, though the details seem confused: I am me, Naomi. But oddly, I am in the Lambert mansion that last night with Beth. I am lifting the phone in her living room, talking into it. I hear Pete's voice on the other end.

"Pete, help me!" I cry. "I'm so afraid."

I mean, I think, "Find us. Bring help." But a strange thing happens. I cease being Naomi. And suddenly, I am Beth.

I, Beth, look down at my hands, and they are young hands, small, and soft. Around my neck is the butterfly pendant I've been wearing because of that silly myth I read about in Naomi's mother's book. I call it silly, but at night when I lie in bed and there's nothing else to think about but the fix I'm in, I kind of hope it's not.

Funny how fast things can change. We started meeting in the woods in October, he and I, and all we did was talk. I didn't even think of him "that way," because back then I had a crush on Travis Hartmann. Well, he couldn't see me for beans, and I knew that for sure when he showed up at my birthday party last Christmas with a date. He didn't even notice how it hurt me.

But Pete did. He held me and comforted me, and that's when I realized I cared about him as more than a friend, someone to meet with and talk to. I knew it that night, out in the summer house.

We were so happy at first. Pete brought me little gifts . . . a dream-catcher—for protection, he said—and once, a pair of turquoise and silver earrings. But then Sally Ann came back home, and Pete stopped showing up at our little place in the woods. And now tonight I hear his voice on the phone, and even though I need him, even though I'm feeling so hurt by Naomi and Dad and my mom, Pete says he has to stay in town because of Sally Ann.

My right hand darts to my abdomen, to the child that lies there. Then I touch the butterfly pendant, half hoping it works and half hoping it doesn't. The Blackfeet used it to prevent pregnancy. Well, it's sure too late for that. But maybe, if I pray real hard, it might help end it?

I know how stupid that sounds.

I hang up the phone, and I am bitter. I am seventeen, I am pregnant and alone. Pete won't be back. I know that now. He as much as told me so.

Thunder crashes. A jagged flash of lightning streams across the windows and, frightened, I grab the phone again. But who can I call now for help? My father? Naomi?

No.

Slamming down the receiver I turn to run to my room. But my hand knocks the kerosene lamp that I lit in case the lights went out, and it topples over. Instantly, the fringed cover on the table ignites. Heat blazes up in my face, burning my cheek. I scream and back away.

The fire spreads so quickly. It licks at the flimsy curtains and streams up them like a snake. I've got to get out. But where can I go?

I run out the front door, down the steps and toward the woods. I know it isn't safe to be in the woods when it's lightning, but I want to be in my place. I'll be safe there, I think, from the fire. Safe with the deer.

I run and run, but the storm seems to chase me. Lightning crackles at my heels, and I can hardly see through the rain. Am I going in the right direction? I'm not sure now, I'm all turned around. For a moment I panic, and then I hear a voice: "Turn right, Beth! Turn right!"

Is there a path there? Yes. My feet can feel it. But is it the right one?

"Just go!" the voice seems to cry. "Run!"

All about me the trees bend and the wind howls. For the first time I feel trapped by the way they surround me.

"Hurry, Beth!" I hear again. I look back, as if there is someone behind me speaking, and then I see, through the trees, flames rising from the house. Sparks are caught by a gust of wind, and several strike my face. I back up, my eyes glued to the flames on the roof. So close. I turn and run deeper into the woods.

"No, not that way!" I hear. The voice is filled with fear. "Not—"

I stumble. My foot catches on a root, and I fall forward. I stick out my hands to break my fall, but there is nothing there. No ground. Nothing but air.

I am at the bottom of the ravine, I think, but the earth is like a cloud, soft and fluffy. I hear the rain, but cannot feel it. Beside me sits a woman dressed in a white robe with strange designs at its hem. I say to her, "Are you Mary? Are you the Virgin Mary?" That's all I can think, because there is light all around her, and she looks like the pictures in my old catechism book, and the statues in church.

"No," she says softly. "I'm Katherine."

"Katherine . . ." The name rolls off my tongue like liquid gold. "Where am I?"

"You are on the bank of the River of Ghosts," she answers sadly. "I tried to guide you, little one. You were running from the fire, and I could see the path before you so clearly. You were almost there, almost safe . . ."

"But I was afraid," I say. "I got confused."

She nods, her eyes filled with sorrow. "And now you are waiting to cross to the other side."

I try to remember what I have read about the River of Ghosts, and the things Naomi has told me about it over the years.

"The River . . ."

And then I know. My eyes fill with tears, and I can't help it, I'm shaking. The woman, Katherine, wipes my tears away with the hem of her dress. Where she touches me, I feel warm. She gives me strength.

"I'm dead," I say. "I'm dead, aren't I?"

"Yes, child," she answers softly. "But I'm here. Don't be afraid."

"I . . . I'm not." I realize, then, that this is true. "It's just . . . what will happen to my mommy and daddy now? And Naomi?"

"They will miss you terribly," Naomi's mother says. I understand, now, that this is who she is. Katherine Wing.

"Naomi says you appear to her sometimes. Will you tell her I'm all right?"

"I'll tell her you are at the River of Ghosts," Katherine says. But she doesn't look happy.

"What is it? What's wrong?"

"Perhaps nothing," she says thoughtfully. "Are you ready to cross?"

I raise my head and look to the other side. There I see my grandmother as I remember her, the tiny blue-gray curls, the dress like a sheath, the stockings and heels. But her face is different; she looks happy now. She reaches out a hand to me, and I see that beside her are both my grandfathers, and my other gramma, too. They reach their hands out, and it seems they are beckoning me to cross the river to their side.

Then, between us, rises a mist. They disappear.

"No, come back!" I cry. "Wait for me . . ."

But in that instant I know. "I can't leave yet," I say softly. "Can I?"

Katherine doesn't answer.

"They have to be all right, first," I say. "They have to know they're not to blame."

"Not even your father?" she says with a trace of anger. And as if a movie has been inserted in my memory, I see the entire story of the troubles between Katherine Wing and my father.

"No. Not him," I say. "And not my mother . . . or Naomi."

"The man, then?" she asks. "Do you want revenge?"

For a moment I hear Pete's last words to me, and yes, I want revenge. I want to scream at him that I am hurt, that he made me love him and then he went to his wife. But it is only a moment. It passes. "It wasn't their fault. They'll each think it was, but I know they all loved me."

"They did their best? Is that what you mean?" Katherine asks, her eyes narrowing.

"I guess so. Yes."

She nods and sighs. "A wise child."

"And my baby . . ." I reach a hand down to touch my abdomen. It no longer hurts, but there is blood between my legs. I know my child will never be born. "Before I can go, I want my baby to be all right."

"What would you like to do?" Naomi's mother asks.

"I'm not sure. I think he should be buried . . . don't you?"

"So his spirit may rest?"

"Yes."

Again she nods. "I will see what I can do."

A thought strikes me. "Katherine, maybe if you . . . if you told them what I said, if you did that for me, then I could go?"

This time she shakes her head sadly. "I wish I could, child. But they can't hear it from me. You must tell them yourself."

"But, how?"

"You will find a way."

I come back to myself. I am Naomi again, and tears stream unchecked down my face. They fall on Susan's back, and I find I am stroking her hair, as if it were Beth's.

Above me, I hear sounds: the screeching of brakes and several voices, one of which I've known nearly all my life. Or have I?

"Naomi?"

I look up. "Yes, Pete."

"Thank God! Are you all right?"

"How can I be?" I say.

EPILOGUE

I stood on the edge of the ravine that morning and watched as the paramedics brought Susan up. They said her injuries were serious, but that in time she would be all right. Adam was there, and he stayed with her all the way to the hospital, and for several hours after. Pete and I remained at the ravine and talked.

"Annie Lowell called the paramedics," he told me, "then she called me and told me what happened at the mansion. She's at Coupeville now, turning herself in."

Annie took complete responsibility for what happened that night. Susan, however, revealed her part in it as soon as she regained consciousness. Then she checked herself into Cloverdale for psychiatric care.

That morning, Pete told me about his affair with Beth. When he was through I felt I'd lost him a second time, if only as a friend. *All the lies.* And for Beth, all that betrayal.

Sally Ann, Pete said, had left him that October before Beth's last Christmas party. "We told people she was back East on vacation with her family, but she actually took the kids and left me. I was hurt, I guess. And lonely. I know it's no excuse, but I didn't think she was ever coming back, and that's when things got out of hand between Beth and me. Up till then we'd just been meeting and talking, you know."

I knew. The same way Pete and I used to meet and talk.

"Naomi, it was strange. She reminded me so much of you, the way you were back in those days. She didn't get along with her mom, and she needed someone to talk to. And it was so innocent, how it all began. I was just out walking in the woods one day, thinking about Sally and missing her like hell. And there was Beth. She was lying on the grass in this little copse, sort of, a clearing in the woods, and she was reading. It was a book you'd given her about the stories of the grandmothers, and I was surprised she was interested. We started to talk about the old legends, and ... I don't know, it just went on from there. The next day when I had some spare time I went back to see if she was there again."

"And she was."

"Yeah."

"And at the Christmas party, it was you with Beth in the summer house. Not Curt Lawrence."

Or Travis Hartmann, as I'd been thinking.

He nodded and looked away, his eyes heavy with shame. "It was the first time we ... well, you know. Beth let people think she was seeing the Lawrence kid, so they wouldn't suspect about us."

"How noble of you to go along with that."

Here he had the grace to look embarrassed. "I didn't see it as noble. But you know how people would have talked. I was still married, legally, I was old enough to be her father, and an Indian to boot. I didn't want her subjected to the kinds of gossip there would be."

The affair went on, Pete said, until late the next spring, when Sally Ann came home and said she wanted to make their marriage work.

"I told Beth I had to at least try. I tried to put my feelings for her aside. I told myself she was young, she'd forget all about me once she went away to school. But then there was the storm, that goddamned storm . . ." He closed his eyes briefly, rubbing a hand over them to wipe away moisture. "And after the funeral, I couldn't hide my feelings anymore about Beth. Not from Sally Ann. She knew."

"That's why she said that being married to you was 'killing' her, isn't it?" I said. "She knows things will never be the same now."

I remember that I too thought I might die when it was over with Pete. But Sally Ann would be all right. Somehow we women manage to go on. And on.

My anger was so terrible that morning on the ravine, I had to move back from Pete to keep from hitting him. "Did you ever stop to think how she felt?" I raged. "She was seventeen years old! She felt alone and rejected. She loved you, she was pregnant with your child, and you left her to deal with all that alone!" I was shaking so hard I thought I might fall apart, and it wasn't all about Beth. I knew that, but I couldn't stem the tide of my fury.

"She wants her baby buried," I said harshly. "She wants him buried properly."

His startled gaze swung to mine. "I . . . I did that."

"You did what?"

"I buried our baby. I was first on the scene that morning, Naomi. I saw all that blood, and I knew right away what it was. I knew I had to be the father."

I was startled. "Are you telling me that was the first you knew Beth was pregnant?"

"You didn't think she told me, and that I let her face it alone? God, no! She never told me a thing. And when I found her like that . . . Naomi, I sat there beside her a long while, waiting for help to arrive. At first I didn't know what to do. Then it was like I could hear Katherine, of all people, talking to me. It seemed like she was saying, 'The baby needs a proper burial. Do that for Beth.' Finally I got up and found some leaves from that big old oak tree over there, and I took them over to Beth."

His voice cracked. "I . . . I cleaned her up in the old way, with the wet leaves, and I said prayers over her. Then I took the leaves and all that blood, and I buried them, Naomi. In fact, I think I must have buried them pretty much where we found you and Susan tonight."

He paused. "I also took her butterfly necklace and buried it in your garden. She said she liked working with you there. I thought maybe she'd still feel close to you."

I walked a bit away from Pete and stood on the edge of the ravine, looking down. "And Gray Steen?"

He stood beside me. "I bribed him, I guess you'd say. I said if he told anyone about the pregnancy, I'd see he lost his job because of his drinking. So he covered, and it wasn't in any of the reports. Except that there was a big hole in the reports, where Gray didn't put anything at all in about the condition of the uterus. And anyone who was smart enough to notice that could figure out what had happened."

"Anyone. Like Travis Hartmann, for instance?"

He shrugged and looked off across the hills.

"Pete. You *did* take those reports, didn't you? Just like Travis said. Except that you didn't take them to protect me, you took them to protect yourself."

"No!" he said angrily. "Never myself, I swear to you. Only Beth. Don't you see? It was too damned late to do anything else for her. The least I could do was protect her from the shame."

I stared at him, wide-eyed, as if I'd never seen him before. "Gray Steen. Did you kill him? Did you run him off that road so he couldn't tell Travis or Susan the truth?"

Pete's shoulders slumped, and as I watched him, it seemed the very life went out of him. "He tried to blackmail me, tit for tat, over the missing records. He wanted money, and I refused. He said he'd sell the information to Travis Hartmann then, and he took off. I was chasing him in the cruiser. One minute I was behind him, and the next my front bumper . . ."

I grabbed his arm. "Did you force him over that cliff, Pete? Intentionally? Answer me!"

"That's the hell of it, Naomi. That's what I've been living with ever since. I just don't know."

Adam and I met in the city, shortly after that incident at the ravine. Susan, he said, was doing well. Making small but important steps, one day at a time.

"She's divorcing me," he said. "She wants to be free."

"For Annie?"

Annie Lowell stood by Susan through her recovery, though she was no longer a practicing therapist. Adam had uncovered some interesting problems in Annie's past. That was why he was out of town those days and nights when Susan had me locked up in the mansion. He was in Minnesota, following a hunch regarding Annie Lowell—who, it seems, had gone over the professional line as a doctor more than once, becoming personally involved with a patient. There are old charges pending against her, and though I've never pressed charges against her for that night, her future is uncertain.

"Actually," Adam told me with a smile, "Susan says she wants to be free for herself."

He also told me about that night at the cabin, when he was late getting home from the store. "I was on my way back, and Susan was standing there in the middle of the road. She saw the car coming, and she didn't move. I slammed on the brakes, and the tires went skidding. I went off the side of the road. But when I got out and looked for her, she was gone."

"Why didn't you just tell me this?" I asked.

"I suppose I was still protecting her. And when I got to the cabin Travis was there, and for some reason I couldn't explain, I didn't want him to know."

As for Adam and me, it is six months later now, and though Susan has divorced Adam and left him free to remarry (at least by civil, if not Church law), there is so much remorse in the way. For though I no longer believe that I stole Susan's husband, as their marriage was over before I appeared, it is probably quite true that I stole her child.

And my nemesis, Travis Hartmann? I did make it to court in time that day. And I did get an injunction finally to stop the sale of formerly Wintu lands to Lambert Enterprises. It's temporary, a Band-Aid, but it gives me time to work something out from my old desk at Robinson-Leigh.

I'm glad I've been able to do this. And I'll do what I can for the Hood Canal as well. But I can't live my life the way my mother did; I can't be bitter because of something that happened a hundred and fifty years ago. That was Katherine Wing's way, and she accomplished much good because of her anger. As for me, I must move forward with love.

This is something I have come to understand just this evening. It is Christmas Eve evening, to be exact. It would have been Beth's nineteenth birthday.

Adam, Susan, Pete, and I stand side by side at Beth's grave. Susan is out of the hospital now, more well than she's been in years. As for Pete, he resigned as sheriff and is doing his best to redeem himself by being active in Native American causes once more. I couldn't find it in my heart to tell anyone what I knew about the way Gray Steen died. Knowing firsthand how justice is dispensed these days in courts of law, I deemed it best to let sleeping dogs—and blackmailing coroners—lie. Pete, Susan, Annie—all of us, including Adam and me—will live with our own special guilts for the rest of our lives. That, I think, is the way it should be.

And who am I, you may well ask, to decide such things? I will tell you: I am Naomi Wing, child of Katherine and Thomas Wing, practicing attorney and full-blooded Wintu. I know who I am now, and what I may one day be.

Meanwhile, we have come here to honor Beth on this day that would have been hers. Adam and Susan have brought their priest, and I my shaman.

Well, actually, I've brought Pete, whom I've always believed had aspirations in that direction. At any rate, he wants to do this for Beth, and I think it is right that he's here. When the Catholic service is over we will burn smoke, shake shells, and tell stories about Beth. My mother, I think, scanning the surrounding trees, must be proud.

When it is over, I ask to stay behind alone a few moments. I sit at the foot of the angel that watches over Beth's grave, and think about my own story, one I have never told anyone else and never will. But I too have ghosts to lay to rest, and as I sit here cross-legged, the pictures become sharp and clear, all the memories I've tried for a year to hold back, to push into a little corner, hoping they'd stay.

I am running after Beth that night after Adam's phone call, trying to stop her. The winds toss the trees about, rain streams down. Catching up with her finally by my mother's hedgerow, I grab her arm.

"Beth, please let me explain!"

She turns, swinging her arm in blind rage. Knocking me down. "Get away from me! I never want to see you again!"

She spins away, running in the direction of her house. I try to get up, to follow, but something is wrong. I've twisted my back. I can't stand.

All night I lie there, crying, not only for Beth but for my own child—only two short months in the womb. For there is pain now, terrible pain. And by morning, my baby girl is gone. I watch as my mother carries her gently in her arms across the River of Ghosts.

I look up, now, blinking rapidly to stop my tears. "It's all right," I whisper. "I don't blame you. And you mustn't blame yourself. I'll be all right now."

For it is this, I know, that still holds her back from crossing: Beth's own guilt. I know this deep in my heart. When all is said and done, I knew her so well.

A light takes shape and forms about me, and though my body stays firm by Beth's grave, my heart flies free. From above, it looks down. It sees everything from here . . . the River of Ghosts, the ancestors, my mother waiting with a child—Beth's little boy, and my little girl—in each arm. Beth hesitates on this side. She looks up and whispers, "Are you sure?" and I nod, or rather my heart, which has become a white sphere of light, seems to nod. "Go," I say.

She sticks one toe in the River, then another, as I remember her doing so many cool summer mornings in the Sound, testing the temperature. I laugh. "Go, Beth! Fly!"

She laughs and flings her arms up, virtually lifting from the ground. Within seconds she is on the ancestor side, reaching for her son. My mother holds the child out, and Beth gathers him into her arms. Beth turns for a moment . . . looks for me, a smile on her lips and in her eyes. *Thank you,* she mouths. Then she says, so clearly, the music of her voice startles me, "Anything can happen, Naomi. Just let it be."

After that I can no longer see, as my heart is blinded by tears.

ACKNOWLEDGMENTS

I would like to acknowledge, in particular, Cathy Landrum, who was of enormous help with research and with stories from her Cherokee past. Thanks for never tiring, and especially for being the best of friends. Thanks also to John Ryan of the American Indian Museum of History in Novato, California, as well as to all the many people who talked with me and sent me information about the Wintu Band in Northern California, and the Snohomish in Washington.

I would like to extend my utmost gratitude, as well, to June Weaver, a wonderful friend and reader. Also to Jamie De La Garza, Francine Cunnie, and Laura Dito, for their enthusiasm and support.

Deepest thanks go to Jennifer Andrews, Janet Rostad, Fran Mc-Goohan, and everyone in the Thursday Wellness group at the Center for Attitudinal Healing in Sausalito, California. You are *so great*. Would that there were more of you.

A very special thanks to the Lehmanns of *Hale Pau Hana*, and to Betty Lindsay and Don Dickson of Koa Lagoon, at whose wonderful homes in Maui this book was completed and the new Hawaii one begun. A *most* lavish thanks to Linda Barron of Koa Lagoon in Maui, whose efficiency, thoughtfulness, and generosity of spirit made so many things possible. And to Keali`i Reichel, whose exquisite music and chant made the days fly by "on the wing of a song."

As always, heartfelt thanks to my agent, Nancy Yost, who understood the dream, and to Jennifer Enderlin, my editor, who agreed, and with her usual enthusiasm, wisdom, and kindness, helped to carry it out. I would like to acknowledge, as well, Amy Kolenik, whose efficiency and good nature never fails.

This book was begun at a very special place, a writer's retreat called Cottages at Hedgebrook, on Whidbey Island in Washington. Hedgebrook graciously provided me with time to write and ponder without outside distractions—no TV, no telephone, and no visitors (except for a welcome lunch that arrived at the door of my cottage every day in a wicker basket, accompanied by wildflowers). I would like to thank a few of the wonderful people who make this opportunity possible for women writers: Nancy Nordhoff, Linda Bowers, Denise Anderson, Conni Brotherton, Kathleen Baginski, Laura Wollberg, Jennifer Rose, Eugene McGunkin, April Davis, Terrie Wallace, Bev Graham, and Sandy Menashe.

I would also especially like to thank my daughter, Robin Weiland, for finding Hedgebrook for me, and for giving her all to help me get there. I will always remember the gifts you gave of time and energy, but most of all your loving heart.

There is one person in particular who has brought great joy and wisdom to my life these past few months, and who has given, in the name of friendship, much more than I ever might have dared ask for. To Lu Wilcox—kind and generous soul—I send my love and gratitude, forever.